LOKI'S WRATH

TROY A. CARRINGTON

Loki's Wrath / by Troy A. Carrington – 1st edition

Cover Art by William Hammock

ISBN-13 978-0-9848889-4-8

Printed in the United States of America

Books by Troy A. Carrington

The Chronos Series
The Hounds of Set
Loki's Wrath

To my wife, my destiny.

"It is not in the stars to hold our destiny, but in ourselves."
-William Shakespeare

"Fate is what brings us together; destiny is what separates us."
-Troy Carrington

"The question that sometimes drives me hazy, am I, or the others, crazy?"
-Albert Einstein

"If two men think alike, then one of them is not thinking."
-Eric the Red

ONE

It was early morning when Alex finally lifted his aching head from the grassy, dew-soaked meadow beneath him. Grass, he thought; boy, I missed it. He squeezed the long green blades between his fingers. A flutter of small birds swooped across the sky in unison, then scattered. The newly risen sun crowned orange above the horizon, barely showing its enormity. Alex felt warm and dizzy, his wiry frame still ached. He knew what happened; he'd been through it before.

It seemed like only moments ago he'd taken the mysterious pendant from around his neck and shoved it deep into the cover of his journal, but there was a problem. He wasn't sure how long ago it was, as the consequence of that action sent him hurdling once again through space and time.

To make matters worse, it wasn't the first time that happened. When he woke then, he was in ancient Egypt. That was no ordinary trip either. Unless getting captured, beaten, and thrown in some dreary dungeon was ordinary. It was in that dark and forgotten place where he first encountered the warrior god Anubis.

The creature stood, much like a man, but was covered in short black hair from head to toe. His head was that of a dog and he was built for battle. He was a living, breathing instrument of war and death with a long snout full of sharpened teeth, razor-like talons for hands, and donned a suit of golden armor. Alex didn't know it at the time, but as strange as Egypt was to him, he was there for a reason.

Egypt was now behind him and history had been set right, but that didn't make him feel any better. The only real joy he found in all of this was that he was finally home.

1

"Home," he repeated. His eyes widened to take it all in. A smile cracked across his face as he savored the moment. He took a deep breath, inhaling all that used to make him sneeze. It didn't matter. All he cared about was that there were no pyramids, no ancient gods, no dogs, and best of all, no stinking sand.

He was confident that any minute he'd hear Matilda announce the coming of a new day. Her cannon blasts were known throughout the region as punctual, if not loud. He paused and listened intently, pushing both near and far for her familiarity, then he heard it; faint and muffled, but nevertheless, a blast. There was something different about it, though; a blast, yes, but familiar, no. His eyes searched for something recognizable. An uneasy feeling washed over him.

The sky above suddenly pulsed with light, but it wasn't the light that bothered him; it was what usually followed. He covered his ears in anxious anticipation. As if on cue, the heavens opened up with a symphony that shook the air around him, forcing him to his knees. His head began to swim.

"Definitely *not* home," Alex corrected himself. His eyes quickly welled with tears at the sudden realization. He tried convincing himself otherwise by playing back his most recent memories; a tent flapping in the wind, a flash of blinding blue light, and his body lifting and twisting, followed by blackness, complete and utter blackness.

It feels like a long time since I've been home, Alex thought, as he wiped his eyes. His mind traveled to the past, of his grandmother. A mere silhouette blurred out of focus in his head. The house on Sandpiper Lane was a distant memory to him now; Mittens, Jackson . . . Tad. Memories that once filled his head were fading, being replaced by fear, loneliness, and pain.

He wasn't sure if the blasts were intended for him, but wasn't about to stand around and find out. Alex forced himself to stand. Every burst landed hard to the ground, throwing up loose dirt and grass into his face. He sidestepped each one as he ran for cover under the nearest tree. It was a massive old oak, well rooted into the ground and made for good protection from whomever or *whatever* currently wanted him dead.

That last part, people wanting him dead, was getting old, he thought. He hid behind the oak's stout trunk, lowering his head to his knees and covering his ears. The sounds were intense, and the ancient tree shook from each impact. The explosions were leaving craters the size of swimming pools in the otherwise scenic landscape. He'd only just arrived and was already panting and out of breath.

I thought I was done with this stuff. I thought I was going home. How the heck did I get here? he wondered.

The blasts, he could handle; but the deed was done. Egypt was saved. It was my time, he thought. I'm supposed to be home. Sitting and rocking with his knees pulled close to his chest, he tried desperately to force the surrounding noises from his head. Streams of salty tears flowed from his eyes as thoughts of his grandmother filled him once again.

"It's not fair," he yelled, "I'm only thirteen!" Ironically, it wasn't all that long ago he raced down the stairs proudly announcing this fact to his grandmother. That was different, Alex thought. I didn't have people trying to kill me. As he wiped tears from his face, Alex winced in anticipated pain, but there was none. His scars didn't hurt. In fact, they were fully healed.

The crack of a whip to a person's face can cause, *did* cause, some serious pain, he thought. He was certain that his wounds would've still been hurting, but the pain was gone, even the blood, gone. His skin did, however, rise in three distinct lines across his cheek. He sat there pondering this, delicately stroking his scars with his fingertips.

How much weirder can my life get? he wondered. He gave a sniff as he ran his shirt sleeve across his nose. He'd been through a lot; in fact, he'd been through more recently than most people have in an entire lifetime. For a moment, he wondered if Egypt had happened at all.

Neither in Egypt nor home, Alex knew he had to keep moving. Stretching his neck, he lifted his head as high as he dared to get a better look. The tree behind which he now sat was one of only three that he could make out in all directions. In front of him was lush rolling grassland that stretched into a fertile field of grain which looked to be about full height and ready for harvest. He could barely make out a narrow pathway that wove its way through the grain and split the field.

The early morning moisture in the air had left the faint remnants of a rainbow rising majestically from where the path ended. It looked odd to him, poised and shooting toward the sky from the horizon, a battlefield for a backdrop.

"Whoa!" Alex yelled as something blew just over his head. The ground shook violently and heaved against his feet. The percussion was so great he needed to steady himself against the tree.

Despite the maelstrom overhead, he thought the view rather peaceful and serene as the grain blew softly in the light breeze. It was what lay beyond that disturbed him.

"No way!" Alex exclaimed as the ringing in his ears subsided. He noticed something incredible; something he couldn't quite wrap his brain around. Impossible, he thought.

An enormous structure appeared to be floating in the heavens above, as if beckoning to those below. Alex rubbed his eyes in disbelief. Must be the heat, he assured himself. "I think I landed too hard," he said, rubbing his head.

The building and its mysteries only served to provide more questions about his current situation. He'd never seen a structure like this. It reminded him of a castle, only different somehow. He couldn't quite put his finger on it.

In fact, he'd never seen a castle at all, other than in his history book. He'd give his left leg for that stupid history book right now, but it was currently serving a different purpose back home as it propped up the end of his oversized bed; but even the castles in the book, he remembered, looked nothing like this.

Well, on a good note, at least there's no sand, he thought; no sand and no flipping death heat. I've had more than enough of that already. If it weren't for the killer explosions threatening to snuff out my very existence, this place would actually be quite nice. Ha.

Just then a sudden reminder of his immediate situation cracked loudly above his head. A large limb split away from the tree as a result of a direct hit and crashed to the ground next to him.

"Or not," he finished aloud. It wasn't all that long ago, in fact, that everything was normal in his life. Well, as normal as it could be. Alex had always been a loner, keeping to himself as he ran about the small harbor town he grew up in.

He was a bit awkward and gangly looking, with a set of oversized feet that he used unwisely for balance. His moppy brown hair hung down in his face most of the time, and it had been some time since he'd gotten it cut. Most of the kids at Peabody-Styers Academy, or PSA as it was known locally, avoided him. It's not that they didn't like him; it was more that trouble always seemed to follow him, and they didn't want any part of that.

In truth, most of his friends were adults, several decades older than his ripe old age of thirteen. They were more of a family than anything. He missed them now, just as he missed the safe warm comfort of his home by the sea. Most important, he missed his grandmother. For as long as he could remember, it had always been just the two of them. They were inseparable. She raised him, and as he grew older and she grew, uh, well, *different*, he took care of her.

There was Jackson, of course; but he could do without that brute. Alex had always been an object of torment for Jackson, the local school bully who'd clearly been held back a few dozen years. Aside from frequently pointing out Jackson's dimwittedness, there were only about three times in his life that Alex could remember actually getting the better of him. It wasn't too long ago he had the pleasure of clocking the thug squarely in his granite jaw. Boy, that felt good. The stuff dreams are made of, he thought, and smiled.

Another bolt sailed past his head. The last time he saw fireworks like this, Captain Shovers was coaxing Matilda awake after her fuse had fizzled one Fourth of July evening. That was a sight. The Captain tried everything to get her to fire, but when he finally dipped a new wick into a can of gasoline and rolled it in black powder, she let out a fiery howl that set the Mermaid's mainsail ablaze.

As it burned, it lit up the sky; all the while the Captain was howling mad himself. It didn't help matters when he tried dousing the flames with a can of kerosene he mistook for water during the chaos. Let's just say . . . it sparked and there was a box of readied fireworks on the Mermaid's deck. Alex chuckled.

He may have laughed, but he was terrified at his current circumstance. He knew he was in a bad spot and in unfamiliar territory. All he could see from his position was the protective oak

6

against which he was leaning, the small grass hill just beyond, and the enormous castle in the far distance.

Maybe there's gold inside that castle-looking thing? *Wait?* What am I thinking? he asked himself. He already knew the answer, but he was pretty sure it was that stinking castle that had something to do with all of this. Alex considered this as he ducked yet another projectile. *Sheesh*. Why go there? Answers, he told himself, I need answers. Oh, wait, there is one more teeny, tiny little question.

"*Am I insane?*" he asked loudly.

"I highly doubt it, my child; but then, only you would know," said a voice. It appeared to have come from the air that surrounded him and echoed in his head. Alex whipped around. Nothing. Oh great, now I'm hearing voices. One of those blasts must've knocked my brain loose, he said. He raised his hand, pretending to knock the cobwebs from his ears, hoping this would fix the problem; no luck.

"What else could go wrong?" he asked rather loudly, trying to drown out both the earthshaking thunder high above, as well as the voices inside his head.

"What now?" he yelled, shaking his fists toward the castle in anger.

As if in response to his last question, an old dredge of a lady appeared seemingly from nowhere and moved from behind the tree where Alex sat cowering. Her sudden presence jolted Alex back to reality and pushed him against the tree. She seemed unaffected by the earsplitting noises from the other side.

The haggard woman before him was hunched over and dressed shabbily in a brown full-length coat of sorts to protect her from the elements. She stood no more than four feet tall, Alex noticed, but he'd been fooled by size before. After all, he'd underestimated Anubis' size at first, too.

7

When they first met, before they became friends, he was hunched over, too, wearing a similar old cloak, but when his friend stood on his two hind feet and stretched, bellowing out one of his tremendous battle roars, he easily towered ten feet into the air.

It was only recently that Alex had experienced something quite amazing by any standards. The discovery of the journal and the mysterious pendant that he now wore hidden beneath his shirt had sent him on a journey beyond imagination. Had Anubis given him the pendant?

Alex had thought long and hard about that same question. He was sure it was Anubis who visited him the night of his thirteenth birthday. He was equally certain that it was Anubis who saved his life from the fury that Jackson was about to unleash on him. Alex had been scared then, too, when they'd first met.

Who'd have thought that I'd ever been besties with a 10-foot tall Egyptian god? *Oh*, did I mention, he looks like a dog, walks like a human, plays with dead things, and is *never* around when you need him? What a dufus. Speaking of ugly; Alex snapped back to the present and stared up at the mysterious hag in front of him. She'd been watching him closely and studying him with great curiosity. He felt a bit uneasy.

Her crooked nose was so long and narrow that Alex thought it looked more like a finger protruding from her wicked face than a breathing apparatus. The wrinkles of her skin were worn and grey with time and had the appearance of the docks down by the harbor back home. Those same docks had weathered both good and bad over the years, and he presumed this woman was no different.

"They aren't angry with you, my child; they're angry at their own fate. With all of their wisdom, they don't understand it's anger that controls their destiny."

The quaking sounds that had filled the air only moments ago suddenly quieted when she spoke. Alex's head felt light. *It's probably from my hard landing*, he guessed. The old woman smiled, or at least Alex assumed that's what it was. Her rotted teeth bore yellow through her thin cracked lips. *Is she doing this to me? Is she making me feel this way?* He shook his head. *How did I get here?* he wondered.

That's twice now this happened, and the last time wasn't exactly a pleasure cruise. In fact, the last time I had to kick evil god-butt. I mean, the dude screeched like a hoot owl whenever he opened his mouth. How do you have a conversation with that? *Oh, and please, let's not forget the demon mutts. Can't a guy at least get a quick nap in?* Anger rose inside him.

"Who the heck are *they* and who are you?" Alex asked, sensing he couldn't trust this stranger. Something was telling him to be wary of her, to be careful and guarded in his words.

"Who I am doesn't matter," she said sharply, eyeing this newcomer. "Who they are, does." Her hard and cracked face softened on her next words. "Why, child, they're the gods," she said simply, her senses hanging on what his next response would be.

"Gods! What? Great. Just flipping great. That's exactly what I need, more gods in my life. As if one ugly looking buffoon isn't enough for me to babysit, now you're telling me there's *more!*" he rambled on, throwing up his hands in disbelief; then it dawned on him, "*Oh*, you don't mean Anubis, do you?" Alex rose and twisted his head from side to side, hopeful.

"Is he here? Where is he? If he's hiding I'm going to . . ." Alex trailed off, only to return his gaze back into the old woman's soulless eyes.

"I know not of this Anubis you mention. I speak only of the

Æsir and the *Vanir.*" She eyed him with her own look of distrust. Alex didn't know why, but he didn't like this woman much, and the sooner he was rid of her, the better, he thought. She gave him the creeps.

"Wh-who are the *Æsir* and the *Vanir?*" he asked cautiously, not sure he wanted to know. He'd been through a lot recently, and he was in no mood to get sucked into another, uh, *situation.*

The old woman looked shocked at this question. It was at that moment that Alex realized a couple of things. First, he was definitely far from home and once again on his own. Second, even though he sensed this stranger wasn't his friend, she'd at least told him one important piece of information. At least this time, he thought, people weren't aiming at him. Good to know. Third, he was confident the answers he needed were in that castle.

"Why, they're both your future and your past, dear child."

"Of course they are," he said as if he knew what the batty old woman was talking about. He didn't. Well, that certainly clears things up for me . . . like mud. Alex figured he needed to get as much information about where he was and what was going on. Being a typical teenager he obviously asked the most important question first.

"Uhhh, you wouldn't happen to have any flesh-eating savage dogs around here, do you?" Alex questioned.

The haggard woman stared back at him sharply. "Hhmmmm," was her only response. Alex wasn't quite sure he liked the way that sounded. His question almost seemed to catch her off-guard.

Once again thinking like a teenage boy, he asked, "Any idea where I can find some grub? I'm starving. I haven't eaten since Egypt." This last part he said on purpose just to see what sort of response he'd get from her. Nothing. Great; a critic, he thought.

10

"I've said it before and I'll say it again, my genius is wasted on you people," Alex said, waving his hand around in a swooping manner much like a visiting dignitary. With the momentary quiet from the skies above, he contemplated his next move.

"I think I'll make my way over to the right, then down . . ." He turned back to where she once stood and saw nothing. Her voice trailed off into the thin air saying, *"Beware of the Bellllfrieeeessss."*

Alex spun his head around. She was gone as quickly as she'd appeared.

"Belf . . . *huh?* Where'd she go?" he asked aloud. "She's gone. Was she even here? Did I imagine her? I must've hit my head harder than I thought when I landed. Wait. Am I talking to myself again? Man, I have to stop that. Like *now.*" Then, remembering what the old woman said, he chuckled to himself. I thought *I* was crazy. That lady was a loon.

"Beware of the Belfries? Yeah, I'll do that, and your bats, too," he added, feeling proud of himself for getting the last word in even though she was gone. He didn't care. It wasn't often he could get the last word in with any female, especially ones at PSA. Boy, they could yap, he thought.

He often wondered if the lights in the town would suddenly dim if those same jabbering vacuums of society ever stopped talking. It was no wonder they're so ditzy; they walked around in a haze of perfume thicker than the last sandstorm I was in. Believe me, Alex thought, *that* was a doozy. In fact, one time Alex swore that their perfume was so thick that it set off the school's fire alarm.

I must've imagined her. With that thought, the sky opened up once again and split the molecules above.

"*Shheeessh!*" he yelled, instinctively ducking his head from the noise. Well, I'm not exactly imagining *that*, am I? I need a plan. It

11

made complete sense to Alex that if this spot was where the raining firefight from above was landing, then he shouldn't, well, be here. Yeah, I'm a genius. He knew what he needed to do. He took a deep breath.

"Oh well. Here we go again," and he was off. Sliding out from behind the oak and giving one last look around for the mysterious old lady, he crawled up and over the nearby knoll and down into the tall grass beyond. He quickly made his way, weaving and hunched over, toward the distant grain field.

The dew was sitting heavily on the green grass, soaking his pant legs through as he pressed on. His sneakers started squeaking and squishing with each step. It still had to be morning, he thought, as the day's sun had yet to dry the grass. The more distance he put behind him, the better he felt, and somewhere along the way he decided that it was far enough from the blasts that he could travel upright.

The day was warming in the rising sun, and he could smell the fresh air surrounding him. This place was beautiful, and for a moment he'd forgotten his longing for home. As the sun lifted, it took the remaining few clouds with it and revealed a vast mountain range far in the distance to his left, beyond the rolling fields and darkened forest.

The noises from earlier had all but stopped, indicating the battle was over and quickly becoming a vague memory. It was difficult for Alex to even recall the last time he actually walked somewhere without being chased. He was always being chased; if it wasn't by Jackson, then it was some dog-breathed demon hound or an evil soul-sucking something or other.

He knew he wasn't out of the woods just yet, but this place was already shaping up to be better than his last adventure, or so he was hoping. He crossed his fingers on that particular thought.

Alex had crossed nearly two entire grass fields when he first sensed it. He wasn't alone. He knew this feeling that had come over him. Usually it was just before Mittens, his grandmother's wicked cat, pounced on him from out of nowhere; pure evil. He'd felt like this back home, that day returning from school. Something had followed him then. He was being stalked.

Why should here be any different? he questioned. Please, just don't let it be one of those freakish slobbering death mutts. I've had enough of those to last me a lifetime.

What was that? He turned and saw only the tall grass moving. What? He spun back around. Nothing. *Hunh?* He looked ahead. Again, nothing. Flashes. Glimpses of color. Am I hearing things? No, it's there. Something's there to my right. I saw it. No, my left. It's moving fast.

Black. Hidden in the green; I saw black. It's going to attack. Alex froze. The warm mid-morning air went cold. The skies darkened. Everything was suddenly still. Eyes.

He saw them through the grass; two small green eyes. They stared back at him. He could barely move, and when he tried to yell, he only gasped.

The low deep utterance of a growl surrounded him completely and echoed into his head, then it moved. Slowly, it pushed through the thin grass line that protected Alex and separated him from certain death. This was it. What the heck? Dang blasted, it *was* a dog. No, not a dog.

A wolf!

Not just any wolf, either; the largest, blackest wolf he'd ever seen. Not that he'd seen a lot of wolves in his life, but still, this thing was big; easily larger than the hounds he battled in Egypt.

Troy A. Carrington

Back then the hounds had been controlled by the evil god Set. Now, Alex couldn't help but wonder who controlled this one. It was scrappy, too, but it kept its distance. It looked like it had been through a lot of battles recently. Well, Alex thought, at least we'll have something in common when he *eats* me.

Through all of this cold, his chest pounded warm, and it was only seconds before it starting burning. Was the wolf doing this? He looked down and saw his shirt glowing, or rather, something underneath his shirt. *Of course!* He moved slowly and cautiously, trying not to startle the beast into a blood frenzy. He thought it might be nice to make it through another day.

Reaching up, he pulled out his pendant from under his shirt. The bright light pierced the darkened sky and the wolf recoiled. Alex liked that response. I wonder, he thought. He raised it even higher, stretching it out as far as the chain would allow. The wolf snarled and ducked back behind the grass, just out of sight. Was it gone? Well, I'm certainly not going in there to find out.

The whole encounter had lasted only seconds when the skies lifted and the sun showed brightly once again. Feeling triumphant over the beast, Alex decided to do a little victory dance. It was the saddest little movement, similar to a seizure with a frightening little kick at the end, but still, with his arms and legs flailing about as they did, it made him feel good to be alive, if at least for a little while longer.

"Who's your daddy now, *pooch?*" he yelled into the grass shaking his fist in the air. "I'll send you back to the pound where you belong, you ugly butt-sniffer." Once Alex had settled down, he recalled the scene over in his mind, then the questions began flooding his thoughts.

Why'd my pendant start glowing? Did it have something to do

14

with the wolf or was there something else? That was no normal wolf. That was a mistake o' nature! A poodle on steroids, that's what it was.

Remind me to *never* get a dog, he told himself. Too much trouble; always wanting to *eat* you. I'm going to look at puppies in the pet store a whole lot differently from now on. Almost makes Mittens look nice. *Almost.* Well, maybe not Mittens, the vindictive little feline fur ball.

With the wolf gone, or so he hoped, Alex cut through the tall grass much quicker now and much more cautiously. There were dangers here, too, just like Egypt. He needed to be on his guard.

Alex had traveled what seemed like a hundred miles and the sun had risen to just about its highest point when he heard a low rumbling noise. He stopped quickly and looked around for more fiery blasts from the heavens above; nothing. The skies were clear, the grass was still blowing in the warm breeze, and all appeared to be right with the world; whatever world this was, he thought.

There it is again. Where'd that come from? Was it the old hag? he wondered, looking around. I hope not. Again? *What the . . .* oh, it's me. He grabbed for his stomach. *That's* what I heard. Alex was getting hungry. Ages had passed since his last meal. When was it? What was it? *Oooh*, never mind, I don't even want to remember, he told himself, as the flash of sucking on a grease-soaked cloth ran through his mind.

"Boy, I have to get something to eat," he spoke out loud.

"*Eat?*" replied a curious voice.

Alex nearly jumped out of his skin. Just when he thought things were fine, voices again. Looking around, there was nothing in sight. He was alone. Man, I must be hungry *and* delirious. Shaking it off as more head trauma from his landing, he started moving again.

"Hey, where are you going?" came the voice with a distinctly foreign accent. Alex spun around toward the direction of the voice.

"*Waaaaa!*" he screamed, stumbling backwards as a dark figure popped up from the tall grass. Was it the wolf from earlier? Had he just been waiting for the right moment to attack?

"*Waaaaa!*" replied the figure back, just as startled by Alex's scream, it, too, stumbled backwards.

"*Waaaaa!*" Alex purged himself one last time, shaking off the fright still bouncing around inside of him. He prepared himself for the attack. It wasn't the wolf, but this thing was just as gruesome and reeked of the foulest of odors.

Alex had only smelled one thing worse in his life; the decaying flesh and rotting organs from above the cavern that he once shared with Anubis. This, however, was a close second. Only bad things could come from this, he thought, as he braced himself.

Alex searched the creature over from head to foot. It stood slightly taller than he and sloshed on its feet in the mud puddle that it currently occupied. It had a strange form and looked, well, lumpy. Its skin slid and moved about as if it had a mind of its own. This thing was horrifying and grotesque, deformed.

"What are you? What do you want?" Alex demanded.

The figure was still swooning from the encounter, but steadied itself in response. It lifted what looked to be some sort of arm up to its head and wiped layers of mud from its eyes. Alex could see it was . . . it was . . . *human?* It was completely covered in a thick suit of mud. It let out a strange noise that sounded much like a, well uh, a burp, actually. It *was* a burp, definitely human; then it spoke again.

"I want to eat, just like you," came the answer. The accent was heavy and thick, but Alex could make out bits and pieces. He didn't like the way it sounded.

16

"What did you say? You want to eat me?" Alex reared back his fist, cocked and poised to land the first blow against this flesh-eating mud sucker.

"Not eat you, eat *like* you. I'm hungry, too." It laughed. Alex slowly lowered his fist and leaned in a bit closer to get a better look, but not so close as to become overwhelmed by the odor. Straining his eyes, he could just barely see that before him stood not a meta-human nor a fierce man-beast as he had assumed, but rather a human. Beneath what were layers of thick grey mud was another boy, just like him. Well, maybe not *just* like him, but still a boy; he thought.

As Alex stood there staring back at this odd person, a million questions raced through his mind. Maybe he has some answers about this place. Does he know where I am? Does he know what those explosions were? Did he know of the old hag? The wolf? Could he help him? Alex wondered.

Probably not, Alex decided as he looked the boy over slowly. This kid was filthy. Sludge was packed into every possible place. It was in his eyes, his ears, his nose, and he was even spitting it out of his mouth. Somehow none of it seemed to bother the lad. His hair was long and ran past his shoulders as the wet sludge slid down his back. He looked lopsided and lumpy like the bog monster that Alex had seen on television during Monster-Palooza Night with Captain Shovers.

For years, he and the Captain had themed movie nights out on the deck of the Mermaid, guy nights. "No dames allowed," as the Captain would say. Could I trust this nut job in front of me? Alex wondered. Do I want to? Probably not.

At that moment, the boy reached up and shoved a finger deep into his nose and became fixated on what he pulled out.

Definitely not.

"Did you fall or something?" Alex asked the boy. "You do realize that you're covered in mud, don't you? What happened? Did you lose something?"

Watching this disgusting oaf in front of him go from bad to worse, Alex likened it to watching the monkeys at the zoo throwing their dung at each other. It was both gross and funny at the same time, yet it was impossible to look away. Oh, and somehow crap went everywhere. Just then the boy flicked his finger and the combination of both booger and mud sailed the distance of about four feet and landed on Alex's pant leg.

"*Auuggghhh! Grooooss!*" he yelled.

Did I mention crap went everywhere? *Did I?*

"I was taking a bath," the boy explained simply, motioning to the puddle of thick muck nearby. Alex watched as a slew of wet snot fell from the side of the boy's face to the ground in a splatter.

"*In the mud?* Isn't that what pigs do?" he asked.

"Yes. Pigs are smart, no?" the boy asked, looking for approval in Alex's eyes.

"No. No, they're not. They're food." Since that fateful day in Biology class with his lab partner Tina Schultz, Alex averted all human characteristics from any animals that would end up on his dinner plate. He loved food; and no flaming Bunsen burner, no queasy screaming cheerleaders, no bursting sewer pipes, and certainly no dirt bike covered in chicken feathers would ever change that. He had Tina to thank for that. She talked him through it.

Alex gave a shudder at the horrific memory. Let's just say Mr. Findling's toupee would likely never return, nor would Mr. Findling; not a bad thing, mind you.

"Well, do you have a name or not?" Alex asked, still not quite sure what to make of the disgusting sight standing only a short unfortunate snot shot away. The thick grey that covered his entire body was quickly shedding off, giving way to brown smudges of remaining dirt in the warming sun. Each slip or slide of the muck peeled off him like a layer of old skin landing in a wet mess at his feet.

The boy stood tall and proud, cleared his throat, and announced himself to all who could hear. Of course, there was only Alex, but the boy amused him, so Alex stepped back and gave him the floor.

"My name is Zacherie Óþveginn Meinfretr."

"Wow. That's a mouthful," Alex replied.

"That's just my first name," he said with a smile.

"Does it mean something important?" Alex asked.

"Zacherie is my father's name," the boy explained.

"And the rest?" Alex responded, mimicking the boy's heavy accent. He looked sheepish at the slip of his tongue. "What does that mean?" he quickly asked, hoping the boy hadn't caught it.

It was difficult to tell beneath all of the dirt and mud on his face, but Alex believed he saw the boy turn red with embarrassment at this question. He dropped his head, trying desperately to avoid eye contact, and muttered something under his breath, barely audible to Alex.

"*Hunh?* What's that?" Alex asked as he leaned in closer to hear, taking care not to get too close to the mud-covered boy.

"It means unwashed stink-fart," the boy repeated a little louder.

"Unwashed *what?*" Alex's head snapped straight. "Did you just say *stink-fart?* No way! You're kidding. Who the heck names their kid stink-fart? That's flipping hilarious!" Alex bellowed. The boy stood quiet. It was too much for Alex, and he laughed so hard that he doubled over, clutching his stomach as he fell to the ground.

19

He immediately realized his mistake. Now the odd boy whom he'd just met wasn't the only one covered in mud. Alex had fallen squarely into the middle of the puddle with a sloppy thick splash. Realizing immediately what had happened, he tried desperately to turn himself over, each time only managing to slip deeper into the puddle.

"That's it," the boy said, watching in admiration. "You must get the ears, too, no."

"I'm . . . *oof* . . . not . . . *ugh* . . . doin-*umf* . . . this on purpo-*udd*," Alex spattered out.

The boy stood to the side watching with a smile. He looked as if he were actually impressed. Of course he was, Alex thought; the dimwit. This is like an Olympic sport to him, I'm sure.

He was getting frustrated. Last time, he thought, it was sand down my pants, this time it's mud. *What the heck.* I need to . . . *oomph* . . . get . . . up. He made one final Herculean effort and pushed himself out of the puddle, rolling to his knees in the drying grass and snapping to his feet, slipping only once at the end.

It took several minutes for Alex to regain his composure, or as he would say, his rawesomeness. It didn't help, for when he finally did, he was quite unsuccessful.

"Can I just call you Stinky or Farty or something?" he asked, trying to muffle a couple of snickers from behind his hand.

"I'd prefer not," the boy responded quietly with his head down, sounding somewhat embarrassed.

"Okay, how about Zach?" Alex asked, deciding not to embarrass him any further. With a name like that, Alex thought, he's no doubt had a lifetime of embarrassment. Could you imagine having a name like Unwashed Stink-Fart and going to school with a bully like Jackson? It'd be unbearable; but he also knew that it was impossible

20

for him to continue calling this person by his full name without some sort of uncontrollable outburst.

"Yes, Zach is good," the boy agreed with a smile.

"Zach it is," Alex concurred.

"Zach it is, what?" the boy asked curiously.

"Never mind." Alex knew better than to travel down that road; he'd never get off. It appeared the boy wasn't all that bright, and Alex wondered how he managed out here all on his own.

"So what exactly do you do?" Alex asked.

"Well, I stand around and let people throw food at me," Zach explained.

"*Ahhh*," Alex smirked. "So how's that working out for you?"

"Not well," the boy responded, lowering his head and shaking it in despair. For the longest time the boys stood, each covered in more mud than the other, staring. Silence fell over them. Neither knew what to do nor say next.

Alex's mind raced on the day's events so far. Let's see if I've got this straight. I wake up in the middle of a spitting match between the gods *apparently*, then there's this weird old lady and her Belfries. Yeah, what's up with her? I say hello to the local mascot who, by the way, is one ugly looking Fido. Again with the dogs. As if that's not enough, now I have this to deal with, he thought, as he looked at the oddity next to him. What's next? I need to find a way home, pronto.

The silence was soon interrupted by the low rumble that filled Alex's mid-section.

He immediately looked around for the wolf; nothing. It was his stomach again, reminding him that it needed to be filled. If he were home, the refrigerator would always be full, and so would his stomach, but not here. He didn't have that luxury. All he had was Stinky, er, Zach, and that was enough to make him lose his appetite.

21

Again, his stomach spoke.

"*Okaaaaay*, this is awkward," Alex said at last. "I need some food."

"There's a village just over that hill," Zach said with some difficulty as he lifted his mud-dried arm and pointed ahead.

"Really? A village?" Alex repeated, once again mocking the boy's accent. The intent of his remark flew directly over the head of his new acquaintance, who was currently busy pulling a wedgy out from his backside. Shaking his head, Alex asked, "Where'd you get your accent anyway?"

The boy stopped everything he was doing and stood straight as a board. His eyes went icy and blank. He looked like he was in a trance. Just when Alex thought things couldn't get any weirder with this kid, the boy spoke, giving Alex a sudden chill in the warmth of the sun.

TWO

A shrill voice parted Zach's blue lips and said, "I'm a direct descendant of the ancient ones." It was no sooner over when the boy blinked twice, unaware.

"What are you doing?" Zach asked, looking puzzled. He was back to normal, or as normal as he could be. Alex shrugged and rolled his eyes. I have no clue what *normal* is anymore, he thought. He looked at the boy in disbelief, shook his head in pity, turned, and strolled off. I don't even want to know, he thought. Besides, I've seen worse.

After his last adventure, Alex figured it would take a lot more than some mud-covered Howler Monkey to get in his way. More important to Alex, he didn't want to be caught downwind of this walking dung heap, so he took the lead. It was the smartest thing he'd done all day; fresh air.

It was past noon and the day only managed to bring about two things, warmth and hunger. Oh, and not to mention a creepy old lady, another flipping shaggy mutt, and *this* guy. Okay, so five things, Alex laughed. The two boys wandered on aimlessly, enjoying the first on that list and hoping to soon satisfy the second.

As the two started out together toward the village and fulfillment of their teenage appetites, Alex had a thought.

"You don't happen to know of any Belfries around here, do you?"

"*Hunh?*" Zach responded, giving Alex a perplexed look.

"I didn't think so. Never mind." They walked on. Several hundred yards of peace and quiet had passed when Alex lifted his head to the sounds of distant thunder. Looking up, he saw nothing but clear skies. The roll of it grew louder with each step they took.

Alex quickened his pace. He'd been in this situation before. In his experience, growing rumbles usually meant danger. This much, he learned in Egypt. Looking rather worried, Zach hastened up closely behind Alex. The noise echoed like a hundred hooves coming up fast behind them. He turned around to find nothing; nothing on the ground, anyway.

His eyes caught a glimpse of something high in the air, several somethings, descending from the clouds now forming from the rumbling itself. A storm was coming, fast; but a storm of what? Alex wondered. The noise grew deafening and the figures falling from the sky grew larger. They moved as one.

Not knowing what he was running from, and at this point not caring, Alex kept moving. He had a dual purpose once again. It was the same as in Egypt; he needed some answers and, more important, he needed to stay alive. His heart pounded harder and harder with each step. Both boys were at a full-out run. Alex didn't bother to turn around and check on the other boy; he could hear Zach pacing behind him and breathing heavy.

Whatever it was, it was getting closer. Alex looked ahead. There was no place to offer protection this time, only the wide open field. He knew what that meant. He knew they'd have to stand and fight.

"Valkyries!" Zach yelled from behind. Alex's heart jumped. *Valkyries?* What the heck are Valkyries? More important, why are they chasing us?

The old woman he met earlier that morning had said, "Beware of the Belfries." Only, she didn't, did she? Not Belfries at all. The boy had said it. No, not Belfries. He misunderstood her. She said *Valkyries,* and apparently they were swooping down from the sky with sharpened spears, canvassing the fields and edging closer.

Closer and closer they rode on the backs of their sturdy winged steeds with thunderous hooves clapping against the air. Battle cries filled both time and space. They moved swiftly and blanketed the field behind them with the mist from their wake. The entire scene was both wondrous and eerie at the same time. Alex stopped suddenly and, when he did, the unsuspecting Zach plowed headlong into him.

"*Unnnghh.*" Zach deflected off Alex and fell to the ground. There he lay, cowering below the cover of the tall grass.

Alex, unaffected by the collision, spun on his heels to face his latest foe. He watched as a wave of white vapor swallowed the field and closed in, chilling the air around them. He could feel the ground tremble beneath his feet. Zach's whimpering was overcome with the roar of the advancing onslaught.

Prepared for battle, Alex spied two of them splitting off from the pack as they approached. His eyes followed the two high up into the air above and past him, only to watch them circle and swoop down at him from the other side. Fast. Super-fast. He was cut off.

His two aggressors slowed their pace and drifted, one behind the other, to within feet from where he stood. There they floated in silence, staring back at this lad in front of them. Upon closer inspection, Alex noticed they were nothing more than condensed wisps of air, not made of anything solid or tangible. They were true visions of beautiful women clad in armor with long flowing hair.

Solid or not, they were real enough to Alex, and he certainly understood they were not to be taken lightly. If nothing else, their shields and spears gave that much away. Alex had always been able to think quickly on his feet, so he reached deep down inside his arsenal of words and shot out the best he could come up with.

"*Hellooooo, ladieeees,*" he said with a wide and cheesy smile. The

25

response wasn't quite what he expected.

A most horrific scream seemed to come from deep in the soul of the spirit closest to him. She screamed with the force of a wind tunnel that blew Alex's hair straight back and turned him ghostly pale. As she shrieked, her beautiful smooth face turned dark and gaunt. Her eyes hollowed and her long flowing hair turned grey. A skeletal warrior now faced him atop the mammoth stallion, and it wasn't happy.

"My bad," he said, his hair windblown from their scream. All he heard next was the scraping of steel on steel, and suddenly there were two long and sharp spears pointed at his chest. The steeds' own massive chests were heaving, pushing out their frigid breath into the air through flaring nostrils. The Valkyries had raised their shields and leaned in, positioning the shafts of their weapons, long and narrow, over their shields and across the necks of their mounts.

Alex knew the time for joking had passed. He concluded that they weren't going to kill him just yet, but the tips of the spears stabbing at his chest indicated he needed to go with them. But how? he wondered. His question was answered when the lead warrior reached down and grabbed his arm, jerking him up behind her onto the back of her beast. Alex was astonished. It felt real beneath him. He could feel the horse's chest expanding with every breath, even feel the warmth of its body, but it was vapor. He could *see* that.

He took a chance to satisfy his curiosity and slowly pushed his hand between the shoulder blades of the apparition in front of him. She was vaporous and his hand felt cool. Pulling it back quickly out of fear, he watched as the moisture trickled off his knuckles and through his fingers. He looked back up at her face, and she was once again the beauty he'd first seen, her golden hair flowing in the breeze.

She kicked her heels hard into the sides of the beast and it bucked, high on its hind legs, causing Alex to slide back. Instinctively, he reached around his captor's waist so as not to fall off. When the horse returned back to all fours, Alex released his grip, realizing what he'd done. She turned and smiled. There was evil in her smile.

"*Eeewwww.* Gross. This babe's got the hots for me. Look, lady, it'd never work out between the two of us," Alex said in his own wisecracking way. "There's the whole age thing, plus, you know, you're uh, well, uh . . . *flipping dead!* You creepy morgue dweller."

With a sudden lunge forward, the beast took off. Frightened, Alex's eyes darted over the grassy area behind them as they galloped away and saw that Zach was nowhere to be found. Where'd he go? Did he run? Probably; the pansy. Where are they tak . . . Alex's thought was cut short.

The horse had reared back again, startled at what stood in its path. Zach, in all of his unclean glory, had appeared out of nowhere several yards in front of them. He must've popped up from beneath the tall grass to surprise them, Alex thought; but how the heck did he get there so fast? That's *impossible!*

Alex's sight was limited from behind the fierce warrior at the reigns, but it was enough to see that Zach wasn't moving and his eyes were closed. He's scared, Alex thought. He doesn't know what he's doing. He'll get hurt, the filthy mud patty. Between flashes of bone that was the changing Valkyrie's ribcage and glints of steel from her shield, Alex saw only one movement from Zach, his eyes. They opened. They were bright red and painfully intense, like a thousand suns. More flashes.

"*Oooff-nnh.*"

Alex skidded to a halt on the ground far below, landing on his backside. The Valkyrie had vanished right out from beneath him. The mist had thinned and disappeared. Rubbing his achy bottom, Alex searched the skies for any sign of them; gone.

His eyes fell upon the boy. The flies had long ago started circling him. He had the most ridiculous expression. It almost looked like a smile. How could he be smiling at a time like this? What just happened? *Did* it just happen?

Standing and brushing off, Alex said, "You'd think I'd get used to this stuff by now. Like most women, they're all cute at first, but then, *Watch Out!* They get all needy, and the next thing you know, you're riding *their* horse, listening to their bones rattle, and getting screamed at for no dang-blasted reason. *Sheeesh.* Soon it's all like, "Does this spear match my horse?" and "Does this shield make my butt look big?" La-tee-daa, la-tee-daa. Who needs it? Who were they, and what did I do to tick them off?"

"They're the winged warriors from above. The Valkyries," Zach explained as he pulled something out of his hair. It began to wiggle, so he flicked it. Alex stared briefly in awe.

"Well, those winged whatevers can kiss my gramma's sweet potato pie. All I know is aside from the death faces they're sporting and those little pointy things they had . . . What do you call them? Oh yeah, *spears!* They're rather pleasant. *Not.* You think you can give me a heads-up next time? Did you see they were made of bones? *Did you?*" Alex asked.

As Zach stood there in the warming sun, Alex wondered how this nitwit could still move underneath so many layers of hardening mud. He couldn't even tell if this kid was wearing any clothes. He was definitely barefoot, mostly toothless, and thin, like Alex, although he was taller by about two inches. As Alex looked over this pinhead in front of him, he felt a strange sensation waft over him.

There's something more here, to him. Was he hiding something? I mean, hey, *nobody* could possibly be that gross, *could they?* Alex wondered. Zach belched, seemingly on cue.

"We need to go before I lose my appetite," Alex stated in disgust, covering his nose with his hand to keep from breathing.

"Yes, tonight we shall eat," Zach agreed.

"Tonight nothing. I'm talking about *today*. C'mon, let's go." He took off running. It took only a split second before Zach was at his side. This kid is fast, Alex thought. "Tell me about these ladies, these Valkyries."

"They're warriors sent by the gods," Zach explained. "Duty-bound to scour the battlefields and seek out the most fierce and righteous battle-dead and take them to the great hall. They're unfeeling, uncaring, and merciless in their task. They're vicious if denied their deed."

"Yeah, that much I know," Alex said quietly, reaching around and rubbing the obvious bruise currently forming underneath his ratty old jeans.

"So, where's this great hall, and what happens once they get there?"

"It's said that the dead are poured endless mead and feast for days," Zach said with a gleam in his eyes.

"Sign me up for that. Wait, I'm here getting my clock cleaned by girly ghouls and they get to have a stinking party. Yeah, that's fair," Alex chided.

"They may enjoy it while they're there, but they're readying for battle."

"Yeah, sounds *real* tough. I'll tell you about tough. Have you ever seen a steel cage match? No? Well, *that's* tough."

"You don't see," Zach said. "They prepare for the final battle.

29

The battle to end all battles. To end the world. They prepare for *Ragnarok!*"

"*Fraggle Rock?* Wasn't that a show on television a while back? No? You remember, little Muppet dudes running around?" Alex could see that he was wasting his time with Zach. What a lunkhead. "After we get something to eat, we should head for that castle-looking thing I saw earlier," Alex said as he turned to walk away.

"You've seen the bridge?" Zach asked, greatly startled. A look of horror struck across his face beneath the smudges and stains.

"Bridge? No, I saw a rainbow and some big castle. *Whyyyyyy-uh?*" Alex asked, hesitantly turning back, not sure he was going to like the answer. "You know, that grunge look went out in the nineties, by the way," he said, not able to resist the opportunity.

"Only great warriors who've died on the battlefield can see the bridge, uh, the rainbow," Zach explained to the now worried looking Alex. It was more the emphasis that Zach placed on the word *died* that had the hairs on Alex's arms standing straight up and left his throat dry.

"Well, that's a load of hogsnot. No offense," Alex offered dismissively. Zach bowed his head slightly, acknowledging the apology.

"The Valkyries make no mistakes," Zach said somewhat defensively.

Annoyed at this point, Alex blasted back angrily, "Look, pinhead, whatever they are, I'm not ready to go. I didn't die in battle. They're *wrong.* They have the wrong guy. I mean uh, *huLLOOOO,*" Alex said, patting himself all over his upper body for effect. "I'm standing right here in front of you, aren't I? I'm obviously *not* de . . .'" He paused, deep in thought, his gaze distant, when a sudden look of fright washed over him. He only now realized something important.

It was Egypt when first he suspected. Set had enslaved the living, turned them into soulless creatures, and used them to bind Anubis; the only being capable of stopping him. They needed to reach Set undetected and there was only one way. Alex didn't like the idea, but he knew it had to be done. It was there in the trench at the foot of the pyramids, there where Anubis sent him to Tuat. In Tuat he was judged pure enough to be accepted as the dead, and move undetected by Set.

"*Crap!* I'm dead! I mean, I'm *still* dead. *Crud.* I can't believe this. Well, that's just perfect. *That's it!* I'm *so* going to smack Anubis upside his beady little eyes when I see him, that flipping good-for-nothing flea-infested, skirt-wearing bonehead. He's lucky I don't carry a rolled up newspaper or I'd land it clear across his drooling snout. I'll turn him into a stuffed rug and put him in front of my fireplace, the idiot. Why, the next time I'll . . . I'll . . . well, I'll kennel his hairy butt. Yeah, that's it," he continued.

"I can't believe he left me still dead. That *moron!* That has to be what happened. Those flying zombies think I'm still dead," he said.

Zach just stood there and smiled that same awkward, thin smile he gave earlier. It made Alex nervous then and it was making him nervous now. He didn't know why, but there was something odd about this lamebrain, aside from the obvious. The sun was lowering in the horizon, and it had already been a long day, so the boys pressed on toward the village, toward the unknown, and most important, toward food.

The village looked small as it came into view at the bottom of the shallow valley before them. The mountain range he noticed earlier framed the landscape in the far distance.

"Glad we're not going there," he said. "It looks cold."

"You should be grateful. It's where the *Jotunn* live," Zach

31

responded incredulously.

"*Jotunn?* Who are they?" Alex asked.

"Oh, um, I think they're what you call Ji-Unts," Zach explained casually.

"Ji-Unts? You mean *Giants?* Ha, I get it. You're loopy, aren't you? You know bonkers, goofy, nutso, daft, gone, wacko; perhaps a few watts shy of lighting the Christmas tree, aren't you?"

Alex dismissed his muddied companion as he would any other minor annoyance and, like most conversations between teenage boys, it was short-lived. Alex had more important things on his mind right now than make-believe; but still, something about what Zach said nagged at him. Mistaking it for more hunger pangs, this, too, he ultimately dismissed.

As they edged closer to their destination, the two boys smiled in unison, both thinking of their stomachs as most boys do. Without so much as a word, they quickened their pace down the grassy hillside toward the village.

It was unlike any place that Alex had seen before. Where he came from, houses were made of clapboard siding; not here. Here they're made of stone and what looked like mud and hay. The houses were small with grass thatch for roofing. Most had a stream of smoke rising from inside.

The dwellings were arranged randomly around a central area that Alex surmised was probably used for gatherings and events much like a village square. Small animals were running loose in the street along with both toddlers and adults alike. If it hadn't been for the now setting sun, the entire scene would've looked quite grey and dismal. The whole place looked *old.* It was the only word he could find to describe it.

As they approached, a small queasy feeling welled up from deep inside Alex. At first he thought it was his hunger reminding him again, but as it grew, Alex realized it was something else. He began longing for something distant, just out of reach. Thoughts of home flooded his mind. The sights, the sounds, even the smells from the small village ahead must've triggered something.

He missed the familiar smells of his own kitchen. Each tasty morsel filled his senses. *Mmmmm.* What he wouldn't give for the comfort of his own home, sitting in the living room by the raging fire on cold nights, the waters of the harbor blowing their cold up against the weathered boards of the old house.

Alex missed his grandmother most of all. Nothing could beat being squeezed to death in one of her hugs. Food may be important right now, but he'd gladly go without eating for weeks if it meant getting one of those hugs. *I've got to start going through my journal*, he thought, as he reached around to his pocket and patted the leather-bound book lightly. *There'll be answers in there, I hope.*

"If you don't mind, I think we'll go in the back way. I need to check things out first. The last time I was around a bunch of people, it was pure chaos. There were explosions, an angry hoot owl screeching god, a whole bunch of crazed drooling ankle nibblers . . . not the kind you can eat, mind you, and my friend Anubis, who's dead by the way. It wasn't pretty. So, yeah, if you don't mind, I'll sneak in the back way, if that's all right?"

"Ahhh, so you're a great warrior, no?" Zach said with a crazed looking smile.

"*Uh*, yeah. I guess so," Alex replied meekly, then beamed with the sudden mixture of pride and conceit. "Yes, I am," he said much more definitively, puffing out his small chest and smiling with his hands on his hips. "I'm Alex Chronos the Rawesome, conqueror of gods, vanquisher of all that's evil, and general all around good

33

looking dude," he said as he flipped his unruly mop back in what was quite a stylish flair. It fell back over his eyes in response.

"I knew it," Zach exclaimed as if he'd won the lottery. "And the gods, they've sent for you?"

"Well, I don't want to brag. Hey, we're here," Alex whispered as they approached the back side of the first structure. He saw Zach's eyes narrow. It gave him an uneasy feeling. Avoiding further discussion, Alex moved on.

The two boys circled to the left of the buildings, along the edge of a thin line of trees. Alex knew they needed to move undetected, but that particular task was proving more and more difficult with each step. The sun had since dropped behind the horizon, and dusk was upon them bringing with it a calm silence.

The problem was, Alex realized, he'd forgotten to tell the meathead who trailed him the importance of moving quietly. Every step Zach took echoed out into the clear night like a twenty-one gun salute, causing Alex to wince. Each breaking branch, each giddy snicker, and every accidental escape of noxious bodily gas threatened to expose their otherwise covert operation.

"*ERRAAUUPPP*," belched Zach one last time.

"*Dude*. Quiet," Alex said, turning toward him and placing his forefinger over his lips angrily. In truth, he couldn't help but laugh a bit on the inside. It *was* a good burp.

In addition to a couple of dozen similarly built houses positioned around the square, an inn sat at the far edge of the village. It was a larger building than the rest, built strong with a covered stable for animals jutting off to its side. That was Alex's destination. If he could get to the stable without being seen, he could find some grub and bed down for the night.

The shelter was just far enough out of the way and would soon be under the cover of darkness. It was a perfect spot for him to try and make sense of the mysteries within his journal. This leather-bound record he held so dear in his pocket was a chronicle of sorts. He had no idea where it came from; why it was, according to Ms. Trudie, *his*; or even understood anything written on its ancient yellowed pages. Every turn of a page led to more questions.

What he knew was that his grandmother entrusted the journal to Ms. Trudie, even before he was born. Unfortunately, that raised more questions. Most times Alex wished he'd never seen it, never walked into Ms. Trudie's store that fateful day.

Despite the grief that this journal had caused him, he knew that it also held many of the answers he was seeking. Once he found food and filled his gut, he needed to take some time to decipher it.

It was the third house they came to that brought them wondrous fulfillment. Alex's eyes popped out of his head, and he immediately began salivating. There, on the rear windowsill of this tiny little house was a feast fit for a king; or at least, that's how Alex saw it. He almost cried.

There was steaming fresh bread, a pie made with some sort of local berries oozing out from its side, and a single wrapping of smoked meat that sat on a table inside, next to the window. Neither knew what the meat was, but neither cared. They had to move quickly.

Alex crept up to the window, listening, stretching to hear any movement from inside. The light from the fire crackling in the one-room structure flickered lightly through the window and across the scattering of trees behind them. Their own shadows danced together wickedly across the branches.

The odors coming from this room were almost unbearable. Alex was virtually seething with anticipation. When he was absolutely sure that no one was inside, he sprang up, pushing a scooped hand into the hot pie. There's no time like the present, he figured.

It wasn't quite scalding, and the berries awakened his every taste bud in a frenzied celebration as he shoved a handful down his throat. Three different colored juices ran down the corners of his mouth and pieces of crust landed on his clothes. All sense of dignity left him. It was too good to be real and too delicious to be concerned. Besides, who am I going to impress? he wondered. The village idiot over here?

No sooner did Alex finish his thought, when he was shoved out of the way by two of the dirtiest hands he'd ever seen. He watched helplessly as those same hands were thrust, wrist deep, into the remaining pie. Zach was now having his turn at the steaming dessert. It was like watching the hyenas after a kill on the hot Egyptian desert. Food was flying everywhere. It was disgusting. That's all Alex needed. Enough was enough.

Alex grabbed the boy by his arm and pulled back hard, sending the stunned, berry-covered pest to the ground. As he sat there staring back at Alex, his expression turned from confused to defiant. Alex was caught squarely in the back of his head with a mud ball.

He wasn't only surprised at the boy's retaliation, but was also impressed that there was still enough wet muck left on him to form any sort of projectile. He must've dug deep down into I-don't-want-to-know-where to come up with that one, Alex thought. *Eeewwww!*

Before Alex could turn around, the boy had jumped back into the window, grabbed the thinner of the two loaves of bread, and began hitting him over the head with it. The loaf was still warm, and it didn't break apart like an older, drier loaf would. Instead, it battered Alex on the head multiple times before he became annoyed.

In the midst of their scuffle, Alex heard a noise. It came from the opposite end of the small room, the door. Someone's opening the door. They both froze.

"Quick, grab the rest of the bread," Alex whispered anxiously as he let go of a handful of crusty hair and motioned to the other loaf still cooling on the sill. Zach pulled the fresh loaf down and, *ulp*, tucked each under a different, *ulppp*, armpit. Alex didn't have time to complain; he had meat to get.

The door screamed as it slowly opened. He had to move fast. His body filled the window as the back of a large woman filled the doorway. Snatching up the meat, he was gone from sight before she turned. That was close. His heart was pounding, trying to get out of his chest. They moved on, down the back aisle, leaving the sounds of the woman's shriek and a whole lot of shouting behind them.

The inn wasn't far, and the commotion stirring behind them as a result of their last visit would draw attention away from them now. Rounding the corner at the last house, Alex's mouth was already watering. He was dying to sink his teeth into the meat cradled in his arms.

After wiping the drool forming at the corner of his mouth, he reached the first window of the stable, gave a quick yank on the shutter, and . . . nothing. It didn't budge. No biggie, he thought, as he moved on to the second. Again, nothing. *Humph*. Well, there are two more, so let's see. The third window proved no better.

Alex was getting frustrated and worried. He set the meat down carefully in the grass, eyeing Zach as he did with a warning. Standing fixed and firm on his feet, he spat in his palms and rubbed them together. He reached up with both hands this time and sent a final glance back at Zach, who by now had lost interest in Alex and was swatting at the flies circling his head.

Probably the same flies from earlier today, Alex thought, shaking his head. Why should the flies bother leaving? They have the one thing he didn't have right now; an endless supply of food.

Redirecting his focus back to the window, Alex tugged hard with both hands; nothing. He tugged again. The animals inside stirred, but the shutters didn't. He wasn't giving up that easily. Wiping his hands on his pants for a better grip, he reached up, preparing to win this battle of strength.

The shutters flew open. The force sent him reeling back, tripping over the meat he'd placed so gingerly on the ground only moments earlier. Somebody had opened the window from the inside. They knew he was out here. He was in the open, exposed. It was too late to hide. All he could do was wait.

A shadowy figure moved into the moonlight, framed by the stable window. Alex's eyes fixed on the shape. What was it? It was monstrous. It was frightening and hideous.

It was Zach! He was inside. But *how?* He was just . . . Alex turned his head.

"How the *heck* did you get in there?" Alex whispered forcefully. Zach just smiled stupidly and nodded toward a fourth window that had been left open. Alex's blood boiled. I've had it with this loser. The first chance I get, I'm ditching him.

Alex thought twice about handing the meat through the window to Zach. It may well be gone by the time he got inside, so he climbed and clamored, shinnied and wiggled his thin body up the side of the stable, the whole time holding onto the edible delight under his right arm. He paused, perched at the top of the sill, half in, half out.

Alex had always been clumsy, constantly tripping over his large feet. He was taller and much thinner than the rest of the kids his age. This made for his awkward posture, especially when he ran, or moved in general. Unruly brown hair fell thick and long into his eyes, and made it difficult to see most of the time. Alex felt it provided some mystery to his otherwise dull life. Unfortunately for him, at this moment, it all added up to one thing.

His grip had only loosened for an instant, but that's all it took, and he toppled inside, landing head-first in a pile of feed. The meat, treasured as it was, fared well.

"That'll leave a mark," Alex said to himself, holding the meat up high as he rolled off the pile. Dry feed had gotten into virtually every nook and cranny. It was in his eyes, his ears, even down his pants, the latter of which would undoubtedly cause him great discomfort the rest of the evening. Better than sand in my pants, he recalled not so fondly. Egypt had been a pain in his butt, so to speak, and so far, this place was running neck and neck with it. At least Egypt had Anubis . . . and Tad. He sighed. They made it bearable.

He first saw Tad in the marketplace. A simple look was all it took and he fell hard. From that point on, it would only be her. There was a softness about her in that harsh land. How long does it take to fall in love? he wondered. He looked down at the meat in his hand and smiled.

"Speaking of love," he said.

Alex brushed himself off with one hand while holding the meat with the other. There was no way he was going to set it down, even for a moment. He eyed Zach, who was now standing unconcerned in a small dollop of manure. When he finally realized it, he reached down with his hand and merely scraped it off.

"You used your bare hand to scrap off horse poop?" Alex asked incredulously. Zach shot back a blank stare. "That's gross, dude, even for you. Don't come near me until you clean that hand off," Alex demanded.

As directed, Zach wiped his hand across his chest, then extended it as if to ask for some meat.

"I didn't mean on your clothes! *Awww*, man. Now I know why they named you Unwashed Stink-Fart. You're not getting any of this unless I pull some off," Alex said as he hugged the meat tighter to his chest.

It was dark in the stable, and as his eyes adjusted, Alex could see several stalls lined against the far wall, but only two were currently occupied. They were both large horses and looked as though they were bred for work just as much as for riding. A few nervous piglets were corralled in a small wooden enclosure in the front corner.

Alex realized that any sudden movements inside these quarters would undoubtedly set off the animals, giving away their presence. He moved cautiously across the floor, dodging an excessive amount of droppings and several small tosses of hay. This place is a mess, even for animals, he thought. It was obvious the stalls hadn't been mucked out in a while.

Stepping over one such pile, Alex made his way carefully toward one of the empty stalls. It was on the end, providing them with the most concealment and the best escape options. He nearly jumped out of his skin when one of the horses whinnied quietly. To him it sounded more like his school band in full marching order. It seemed to echo through the stable, out the windows, and across the valley.

Collecting his wits, he tiptoed past the piglets, and something caught his eye, a glint of the moonlight that now shone brightly through every crack of the stable. It was cold and clear tonight, and Alex was glad to be inside. What was it? He moved in to get a better look. Horror washed across his face and he gasped.

There, on a post next to the corralled pigs, were hanging all sorts of metal cutlery and crude farming devices. Most still had, *ulpp* . . . They were covered in fresh blo . . . *urp* . . . *uummpff* . . . Alex brought his hand up to his mouth in fear of projectile vomiting. It was horrible. Medieval torture instruments are more like it, he decided, too late.

Alex let loose. The one thing he'd eaten for as long as he could remember was the handful of pie just moments earlier and now on the floor. It only took once; he wiped his face and was hungry again.

He slouched against the corner and dropped to the floor. The animals in the stable were still. Only he and Zach made any movement, and that was to ready for the pending feast. Alex pulled at the meat with his grubby hands.

Suddenly he was feeling a bit guilty about the pokes, both physical and verbal, he'd taken earlier at Zach, who was now sitting across from him waiting anxiously with a gleam in his eyes. As much as it was killing him, Alex leaned over and handed the first piece to the boy.

He watched with an odd mixture of amusement and revulsion as Zach snapped at the meat and devoured it. The guilt Alex was feeling abruptly disappeared as the boy tore at the meat like the flesh-eating vampires during movie night.

He'd already been sick once, and if he continued to watch the scene unfold in front of him, he would certainly blow chunks again. Not wanting the only food he'd eaten in days to end up on the floor again, Alex focused his efforts downward at the remaining slab of meat in his arms.

It was large, still warm; cooked to perfection, and it was gone. There was no time for savoring the delicious flavor. No time for taste. Moments later, both boys were leaning back against the wooden walls of the stall, each rubbing their bellies and dreaming of how wonderful the meal had been.

"The bread!" Alex remembered. Suddenly their feast was more, lasting. This was too good to be true. Is this Utopia? Shangri-La perhaps? Alex wondered. If Shangri-La had a feeling, it'd be this, he thought. Zach pulled the two loaves from under his arms and held them both out to Alex. He took them both, weighed them in each hand, reminding him a bit of the scale used in his recent visit to Tuat, the Egyptian equivalent of a place of judgment.

Both loaves were somewhat dirty, their heavenly odor replaced by the stench from whatever grew underneath Zach's armpits. One, however, looked far worse as a result of being battered over Alex's head earlier that evening.

"This one's yours," Alex said, throwing the tattered loaf back to Zach.

He did his best to eat the second loaf. Pinching his nose between his fingers, he swallowed bite after bite until it was no more. With the moon teasing its light across the backs of the beasts in the next stall, his mind drifted to past places, earlier faces, and events already told. He remembered his grandmother, first and foremost. She was always in his thoughts. Visions of Tad and Anubis drifted lazily through his mind. He'd see them again one day; he had to.

THREE

Alex didn't know what he was doing here in this strange and unfamiliar place, but he was certain he'd get back to those dear to him one way or another. If only he knew *how*. If only there was a clue. *If only I wasn't so dad-blamed uncomfortable.*

What the heck am I sitting on? Alex reached around and felt his way through the darkness. That's it! The journal. It can help me. He pulled the book out from his back pocket. *Aahhhhh*, instant relief, and he settled back down.

It was some time since the journal had been last opened. Only a few clues were ever deciphered from its pages. Most of the information it contained between its leather-bound covers only led to more questions. He rubbed his hand over its surface.

Thoughts of his last adventure now flooded his mind. An evil Egyptian god had taken over all of Egypt, exiled its true and beloved ruler Osiris, and made Egypt's people his slaves. Devoid of life, they were trapped, doomed to suffer; suffer, that was, until Alex freed Anubis, God of the Dead. As strange as it sounded, the two of them had quickly become close friends. A common enemy on the battlefield does that to warriors, Alex thought. Together they fought Set, side by side. Well, actually, I did most of it.

They'd been through a lot together in such a short period of time, especially having to fight all of those hounds, the marketplace, *the Sphinx!* Yeah, that last one was a doozy. Who'd have thought a million tons of angry stone would suddenly spring to life and chase me? he wondered.

Zach had fallen off to sleep. Now was as good a time as any. The moonlight where Alex sat was, with a bit of shifting and wiggling,

Troy A. Carrington

just about right. He cracked open the journal. The figures and drawings covered the pages. There seemed to be more than he remembered. He saw the familiar forms of Osiris and Isis. He smiled as his fingers gently brushed over them. Although he'd never seen either of them, they were a part of him now.

There were others he didn't recognize, other couples somehow significant to all of this. Most were drawn in long flowing garments, some with headdresses, some without, but they were always drawn in pairs, a man and a woman.

He flipped through the thin leafs slowly. There was finally time. Zach stirred, rolled, and drifted back off to sleep, snoring obnoxiously. It took all of Alex's concentration to get past the noise and through the task in front of him. He discovered something the last time he turned these pages. Not only was there a repeating pattern of couples throughout the journal, but there was also a second symbol illustrated on several sheets of yellowed paper. A shiver went down his spine. Man, why's that always happen? he wondered.

A serpent, large and evil, covered multiple pages as well. What's its significance? There was the serpent carved around the entrance to the outer cavern in Egypt, under several tons of sand, then there was the ghostly-white sea serpent that destroyed his boat on his perilous journey to Tuat. Did he see that or imagine it? It all seemed like a dream at the time. Adam and Eve had a serpent. *Yikes!*

Reaching under his shirt, he pulled out the pendant that hung around his neck. Strange little thing; it had a carving of a man and woman on it as well, not Osiris and Isis, though; a different couple. Alex glanced over at the boy across from him, who moved restlessly in the hay. The pendant also had a serpent on it that wrapped itself tightly around the tree in the center. This was the key to everything.

The journal was, well, information and clues, but the pendant, well, that was the key. It had to be.

As Alex held it high in front of his face, it glowed, and when he swung it, dangling from its chain, into the moonbeams scattered against the walls, it spun uncontrollably. It was just like in the cabin of the Mermaid. The stable burst with a pulsing light that danced off the walls, throwing strange shapes and figures all around. He was surrounded by pictures, clues, questions. Not here, not now; he couldn't risk being discovered.

Alex got nervous, fast. Was that a movement? His eyes darted around through the blasts of light. It was rather intense and blinding at times. The pendant was quickly tucked away in its hiding place beneath his shirt. It would have to wait until later, when he was alone. The light disappeared instantly. Only the moonlight remained.

He returned to the journal, three wavy lines. These, I remember. Could it be real? He dared to dream. According to his interpretation, it was the center of everything. It was all there in the Hall of Records. That'd be cool, he thought wildly.

What's that? Alex's eyes landed on a strange word he hadn't seen before.

"*Gleipnir*," he whispered. His eyebrows raised, and as he sat straight up against the wooden boards of the stall, a sound caught his ear. It was muffled, but near. No, it wasn't muffled; it was a scuffle.

Some*one*, or some*thing*, else was inside the stable with them. Had it seen the light that stretched across the old structure and emanated from his pendant? Had his own pendant given him away? There it was again. Alex froze. It was getting nearer.

Zach stirred slightly, and Alex jumped. He couldn't say a word to warn the boy, not even a whisper. All he could do was hope that Zach wouldn't move anymore. It was edging closer. Alex could hear its breathing. It wasn't human. It was . . . it was . . . *Oh no*. Zach moved again. No. Stop!

"Don't!" Alex yelled without thinking. Too late. Zach woke with a start, and whatever it was definitely knew they were there now. A large shadow cast across the far wall. Alex shrunk into the darkness to hide.

It was a *goat!*

"A flipping goat. Are you kidding me?" he said in a hushed tone to Zach, grabbing at his pounding heart. In response, the goat announced itself to the boys in its familiar utterance as if to say, *Feed me.*

Alex rolled, grabbing a handful of loose feed off the stable floor, and held out his hand to the intruder. The goat took three hesitant steps and was eating out of his hand. Alex snatched the short rope lashed around its neck and pulled the goat in close.

"You know, we can drink . . ." Zach trailed off, pointing at the underside of the goat.

"*Eww*. Gross, dude. I'm not drinking that," Alex returned, petting the goat's head.

"I will," Zach responded, and with one swift motion was on the floor with his head alongside the animal and his mouth wide open. It wasn't long before the milk was spilling out of his mouth and onto the ground. All Alex could do was sit and watch in disgust. He thought he could avoid the whole thing if he just closed his eyes and caught some sleep.

It was less than three seconds when a stream of milk arched through the air, across the stall, and landed against Alex's forehead. The thin white liquid ran down into his eye and along his nose, caught the corner of his mouth, and dripped off his chin.

"*Hey!* What the . . ." Alex sat up, surprised. He pushed Zach out of the way and grabbed at the underside of the animal. Alex was a novice, but this was war, and it didn't take long before the other boy was soaked.

"Take that, you walking trash heap," Alex responded. They laughed and rolled together, taking turns squirting each other. The goat itself was getting quite agitated.

When they were both done and the goat quite exhausted, it scurried off to find itself a safer and quieter part of the stable. Alex settled back on the hay bedding and leaned against the wall. The day's events were catching up with him, and he lowered his eyelids.

He was deep into his favorite dream involving an ice cream truck and a skateboarding Yeti when something woke him. Both eyes lifted to a much darker stable. The moon had drifted beyond its reach. There was a commotion outside and people were yelling. He was either still groggy and half asleep or they were speaking a language he couldn't understand. Both were possible at this moment, then it dawned on him; he was alone.

Where's Zach? Alex searched, quickly darting his eyes across the end of the stable. He slowly rose to get a better look, peeking over the top of the stall. It didn't help. He still couldn't see anything. The yelling was muffled, and Alex guessed whoever they were, they were moving away. Away was good, he thought. Where the heck was Zach? he wondered.

The goat let out a quiet sound, cracking the otherwise silent interior of the stable. Alex jumped in response, then quieted himself.

Nothing; he must've left. Alex was on his own again. Good, I like it that way, he thought. Settling down, he pulled out the journal and returned to his decoding. Might as well, I'm awake now. He flipped feverishly to the page that he'd seen earlier, the one with that symbol. Interesting. There were other symbols like it on these pages, but this one was slightly different. I can't believe I didn't see this before, he thought.

As he sat there and stared with his nose pressed close to the paper for confirmation, a heavy feeling washed over him. He felt a presence nearby, the kind of feeling he would get when he was walking home alone late at night, looking over his shoulder. It was the same feeling he had on his thirteenth birthday, before everything had happened, like someone was watching him. He wasn't alone.

A dark figure stood off in the shadows. Alex could barely make it out. He strained his eyes to focus. He wanted to know what his opponent looked like. As it passed by the open window of the stall, Alex could see it moving toward him. There was nowhere to hide. His fists clenched, Alex was ready to strike.

"*Yaaaaaa!* You again! Don't you people knock?" Alex grabbed at his thumping chest to push his heart back down into its resting place.

"Miss me, did you?" he asked as he closed the journal and quickly hid it back in his pocket. It was the old hag from this morning.

"You've already met the mischievous one. He's now part of your past, he remains in your present, and determines your future," she spoke calmly.

"*Whatever,*" Alex responded, sounding a little too much like the same teenage girls he so often ridiculed back home. His face reddened at this. He noticed immediately that her feet were about three inches above the dirt floor of the stable, floating.

This would've frightened anyone else, but not Alex. He'd seen this before, several times, actually. He was getting used to this kind of stuff. It wasn't normal, but then, Alex thought, *normal* hadn't come to visit me in quite some time.

"Why do you people insist on hovering?" he asked, waving toward her feet. "Did you get lost on your way to the rubber room? Are the men in white coats looking for you?" Alex asked mockingly, looking around the dark stable for effect.

"Hey, if I drank from a milk carton, would I see your face on it?" Alex jibed one last time. Given the fact that there was one ugly old witch hanging inches above the floor in front of him, he thought he was handling the situation rather well. His cheekiness was suddenly broken when a burst of raucous laughter rang out from inside the bordering inn.

"Aye. Showed him," he heard through the thin walls. More laughter echoed across the stable walls. When he looked back, she was gone. He glanced around, twisting his body and head, just to make sure. Yep, gone. Freak.

What did she say? Mischievous one? I've already met him? I haven't met anyone. No, wait. The wolf; she meant the wolf. Yeah, uh, okay. Now what?

In response, the voices coming from the inn grew louder and more frequent. Sounds like they're having a party, he thought. He knew he wasn't going to get anymore sleep. Might as well go see what all the fuss is about. Besides, I could use some information. Alex brushed himself off and took one last look around, hoping that he wouldn't actually see the woman again. It's not that I'm afraid of her; she's just sort of, well, creepy, Alex thought.

Thinking it through for a few seconds, he decided it would be much wiser to crawl out the same window he fell through only a few short hours before. Sometimes, he figured, it's better to hide right out in the open. I'm going in the front door. Gingerly stepping over one tired goat, he once again struggled with his gangly arms, pulling his thin frame up through the window, and once again he fell.

"Oommf."

He shot up from the tall grass like a gopher. The cooling night air had caused dew to form on the edges of the green blades and his pant legs were wet again. Alex worked his way around the back of the stable and out into the night, temporarily exposed. He was no longer confident that this was such a smart idea.

The front door of the inn burst open and a rather large, unshaven and particularly rough looking man stumbled out of the opening with a much smaller woman under his arm. The two were laughing as they held each other upright. She, Alex noticed, was doing most of the work.

They spilled out into the dirt street under the moonlight, unaware that anyone else was there. Alex dove into the shadows and froze. When they finally staggered off, he made his move toward the door.

Dim yellow light flickering from inside poured out through the windows and bounced against anything in its way. He could hear the laughter and loud conversation coming from inside; not much peace and quiet here.

The horses in the stable were restless, but well fed. It was as if these people cared more for their livestock than themselves, he thought. It was a hard life, having to wake up at the crack of noon to do all of that pillaging and plundering. He laughed quietly.

"Just when you thought you were safe, someone up and ransacks your hide and steals your goat. Suddenly you're goatless. That sucks," Alex joked quietly. It was risky, but still, he needed to go in. He needed information.

The door was opened only a crack, but it was enough for Alex to squeeze inside undetected. It took a few seconds for his eyes to adjust, but when they did he scurried off to his right to find a table hidden in the shadows of the heavy beams and low light.

Everything inside was wooden and rough. The thick warped floor cut from the highland pines had been worn smooth from years of large rough men just like the one who left a moment ago. Men of war; they weren't easy on anything.

The bench he sat at was cold and hard, made from a log sawn lengthwise. In the flickering light, Alex could see that the large hand-hewn beams supporting the roof ran across the tops of four hefty posts set along the middle of the open room, all in a row. With each dance of the flame, the beams showed their whitewashed stains from the pigeons cooing above.

In fact, the only thing in the oversized room that wasn't made from wood was the stone fireplace set against the left side of the room. Alex was too far away to enjoy its giving comfort, but still, it was better to lay low.

The same stout rectangular table was positioned several times along the outer walls to the left and right of the room, with occasional round cut tables strewn about in the middle surrounded by all fashions of stools and chairs. No two were alike.

There was a second door to the rear of the building, and Alex surmised it probably led to the kitchen. The last door, only a few feet away from where he sat, led back to the stable. He could've entered that door earlier, but he would have been noticed for sure.

From where he currently positioned himself, Alex wasn't quite sure whether the odor he smelled came from the beasts in the stable or the men who sat only a short distance away. Maybe even the food, he thought suspiciously, as a rather portly woman with an apron moved across the floor carrying several plates of the night's offerings. She was plain looking, and Alex guessed that the poor lighting was probably an ally to this woman's beauty, more so than any beauty cream could ever be.

There were at least a dozen or so guests that dark night, all of whom looked like slight variations of the last. Not much in the way of expressing their individuality, Alex thought.

Each man was large, easily over six feet, and had to duck below the low beams when they moved about. They were all clad in similar attire that consisted of some sort of animal skin or fur, scatterings of armor or leather around their wrists, and fur boots wrapped in leather strapping to below their knees; simple, sturdy, necessary.

They ate with the same ferocity as the hyenas under the hot Egyptian sun. They coveted their food, protected it from the others. They were hungry.

Alex watched as one man, one of the larger in attendance, purposely allowed the drippings of what he ate run down his long mustache and beard, saturating and staining it dark. *Gross.* His toothless laugh opened widely, showing the remaining chunks still half-chewed in his mouth. *Did I just see bone in there?* Alex wondered. *It must've been chicken or some other bird.*

Alex looked up. *No, couldn't be,* he thought. The pigeons did seem a bit edgy. *How smart were they anyway? Mmmmm, tastes like chicken.* Alex smiled.

Two other men sat together, just off from the crowd. Alex thought this a bit odd, given that everyone else was deep into the frivolities of the evening.

Alex always had a keen eye and paid close attention to his surroundings, a trait, he believed, that evolved from years of trying to avoid Jackson, or more precisely, Jackson's fist; a trait he needed to use from time to time, especially recently.

These two men were slightly smaller than the others, but not by much, and being obviously younger, were also far more muscular than the rest. In certain waves of light, they looked like brothers, twins even. Neither was old enough to have grown the same frightening beards of their companions.

Alex noticed right away that something was different about these two. They seemed jittery and nervous, he observed from beneath the corner shadows. He watched as they leaned in when they spoke, as if the words weren't for the rest to hear. Fortunately nobody had noticed him, including these two, so it was easy for him to steal a word or two from what was obviously a private conversation.

The inn was loud and filled with stories of great battles and triumphs. In any other situation, any other place, Alex would normally cast his doubt on the tales he heard, but not here. Here, they actually might be true. Each time the stout old maid delivered back and forth to the tables, Alex hunkered down into the corner darkness, out of the way. He needed concealment.

The two younger men looked distraught by their discussion. This intrigued Alex, who was straining his ears, stretching them to great lengths to filter out the boasts and meaningless chatter from the crowd, trying to focus on only the words between these two. The inn was loud, and this proved to be quite difficult for Alex who could only catch unconnected phrases and disjointed jargon, in an already heavily accented tongue.

It was clear to Alex that these two had been enjoying the ale a bit too much as they swayed back and forth in rhythm upon their seats. It must've also affected their ability to whisper, as was evident by the occasional "*sshhh*" from one brother to the other and back again.

"Yes, low-keyed. Yes," the first one said, under his furrowed brow.

"Cast out," continued the second brother, shaking his head as if he were ashamed.

"Yes and his brood with him," replied the first again, only much angrier.

"*Ssshhhh*, dangerous," hushed the second.

"... plots ... gods ... *sshhh*. Yes," agreed the other.

Whatever they were talking about, it was dangerous enough to make two overly large men scared. They said they needed to keep it low-keyed and quiet, something about the gods and a brood. That's the third time in a day someone mentioned the gods, Alex recalled.

Questions flooded his mind. What gods? Who are they? Why's it dangerous? I mean, does it always have to be gods? *Again? Really?* Instead of gods for a change, why couldn't it be something like oranges? I *like* oranges, except, of course, when the juice gets on a cut, then, not so much.

The conversation paused momentarily for some additional thirst quenching followed by some laughter and concluded with a head butt. It was executed with such great force that the resulting noise that echoed throughout the room caused a flutter above with what was likely tomorrow's meal.

The pigeons overhead exploded in a symphony of flapping and whooping. As Alex leaned in to hear more of their conversation, he was met with a first-hand introduction to the panicked birds.

"*Awwww*, crap!" Literally; in all of the excitement, the entire squadron of pigeons let their fear go, right down on top of Alex's head and right shoulder. White covered the entire side of his face. It was time to leave.

The front door was currently occupied with several more large, fur-covered night dwellers, each boasting his tale of bravery, and the kitchen was too far away to hope to make it undetected. The last door, the one to the stables, was his only option, but Alex needed to move undetected, so he did what most teenagers do best. He slouched. In fact, he slouched all the way down to the ground, sliding between his wooden seat and the colossal table.

This plan would've worked beautifully if it hadn't been for a rather large sliver of wood that had split from the bench and lodged itself into his lower back. The initial pain was quick and sharp, but when his momentum carried the full weight of his body downward to the floor, the spike carried its vengeance the entire length of his spine, tearing flesh from bone, or at least, that's how it felt.

When all was done, Alex rolled and rocked quietly under the table, with his arm twisted up behind his back, trying to reach that unreachable spot between his shoulder blades. Why . . . *oommff* . . . does this stuff always . . . *mmmuuhh* . . . happen to . . . *unghhh* . . . me?

His shirt was now torn, and when he pulled his hand back around, it was colored red. Alex was still in pain, but after all of his effort, he held in his hand a bloodied bark-covered wedge.

"*Sheesh*. I could surf on this thing," he whispered to himself, tossing it to the ground. It was obvious to Alex that this wasn't going to be as easy as he hoped. On all fours, every move he made twisted him up in pain from his open wound. I have to keep moving, he told himself. I can't stay here all night.

There was only a short distance to cover, but in that short distance, there were three sets of tables and chairs to navigate, and each was occupied. The expansive distance between the tables didn't make matters any easier either.

The searing pain between his shoulders radiated outward, and his body began to ache. Alex pushed and pulled himself under the first bench, careful not to scrape his back on the underside of its roughened bark. A move like that would send him screaming, and that's something he was desperately trying to avoid right now.

Now a gap; there was about three feet between his table and the next. It may as well be a mile, he thought. How the heck am I going to cross that without being seen? He waited. This group's a loud one and would hide any noise he made, but it wasn't noise he was worried about. Alex looked around for something, anything that could help. There, against the wall. That's it.

Alex moved sideways as far as he could before the table legs got in his way. He stretched his arm, reaching toward what looked like a dinner roll from last week's meal. Just about there. Almost. He paused.

Someone kicked a stool nearby and it rolled into his foot. He didn't dare move, not now. Alex closed his eyes, held his breath, and waited. He heard yelling and felt the stool move. Weeks seemed to pass as Alex waited. Slowly his eyelids opened. Nothing had changed. The stool had been placed upright, but he remained hidden, his arm still outstretched, his fingers extended beyond their limits. Got it.

It was slightly rounded and about the size of a softball. It weighs a ton, Alex thought. I feel sorry for the person who was going to eat this thing. Actually, *he's* the one I feel sorry for, Alex thought, as he spied his target. An older man, looking like his road was much harder traveled than the others, had made the mistake of drifting off to sleep near the warmth of the fire, and Alex had zeroed in on him.

It had been a while since Alex last held a ball in his hand. This wasn't a ball, but it felt nice. The angle wasn't perfect, but there was no choice. There was no room to wind up, so he had to throw sidearm. Three . . . two . . . one.

Alex beamed brightly. Nailed it! The moldy bread had sailed directly to its intended mark. It hit the nodding man's mouth and jaw with such force that it sent his drooling face backwards, sliding off his palm. The man woke with a sputter, jerking his head with such power it sent him over the back of his stool, cussing as he went down. He landed hard next to the fire, sparking his arm into a blaze.

"AAAAAARRRRHHH!" the man screamed, waving his burning arm around like a flaming pinwheel. Silence fell across the room, followed by an explosion of chaos and laughter as the maiden rushed over, wailing, and doused the aged warrior with a pitcher full of a thin white liquid. That poor goat, Alex thought.

Perfect; well, for him anyway. Not so perfect for the old man. Alex tried hard to keep from laughing at the product of his good aim. He couldn't help but let a couple of chuckles loose; fortunately, the roar from the others buried the sound. All eyes in the room were on the opera playing out next to the fireplace. Now's his chance.

Yep. Baseball. I'm joining the team this year. No question about it; time to move.

Hand . . . knee, hand . . . knee. He was out of harm's way for now. Alex looked over at the small gathering and decided to keep moving. Hand . . . kn . . . Alex paused.

Uh oh. One of the men had returned, blocking Alex's path. *Crud.* This was going to be tricky. He used all of his resources on that last episode. He was stuck unless he could think of something else. Think Chronos, think. He had nothing. *Man,* these guys smell, he thought; smelly, loud, and hairy. Wait, yes, of course. *Hairy!*

Cautiously and quietly he worked his way underneath the now crowded table, dodging two of the hairiest legs he'd ever seen. It didn't help that this guy was also giving off a foul odor. It burned his nose hairs and almost brought up his evening's meal. He had to act quickly. One pull and he'd be off. Reaching slowly up, Alex grabbed a handful of the man's leg hair and ripped.

"Yaaaaahhh!" the man yelled, grabbing his leg as he shot up out of his roost.

Alex looked down. He still had the man's clump of leg hair clenched in his hand. The towering man's face grew red and hot from embarrassment, so he did the only thing he could after that rather girlish shriek. He cocked back his hammer-like fist and landed it on the backside of the nearest head. It sounded like someone splitting wood.

The unsuspecting recipient had been laughing at the time and was sent, unfortunately, mouth wide open and face-first into his bowl of gruel. When he lifted his head, all sorts of questionable things ran down his face. Underneath all of the mess, Alex could see that he was angry.

The scourge of a man didn't dare retaliate, however, as his attacker easily overshadowed even *his* large stature. The room again erupted in laughter. They all seemed to take pleasure in each other's pain. Great, Alex thought, I'm in a room full of Jacksons.

Alex was getting both desperate and anxious. He couldn't wait around for the next act of this comedy to play out. No, he had to keep moving. When the man with the now patchy leg had his back to him, Alex rolled in his best ninja-like maneuver underneath the third and last table next to the door that led to his freedom. I'm practically home free, he thought. He sat for a moment to catch his breath. His heart was thumping like a drum.

At one point, he made the mistake of passing too close to a large beast of a man. As he did, he brushed against the hulking figure's leg. He paused, not moving. Had the man felt him?

Suddenly a freakishly large hand came down and rested on the top of his shaggy head. Fat fingers moved through his unkempt mane. No. *No way!* Am I being petted? Like a dog! He thinks I'm a dog. Are you flipping kidding me? What am I, the family pet? All he could do was keep still and endure the humiliation. This is just plain wrong, he thought, as he gritted his teeth. No way will Anubis ever hear about this. Not ever.

Alex waited patiently until the man lifted his hand. *Now.* He slid sideways under the table and toward the door, still on all fours. Pushing it open quietly, there was barely enough room to slither through and stumble down to the damp earthen floor of the stable.

The only thing the surprised man would've seen when he looked down was the door to the stable closing and something scampering inside. As if giving it no more thought, the burly man turned back to his meal and continued to fill his round face.

Safe. Maybe. Alex continued to move hand to knee through the darkness until he bumped head-first into a wooden bucket. The hollowed noise echoed through the night, and the animals that were fast asleep now stirred inside their stalls.

"Hey. What am I doing?" he asked himself as he stood to brush off. He made his way through the night to the same familiar corner of the last stall. The once bright moonlight that earlier flooded the stable was now gone and a cool fog had settled in, indicating that morning was approaching. The last thing he remembered as he slumped down and drifted off to sleep was feeling quite alone.

Alex tossed in the early hours of the morning, half asleep and desperately trying to figure out what the heck was poking him. *Ouch.* Restless and turning, he hoped he could pick up where he left off with his last dream, but instead visions of a great fanged snake flooded his mind. It was so enormous that it slithered and wrapped itself around the entire earth and began twisting and tightening, squeezing all life from the world. It was snapping its blood-covered fangs at him and landing each bite. *Ouch.*

He knew he was dreaming, but it felt so real. *Ouch!* Alex shot up, wincing in pain and shielding his eyes from the bright morning's sunlight edging its way through the window, only to find a wooden pitchfork stabbing at his ribs.

"*Owwww!* What the . . ." Alex blurted out. As his eyes adjusted, he could see that the bearer of this weapon was none other than the portly lady from the inn. She was screaming at him from the other end of the pitchfork, and it wasn't long before Alex heard the muffled sounds of bedlam rising from behind her.

It sounded like a bull running through the room and reminded him of the story Elsie Quinn told his Current Events class about her vacation to Spain. Apparently, the people of that country thought it was fun to funnel hundreds of angry bulls through the streets and try to outrun them. Yeah, that's a bowl of laughs, Alex thought sarcastically. Whatever you do, don't slap the baby bull, he thought, remembering a particularly sobering part of her story.

Just as his mind had drifted momentarily to humor, he was brought back to reality when an unusually large figure smashed through the door that led to the inn. Catching himself as he stumbled into the stable, the man gathered his wits and let out a growl that shook the wooden walls and spooked the animals. Almost on cue, the beasts erupted into a concert of barks and grunts.

This was all the distraction that Alex needed. He rolled out from under the sharp points that were starting to pierce his skin and scrambled across the stall. It was no use. The man reached a large club of a hand from behind the lady and wrapped it tightly around Alex's neck. As the man lifted him clear off the floor, Alex noticed a patch of bare skin on the grizzly man's leg. Oh great, he thought, as he choked for air.

The brute moved quickly for his size. His other hand grabbed Alex at his belt loops and hoisted him up horizontally. Before Alex could yell, he was airborne and sailing across the stable. It was in mid-air that his foot caught one of the posts and it spun him around like a helicopter, sending him crashing through the same sunlit window and out into the pen. He landed in the dung pile with a splatter, taking the lower half of the window and its sill with him.

The horses kicked and whinnied, sending the nearby piglets into a frenzy. A flutter of foul flapped through the window following Alex into their release; and through it all, Alex could hear the goat crying out.

Struggling to get up, Alex responded, "Unnnghh. I feel your pain, dude." The twinge in his ankle hadn't hit him until he stood. The throbbing told him it was swelling fast.

"Ow. Ow. Ow! Ow! Owwwuuhh!" Alex whimpered loudly. He was outside and in pain, but it was far from over. The patchy-haired mountain burst through the wooden wall of the stable, sending splinters and hay flying everywhere. Dust filled the immediate area, and the morning light dancing off the particles temporarily blinded Alex, causing him to slip backward into the pile of slop.

The man was on him again. He lifted Alex like a sack of potatoes and hurled him out into the square. The commotion woke those who hadn't already risen, and people flowed out from the lazy warmth of their homes to see the scene unfold.

Not one for words, the man mostly snarled, which made Alex want to catch the next horse out of town. He felt the tightening grip of a hand constricting around his thin neck. Much more and it'll snap, he thought in desperation. There wasn't anything he could do with a sprained ankle and a vice clamping down on his throat.

He was led by his narrowing gullet to the center of what Alex thought only yesterday was a quaint little town. Under the current circumstances, he was having second thoughts. He was dragged, kicking, and swinging, up onto a small platform where two wooden blocks stood, anchored and domineering. Alex couldn't help but notice how archaic and medieval they looked. Like flipping torture devices, he thought.

Some unfortunate sap, slumped over and sleeping, currently occupied the first one. The poor wretch had been positioned on the cross brace of the pillory while a second, equally massive board was swung down and placed over the top. The apparatus allowed for a person's head and hands to protrude through, locking them in place and rendering them immobile. Alex quickly surmised that although this was how it functioned practically, its true intention was to publicly humiliate the occupant.

"So I got *that* going for me," he muttered to himself. Hearing Alex's muffled voice, the man responded with a quick jerk of his hand. It was only moments before Alex found out how right he truly was.

A pungent, slightly familiar aroma filled the air and grew stronger as Alex approached. He slipped twice before realizing that garbage, complete with all the trimmings of rotted food, was strewn far and wide. It was on the platform, the pillory; heck, it was even on the poor fool next to him, whom, oddly enough, didn't seem to mind much.

Several stray dogs were lapping up anything they could from the scene to fill their empty stomachs. One such stray had taken to licking whatever ran down the prisoner's leg. He remained unfazed. As they drew nearer, Alex's sentinel gave a sharp kick to the ribs of the nearest mutt, sending it tumbling into the others with a series of yelps.

Despite his rather bleak situation, Alex chuckled to himself as the pack scampered off. "I remember that noise, real well."

Several of the villagers gathered in the street just in front of the platform. The looks on their smudged faces said everything. They were anxious and excited; some appeared to be salivating. Their anticipation was building as it typically does in crowds, feeding off one another. Their voices grew louder while their children ran wildly through the crowd laughing and playing. It was like movie night to them, Alex thought. The only thing missing was the popcorn. From the corner of his eye, he caught a couple of younger lads carrying baskets. Curious.

As he was wrangled around the second pillory, Alex passed the pathetic soul who stood cast in the first and saw something familiar. *Ahhhhh*, so this is what happened to him, Alex realized. It was the rather odd boy he encountered earlier in his travels, his rather annoying companion of yesterday. It was Zacherie. Mystery solved.

Doubled-over with his weight on his good ankle, Alex felt the heaviness of the unforgiving swing arm come down hard, landing with a thud around his neck and wrists. Although he couldn't see it, he heard the sound of a pin being driven down through the chain for good measure. He was stuck. What now? *I know I keep asking this, but how the heck did I get here?*

He stood hunched over and staring at his feet. They were unusually large for someone his age and were always getting in the way. His grandmother would always sigh when she bought him new shoes. She'd say, "You're growing up too fast. Quit it." *Boy, I miss her,* he thought. *Wonder what she's doing right now?* His thoughts were interrupted.

The crowd roared with laughter as something soggy landed squarely against the pillory that Alex now occupied, sending rancid juices spraying up against the side of his face and into his hair. Cheers echoed across the small valley.

With the coming of new entertainment, so to speak, and the welcomed opportunity of newfound torment, the villagers closed their ranks and let fly a barrage of rotten projectiles. Alex was covered . . . and foul. There was a slight pause for reloading.

"*Unnfff.* That last one must've been Sunday's dinner," Alex joked. There was nothing else he could do but to make light of it. Eyeing one young mother handing her child what looked like some sort of brown something or other, he yelled.

"*Sheesh*, lady, can't you just get her a puppy or something?" Alex turned slightly toward Zach and spoke more softly, "I blame poor parenting."

Unfortunately for Alex, the child had unusually good aim. He stood there unable to move, with the over-ripened liquid of last week's meals running through his hair.

"So how's that working out for you?" Zach asked smugly. Alex guessed the boy had been waiting all day to throw that line back at him. He felt sheepish.

"Not well," Alex responded quietly in his best Zach-like accent.

Another assault landed hard against his cheek.

"Not well at all." He would've never guessed tomatoes, but as the liquid dripped from his nose, he couldn't mistake their pungent smell when he unwillingly inhaled the stinging acid, burning his nostrils. His eyes began to water as he licked the food from around his lips; not the way he wanted to get his next meal. Gross, he thought, but effective.

The thrill of humiliation seemed to have left the crowd, or

perhaps they simply ran out of food to throw. Either way, they gradually dispersed and left the boys to suffer through the remainder of the day. At one point a raven, black as coal, perched itself on Alex's pillory, pecking at the drying food until it landed one sharp beak into his skull.

"*Oww!* Hey, git!" Alex yelled, shaking his head furiously. The bird flew off into the distance cawing the entire way and cussing back at Alex.

It was midday and the sun was at its highest, beating down on his head. Sweat beaded from his temples and rolled to the tip of his nose, hung for a moment, then dropped to the ground. Hours ago he discovered the best position to stand without placing pressure on his sore ankle. The only problem was, now, it was asleep. His whole leg had gone numb from the tingling.

Meanwhile, the clueless dimwit next to him had taken to humming to pass the time. It had gotten on Alex's nerves. *About two flipping hours ago!* he thought. I swear he's doing it on purpose. If I ever get out of here, I'm going to pull his bottom lip up over his head. Let's see what sort of noise he makes then.

The sky was still bright, casting shortened shadows down to the ground indicating the sun was high, but Alex's thoughts of pummeling the boy next to him were cut short by the sound of distant thunder. It rolled off the far mountains and echoed through the village. It doesn't look like rain, he thought for a second.

As it shook, the little stone houses rattled to their foundations. The vibrations sent all manner of beast, four-legged and flying, spilling out from the stable. Suddenly the street, the entire village, was alive with fear. Mothers gathered their children and ran inside. Men frantically scrambled for their weapons, readying for the unknown.

This isn't any old thunder, Alex thought.

"Oh crap!" Alex said aloud as he realized the hooves of a thousand ghostly steeds rained down from the heavens, heading for the village. They were at the foot of the far hill, coming fast. He couldn't see much, bent over as he was, but every now and then if he careened his neck just right, he could see their formations. They were almost military in nature, yet different somehow. They were vicious and uncaring, and they were dead.

"*Valkyries!*" Alex yelled. On this, the village went quiet. Every head turned and stared at Alex.

FOUR

"*Uh*, was it something I said?" he mocked, staring back into the confused crowd.

These were strong men, powerful men of battle. Pain and suffering came natural to them. Blood was frequent in their lives, but *this*, this scene that unfolded before them, they'd only heard of, spoken of, until now. They were scared, and Alex could feel it. They aren't the only ones, he thought.

A surge of pure energy burst outward from the farthest house at the edge of the quiet village, breaking the momentary silence. Stone and timber was sent everywhere as the first of the advancing Valkyries entered the village. Screams filled the air and hung, only to be replaced by more. Panic.

A flank of wraiths rolled out and surrounded the once unimportant village and closed in, tightening their ranks. Hundreds of heaving mounts, held barely under control by the demon-beauties at the reigns, stomped restlessly just outside the village. They wanted in. This is what they do. This is why they exist.

The tiny village was laid out with houses in two semi-circles bowed around the center platform on which Alex currently stood. He didn't have much of a military mind, but thought that this particular design was probably for protection from invaders. He found it ironic that this same design was what now kept the villagers imprisoned and virtually helpless, like fish in a barrel.

One by one, the same fierce she-devils from yesterday swooped down upon the village, casting fear in front of them and leaving destruction and waste behind them. Covered in gleaming armament, the second two riders split off at full gallop chasing down a particularly repulsive looking man who had broken off from the crowd and ran wildly into the nearest house. It was only seconds before they were on him.

With a slight flick of the reigns, the forward Valkyrie coaxed her steed onto its back legs. The beast tore madly at the door, disappearing inside; her companion calmly followed. Eerie howls bled out through the windows.

As much as Alex hoped they were the Valkyries merely bellowing out their war cry, he knew better. All else in the village remained quiet, as if stunned by what was happening. The bulk of the enemy's force remained paused in silent vigil just beyond the houses.

A muffled cry for help came from inside the house, a crash, a thud. The roof collapsed from within, sending dust mushrooming upward through the rafters. A flicker of flame found its way through those same rafters. The house was suddenly on fire. *Get out now, you idiot!* What's *wrong* with these people? The clatter grew louder.

Alex wondered how much more destruction could be done to such a small house. He watched out of the crook of his eye as the flames grew higher. The battle-ready horses whinnied and bucked. Even they, dead as they were, didn't like the fire.

Terror screamed out. Alex jerked his head in a twist toward the grisly sound. When he did, the man who'd been chased inside was thrust back through the wreckage, lifted, and carried upside-down on the tips of two sharp spears.

As the two specters carried him through the undersized entry, dangling him like the spoils of a victory, the army of phantoms that waited beyond roared in a rally of high-pitched shrieks, banging spears on shields. The noise cracked across the sky with thunder. That's not good, Alex reflected.

The man hung about four feet above the ground by a single fur-covered boot, trembling and muttering incoherently to himself as if he'd snapped. Women in the square cried out in horror. In truth, Alex thought, it was much more embarrassing than horrific, but to men like these, which was worse? I mean, come on, beaten up by two girls on ponies? I'd hate to be that guy, Alex decided. Pansy.

This had no sooner played out when the next champion of vapor and mist began her ride down through the center of the village. As she approached, a long steel chain dropped from her side and unfurled a spiked mace at the end. She jerked it up above her head and began to whip it wildly about. After three turns of her weapon, she let it fly, sending it sailing through the nearest window, her stallion at full run.

As she urged her ghostly steed past the first house, she leaned forward into its mane and straightened the long chain with a tug. It went rigid and locked itself around one of the massive beams that supported the outer walls.

The house collapsed in an eruption of straw and splinters, bringing roof and timber to the ground in a heap.

"Hey, that was somebody's home!" Alex cried out. Despite how these people had treated him, it had been some time since he'd seen his own home and he somehow felt sympathetic for them.

With a second jerk, out snapped the mace from under the debris, searching for its next target. It found one when it smashed through the stone wall of the same inn that only hours earlier Alex shared with both man and beast.

A chaotic symphony of noise rang out from inside the stout structure. Two and four-legged creatures alike scurried out through every crack and crevice made available from the onslaught. Piglets ran squealing, anxiously looking for their mother. A sea of feathers fled the stable clucking in angry unison. From the inn, the once brave men were now stumbling over each other in fear. It was hard to tell which was making more of a raucous.

The Valkyrie howled in triumph. She continued on through the street, through the scampering masses. These people were scared and they had every right to be. It's not every day that angry howling female barn swallows come knocking on the door, Alex thought. They're here for a reason, and it wasn't to borrow a cup of sugar.

The plump woman from the inn ran screaming and half-crazed across the once quiet road, kicking up a dust cloud as she went. Alex felt helpless as he watched her dart aimlessly back and forth until one of the small burros from the stable made the mistake of getting in her way. Alex gasped as she fell head over heels across the top of the diminutive beast.

The burro, which had been quite content quietly pulling down loose straw from the now exposed walls of the stable, was taken by such surprise that it started bucking, coughing with every jump it took. The unfortunate waitress who was now busy steadying herself and pulling her stained apron down from over her head looked up at exactly the wrong moment from where she sat.

The burro landed a wild hoof to the side of her head and she was out cold. For a second, Alex thought he actually saw little birds chirping around her head before she hit the ground.

"*Oooohh*, that'll leave a mark," he spoke aloud.

Both specter and mace were approaching fast. She unfurled her rage yet again, this time dragging it behind her, purposely letting it leap and skip across the dirt road, causing obliteration with every movement. Her eyes locked on Alex as she kicked her bladed heels into the exposed ribs of the massive creature beneath her. She let out a bloodcurdling cry announcing her intent.

"Oh crap," he muttered to himself. He looked around frantically from his rather precarious position still stooped in his restraints. Nothing; no means of escape. Suddenly, tomatoes to the face weren't so bad.

She was upon him in seconds. The beast below her was restless. That same beast knew what was coming, and so did Alex. Well, it's all over now except the crying, he thought. He could see the familiar hollow of her eyes as she closed in on him. It was that same vision of death set deep within her that he'd seen before. The souls of her conquered were welling up inside her, haunting her, driving her. She was every bit a warrior, fierce and relentless, and now those same eyes were locked on him.

The monstrous stallion reared back on its hind legs in anticipated triumph. The Valkyrie snapped her wrist and the mace began swirling high above her head. The noise cut through the screams of the crowd. Alex needed to buy some time, so he did what he does best.

"Maybe we can sit and talk about this? You know, over some hot cocoa. No? Come on, you obviously like me. I can tell. I can see it in your, uh, *bones?* It's my hair, isn't it?" he remarked and did his best to flip it to one side. "The ladies dig the hair. No? My eyes then?" he asked, batting his lashes at her. "I know, I know, it's just my overall rugged good looks, isn't it?" he quipped as a mass of thickened gruel slid across his brow, down from his hair and ran into the corner of his mouth.

She wasn't amused and let out a scream defining her displeasure.

"Soooo, that's a *no* then? Really? Because I felt something there for a moment, didn't you? I'm pretty sure there was a connection, a spark. Well, I guess it could've just been gas."

As Alex lowered his head in defeat he caught a glimpse of movement to his side. Zach? What the heck's he doing now? Alex's

71

heart pounded and the Valkyrie seemed to sense it, perhaps even feel it. He had this feeling once before and didn't much like it, not at all.

An overwhelming sense of helplessness flooded his mind as his thoughts were suddenly swept back to Egypt. He remembered lying there on the cold slab, immobile, Anubis ignoring his screams. Ammit had entered, thrashing her vile tongue and edging ever closer. She wanted to feast. She wanted his heart. He was alone then, he's alone now, Alex considered quite clearly. This same clarity quickly brought him back to the present. His time in Tuat wasn't pleasurable, but he survived.

Alex heard it land. How could he not? It startled him much like Matilda did every morning before school, steel on wood. The outcome was predictable; the mark wasn't. To Alex's surprise, the mace had landed with such force it shattered Zach's pillory loose from the post and platform.

"What the . . ." Alex blurted, still dazed at what he'd seen. For a split second, joy had replaced his fear. He wasn't sure how, but she missed. There's no way, he thought.

The scene played out before him, a pile of debris, the backside of a retreating warrior, and his uncommonly foul acquaintance still locked in restraints at the arms and head, fleeing for his life. She must've struck the wrong one; and he, Alex glanced at Zach, *survived?*

With the immediate threat over, Alex watched in utter bewilderment at Zach, who was now running in circles in the middle of the road unaware of the danger that surrounded him. The pillory bounced off anything in its path, each time sending him flailing to the ground.

It was hilarious actually, Alex thought, seeing him run around with such a bulky device strung across his neck and arms. The imbecile. If it weren't for his own current predicament, he might actually laugh.

Miraculously, the schmuck actually made it past the Valkyries and down the nearest alley unharmed. They weren't concerned with him; they had a mission, and Alex had already guessed what, or who, that was.

"Does this mean we're not dating anymore?" Alex yelled after the Valkyrie. "Look, I'm sorry, but it's not you; it's me. Well, actually, I'm pretty sure it *is* you, you bleeping bird-brained banshee!"

The skeletal vanquisher galloped away, mace still spinning above her head. It was loose once more. This time it blew a hole through the nearby drinking trough, sending about a hundred gallons of murky water spilling out onto the road; instant mud.

Alex looked around, half expecting to see Zach come out from the shadows and take a swan dive head-first into the fresh soup. No luck. Where the heck did he go? The coward.

With all that happened in the past several moments, Alex had almost forgotten about the panic that swept over the townspeople. All forms of color had left the day. The advancing Valkyries had brought with them a fog that settled on the town in a thick grey blanket. From the fog would only come death in the form of more demon warriors.

The Valkyries drifted feet above the ground, fixed in their leather-worn saddles. The clouds above clashed in their own battle, egging on what played out below. Rain fell from the sky in taunting fashion, and the warrior legion's once gleaming armor dulled in the haze of the day.

As the beasts in the herd snorted in disgust, warm steam pushed through their flaring nostrils, rising from the cold depths of their soulless forms. Wet and dismal, Alex shivered as a chill ran up his spine. *Man,* could this day get any worse? he questioned.

Bad move. The Captain would always say, "If you have to ask the question, you already know the answer." Yes, yes it could get worse, much worse.

Sure enough, another Valkyrie broke rank and raced through the town. This one was smaller than the rest and wielding an enormous double-bladed battle axe, easily her same height. *Great,* Alex thought, just what I need, a flipping fairy with a Napoleon complex.

She may have been small, but her yell was just as piercing as she held the axe high above her head. She rode on, dropping her arm to her side allowing the axe to slide through her hand, blade down. Her eyes locked, just as the last warrior's had, on Alex.

"Crud. They're taking turns," he spoke to himself. "Look," he yelled, "I don't make it a habit of dating more than one girl, *uh,* or whatever the heck you are, at the same time. It causes, umm, you know, complications. I mean, I don't need you ladies fighting over little old me."

With a flick of her wrist the axe spun high and came back down, driving its blade deep into a nearby hay wagon, her eyes still fixated on Alex. Her steed didn't miss a beat; he continued to advance.

A second flick and the blade lifted the wagon, a third and the axe released its grip sending the wagon and its contents spinning through the air and crashing to its side, cracking several spokes from its wooden wheels. It was easy to see that her job was to terrify her enemy through destruction. It was working.

"You're lucky I don't have a huge fly swatter or a jumbo bug zapper," Alex threatened out loud, his fist clenched. The Valkyrie hissed in response, but still she charged ahead.

74

If changing back and forth between girly and ghoulish was any indication of how angry they get, then this one was ticked, Alex thought; *but then, I have that effect on most women.* She was approaching fast, her mount plowing through anything that dared get in its way.

It was then that Alex saw it. He had to blink twice. Why, this had to be the dumbest thing he'd ever seen. Well, maybe not the dumbest, his mind racing around recent memories of Zach, but definitely up there. The hulking twins from last night stood side by side in the path of the oncoming attacker. *Are you nuts?* Alex wondered.

Unfazed, she leaned low in her saddle and kicked her heels. The beast beneath her lunged forward, pushing swirling clouds of mist up behind it. The twins couldn't get out of the way fast enough. Their hardened muscles may have been enough to battle most enemies, but this was no ordinary foe.

"Get out of the way, you knuckleheads!" Alex yelled at the top of his lungs.

Too late. One of the brothers was caught against his chest with the full force of the charging animal, sending him spinning laterally through the mist. He landed face-first into the mud, dazed.

His brother was less fortunate and caught the top of the spirit's armored boot squarely with his lower jaw, cracking it and driving it into the teeth above, shattering most of those he had left. Blood ran from his mouth as he wailed uncontrollably, grasping at the pain. Unaware of his surroundings, he spilled over into the town's well and disappeared.

Unwavered, the abomination drew closer. The pounding of the approaching hooves echoed in Alex's head, louder and louder. *Strange,* Alex considered, *since they're riding on vapor.* Regardless,

75

one thing was for certain; she was coming for him.

Her axe was free and again dropped to her side. The cold steel sang as it cut through the damp air. The Valkyrie screamed. Deadly accuracy sunk the blade deep into the pillory. The crazed mount grunted and heaved. Again, it urged its master. The blade was splitting the air once more. It landed the only way it could, with force.

Alex's restraints, the thick wooded pillory that held him so securely, had been torn from its post. Freedom . . . sort of. His ankle was sore, and much like his friend, the top half of the pillory was intact. Still, he could move, though.

He was good at running, just ask Jackson. Back home, his curse was to deal with the likes of Jackson. Alex, of course, was his favorite pawn. So, at an early age, Alex became skilled in the art of evasion.

Jackson was easily twice his size, having been left behind a grade or two and rarely ever travelled without his crew of minions. Out of necessity, fear more so, Alex took to running. He was always safe as long as he could get in the open and run. *Wait. That's it!* I need to get out of here, out in the open.

Using his one good ankle, he jumped off the platform that only a moment ago held him fast to the ground, feinted to his right, and dodged the next falling blow from the razor sharp battle axe. He moved as quickly as he could past his attacker, causing her steed to rear back and redirect the swing of her weapon.

He caught her by surprise, and the resulting blow passed through her mount like a knife through air. Alex knew he didn't have the luxury of pausing to assess any damage. He needed to keep moving.

Unsteady on his feet with the weight of the remaining timber strewn across his back and bearing down on his ankle, Alex had a sudden understanding for Zach's escape. The shifting weight on his shoulders was awkward and cumbersome, but he wasn't about to stop now. Each tortuous step drove stabbing pain up through his leg and the massive beam down onto his wiry frame.

The pain was growing, but he had to keep moving. Alex slowly lifted his head to survey his options. This would be easy if it weren't for the flipping tree trunk on my blasted neck, he thought.

The tip of the beam he carried caught the temple of a misfortunate soul trying to escape the chaos in the muddied lane. The impact twisted Alex's body around as his feet stood firm, buried in the muck. He felt his ankle give way and pop. Suddenly the pain was gone, and all that was left was a warm numbing sensation. I'll take numbness over pain any day, he thought.

The lesser fortunate man was unconscious, face-down next to him. Alex fought to keep the world around him from whizzing by, but it took a moment for the dizziness to leave his head.

"Thanks, dude," he said, looking down at the man. His thought was quickly interrupted, and his eyes slowly lifted from the vibration. She was at the opposite end of the village, but that didn't make her seem any less frightening. Her steed reared gracefully and crashed to the ground, pushing ripples of movement across the vast space between them. The earth around him quivered in response, sending tremors through his body.

Having just broken free from the rage of the last death moth, Alex noticed this new one had peeled off from the pack and began charging. She was next.

"Well, at least they're polite," Alex shouted. The weight of the beam dug deep into his shoulders, rubbing until blood began seeping through his shirt. It felt unusually warm in the surrounding air, and he could smell the iron in it. Still, it was nothing compared to what would happen if they caught him, he considered briefly. With so much debris in his way and an unsettling mist blanketing the village, Alex knew his only route was a direct one.

He moved toward the dark unknown. Each gained speed, edging faster and faster toward the other, opponents in a game of chicken, wondering when the other would pull away, scared. Neither, however, strayed from their course. Alex leaned into his run, gaining momentum, then at the last minute executed a perfect spin using the weight of the timber to glance off the charging mount, deflecting its force to his left, sending it and its rider to the ground in a puddle.

"Nothing but wet," Alex said.

He didn't have any time to waste being smug, and he knew it. With that, he ran off, dodging the ruins of what was once a small quiet village. Destruction lay at his feet. For a moment it reminded him of the marketplace back in Egypt. He went there to find the ingredients he needed to travel to Tuat. He wasn't alone; the demon hounds had followed him there. That, too, had been a battleground.

Was that it then? he wondered. Are death and destruction going to follow me everywhere I go? Is it my fault? Am I responsible?

Passing the remnants of the last stone wall, Alex headed out, away from the village and toward freedom.

"Ooof." Well, sort of, he thought. The weight of the timber upon his shoulders had become so unbalanced that he fell to his knees. The pain was growing. He needed a way to free himself.

Struggling to get up, he headed for the cover of the nearby trees, just beyond the village and its invaders. The mist was lifting, and Alex suspected that, without him around, the Valkyries would eventually leave the village and return to whatever nesting ground they came from.

Just steps from presumed safety, he turned back for one last look. The Valkyries were indeed leaving, but being right didn't make him any happier. From this distance, he could see the village had been leveled. Encountering the Valkyries was like having relatives come for a visit, he thought; nice to see them, but, man, I don't want them hanging around too long. Alex knew it wasn't over.

FIVE

The dark woods seemed to beckon him. Strange, he thought; but he'd seen stranger. Zach was long gone, and Alex knew he had no chance of finding him in the dense forest. Alone again, he hesitated there at the small opening, wondering what this path ahead held. Would the forest embrace him, protect him even? Was it the way home? Or did it hold a more sinister plan?

The footpath forced its way through the thick woods, making it difficult for Alex to maneuver with his heavy load. He searched for something, anything that he could use to remove the weight from around his neck. A few steps away he noticed a large tree that split at its trunk. Perfect, he thought.

As Alex turned and started off the path, the dangling chain that still secured him to his plight caught on a low-hanging branch, suddenly jerking him back similar to a barking dog on a leash. He landed flat on his back, moaning.

"Who puts a kid in a contraption like this?" he asked. "Like I said, poor parenting," he answered himself. His words danced through the woods in an echo. There he lay, looking up at the green canopy above. Strangely, for being in the woods, he noticed no sound. The trees weren't only silent, they were still. This made him a little uneasy, and the more he thought about it, the less he liked the idea of staying here.

He rolled from side to side in an awkward jerking motion that left him looking and feeling quite like a turtle on its back, but it worked. He was up, if only for a moment. He stumbled slightly and fell again, this time unintentionally wedging the pillory in the notch of the tree. The force of his fall split the two massive pieces apart, pulling the chain from the wood. He was free!

Freedom, however, didn't make his neck feel better. Freedom didn't make his shoulders stop bleeding either, but it was freedom nonetheless, and it felt good.

Sliding back to the ground and feeling a bit dazed, he looked at the pillory and uttered, "I meant to do that."

It was now, finding himself surrounded by the vast forest, that he realized he was alone; not just because Zach was nowhere to be found, but alone much like he felt in Egypt. He always kept to himself back home, but being a loner and being alone are two different things, he thought. He was forever grateful for his grandmother's love and affection, then, in Egypt, for Anubis; but neither was here now.

It was this feeling that forced him to stand, take a deep breath, and pull the twigs from his hair. Any direction's as good as the next, he thought, so he began walking, edging farther into the thick forest, farther into the unknown.

As he moved forward, the once still trees creaked and swayed to life. He felt no breeze, but the great firs that towered above him moved almost violently. Were his eyes playing tricks on him?

Alex heard Zach's faint laughter buried in the thickness. "Where'd that loon run off to now?" he asked himself. The laughter grew and echoed in the woods, each tree redirecting it. It was a laughter that hastened toward the maniacal.

"That dude's loopy," Alex said aloud, mostly to keep his wandering mind company.

The path narrowed ahead, and he could see it would be difficult to navigate the farther he went in, but he had to. He knew what was behind him, and the urge to move forward was rising inside him. Either that or I'm hungry again, he thought.

81

Pushing through thicket and low-lying brush, dodging limb after limb, it was as if the forest was pushing back, trying to stop him from going any farther. At its thickest, Alex stopped. He could move no more. The limbs, the forest itself, were clawing at him, grabbing and holding him. With every attempt, their grip tightened. They wrapped around his neck, his legs; there was no use in struggling, but struggling was just what he did.

Zach's laughter was all around him now. Am I going crazy? he wondered. His chest pounded and grew heavy. He was out of breath. A sudden flash of light and heat surrounded him. Grabbing at his chest with his free hand, he knew what it was. He'd felt it before. A heart attack! It had to be. No, wait, he thought, feeling slightly embarrassed. The pendant! It was glowing white.

Alex quickly removed the necklace from under his ripped shirt and held it high in front of him. The tree limbs clawed at his arm, pulling at it, as if they knew. Seeming to sense the danger, the pendant grew brighter. Limbs and vines recoiled, shrieking as they shriveled away into the safety of the forest. Alex grabbed at his throat, rubbing it while he coughed away his own fear.

He took a single deep breath, then did what any mature, self-respecting thirteen-year-old man would do. He kicked at the retreating vines and limbs feverishly, until his feelings of fear turned to those of victory. Confident he'd won this battle, he gave one last kick for good measure.

It proved to be one kick too many. Again, he lost his balance, tumbled head-first into the brush, and somersaulted through to the other side. It took several moments for his head to stop spinning. His bruised body ached as he rubbed at his side.

He landed on a flattened patch of grass where it appeared as though some animals had recently bedded down. Good idea, he thought, as he crawled on hands and knees, collapsing flat-faced onto the soft grass. He was asleep in moments. Visions flooded his mind. His grandmother, the journal, Tad, Anubis, even flashes of people he didn't recognize danced in and out of his head.

Something, a noise maybe, perhaps a feeling, slipped into his dreams as he slept unaware. He awoke with a start, wiping the drool from the corner of his mouth. The woods were dark and quiet, letting him know that night had come.

"Must've been dreaming," he told himself. Alex slowly stood. The pain from his shoulders shot up and down his arms as his shirt pulled at the dried blood. Now's not the time for pain, he thought, rubbing his arm. Something's out there, watching, waiting. He stood, pressing his gaze into the darkness. He knew something was there, just beyond the black, something hidden, frightful.

Alex didn't dare move. I know how these things go, he thought. I've seen the movies. I get chased through the woods, trip over nothing, then get pulled back into the darkness by my feet. All that's left are my howling screams cutting through the night. Next scene, some dude in a hockey mask is skipping through the streets. A chill ran through his body. I'll pass, he thought. Focus Chronos, focus.

Somewhere close, a twig broke. The hairs lifted on his arms. His body went rigid. A low gurgle rolled out through the brush in front of him. Something moved. His heart raced, its beating echoed like a drum through the woods. He was certain the noise would give his location away.

"No, boy, not the noise, your fear," a voice responded to his thought.

Something big had launched itself through the darkness toward him. A wild roar rung out, piercing the silence. Alex could only see shadows, darkness upon darkness moving. Just before he felt it, he saw eyes, green and evil. Everything seemed to move in slow motion. This happened to him once before, in Egypt. He needed to react, to . . . too late.

The impact sent him tumbling backward into the thickness of the forest. As he rolled helplessly, his head glanced off a small tree sending a flick of blood from his eyebrow and through the air. He skidded to a stop on his stomach, across the floor of the woods. It felt like road rash on his skin.

He cried out in pain. It felt like someone had peeled the flesh from his muscle. His shoulders were no longer his biggest worry. He had to get up, to force himself to face whatever had attacked him. Pushing up from the ground, he steadied himself on his knees. Slowly he turned to see his enemy. A squirrel chirped and darted into the brush in front of him.

"Are you flipping kidding me? I just got my butt handed to me by a stinking mutant rodent? For real?" he shouted. He caught movement again from the corner of his eye. This time he reacted. From his knees he spun around, kicking his legs out from under him.

Quickly rolling backward, lifting his left leg and enduring the pain both old and new, he caught his assailant in the ribs with a sharp kick. His timing was perfect. His foe let out a yelp and the momentum carried it back into the darkness.

Alex was back on his feet, poised and ready this time. From beyond the trees, he could hear rustling, utterances of pain. He listened carefully as that pain turned to anger, and anger grew to rage. The trees awoke from their silence. They bent and swayed in fear. Something was moving them, something big. No, not big, huge. It was mad, and it was definitely *no* squirrel, Alex thought.

The moon was high and had found itself wandering across the

sky. Its light started to trickle down through the canopy and dapple the dew on the forest floor. New shadows were being cast and mocked Alex where he stood. Every movement, every play on light, was his enemy attacking. His nerves were heightened, raw.

Alex heard it rushing toward him, crushing everything in its path. If only I could see, he thought. The ground began to shake. Alex stood his ground. He had nowhere else to run.

One of the trees in front of him danced and trembled. Something was pulling at it. He heard it groan and crack as it was torn from the ground. What the heck could do that? he wondered. He soon had his answer.

Its eyes appeared first, enraged and maddened. An enormous black wolf stepped from the night, tree between its jaws. It stood across from Alex, and he could see the froth gathering from around its mouth. He recognized the signs. He'd seen this before, in Egypt. Alex knew he needed to try something, anything.

"Look. I don't have time to play fetch with you, Fido," Alex mocked. The beast clamped its jaw down hard on the tree in response. It crushed under the force, sending daggers of wood hurdling through the air. A rather large one flew straight at Alex's head, narrowly missing his ear.

"Hey! Watch it, pound puppy, or I'll have you neutered!" he yelled. The wolf stood, chest heaving in much the same manner as Anubis did before battle. This realization alone frightened Alex. That bird-brained beaver beak's never around when I need him, Alex thought of Anubis. What good is it to have a god for a friend when I can't ever use him?

The wolf was easily twice the size of the previous hounds he battled and likely twice as strong. It took to pacing slowly back and forth, keeping its distance. Alex knew it was sizing him up for the attack and couldn't help but feel a little like the *All You Can Eat Buffet* at the Dockside Grill back home. All those hungry sailors. *Yikes.*

The wolf licked its lips as if sharing that same thought. It was different than the beasts he fought in Egypt. It wasn't only larger, but somehow it seemed more desperate. Its fur was shabby and matted in places. Alex was certain this was the same wolf he'd seen in the field. Had it been following him this whole time? he wondered.

Without so much as a twitch, Alex looked around for anything he could use. The area was lined with trees and shrubs; it looked hopeless, and he knew things were only going to get worse. Story of my life, he thought.

His mind raced, analyzing thoughts of both past and present. It's not like before, in Egypt, he recalled. At least in Egypt all I needed were some chemicals, a roll of cotton, a couple of stones, oh, and a 10-foot tall warrior god. Now I have nothing, except maybe the stones.

"Except the stones," he said excitedly as he slid his hand into his pocket, rolling the two objects between his fingers. They're still there. How? he wondered. More important, how can I use them? Alex narrowed his eyes with new intent. The wolf had stopped pacing, watching every move he made. The quiet of the moment made Alex uneasy and he shifted nervously. Pieces of wood from the broken tree cracked beneath his feet. He tensed; too late.

The wolf lunged. It was in flight with open jaw before Alex could move. He had just enough time to turn his head, barely avoiding what would've undoubtedly been a life-ending swipe of the creature's deadly claws. He fell to the ground, pinned beneath the beast. The wind had been forced from Alex's chest; the monster's claws were sinking into his bloodied shoulders, gripping. Its weight on his chest kept his lungs from inflating, and Alex desperately gasped for air.

The wolf growled hungrily at him as saliva fell from its mouth. It moved close, inches from his face. Alex smelled the familiar stench of death on its breath. He'd gotten way too familiar with that particular smell. Pain, blood, disgusting dog slobber; it was Egypt all over again.

Reaching desperately to his side and grasping at the ground beneath him, Alex was searching for anything he could use. His head was pounding, his sight dimming. Things were going black. He felt his fingers curl around something.

A second later he heard a deafening howl, and air rushed into his lungs. The weight was gone. Alex sat up grabbing at his shirt, coughing and wheezing. His chest burned with pain as the coldness spread inside him. Blackness was replaced by light. He could see again. He could breathe.

The cries remained as Alex stood and slowly turned toward the bellowing wolf. Regardless of the pain, he wasn't going to miss the next attack. A mix of whimpering and growling came from the enormous mass of fang and fur. For a moment, Alex felt sympathy for the wounded beast, but only for a moment.

Despite his agony, despite almost losing consciousness, he managed to fight back. The beast now danced in pain at the edge of the clearing, stumbling and clawing at the wooden stake set deeply into its eye, blood flowing from the wound.

Alex stood motionless. He knew he was physically out-matched in every way. He also knew that any wolf, this wolf in particular, as large as he was, had always been the predator, never the prey. His only chance was to outsmart the beast.

Fido expects me to run, he thought. Heck, I expect me to run. What would Anubis do? Truth is, he'd attack, Alex told himself.

"Man, I miss Anubis," Alex said aloud as his throat choked back more tears.

He clinched the small stones, one in each hand, and took off toward his aggressor, toward his destiny, and likely toward his death. His legs may have been moving with purpose, but his head, however, was questioning his latest decision. What are you, nuts? he thought. The wolf growled and snapped. With a single step it became airborne once again.

It wasn't until the last possible second that Alex spied the pillory, still wedged and broken in the notch of the tree. Hunh, I've come full-circle, he thought. Must've got turned around. Leaning in shoulder-first, a maneuver he'd likely regret later, Alex chipped the two stones together, throwing sparks into the wolf's good eye.

The act didn't quite play out as intended. The sparks caused the wolf to jerk its massive head away to the left, while Alex deflected off the animal's ribs to the right, catching both beast and boy off-guard. Its momentum was too much, and the wolf slid to a halt as Alex rolled hard against the tree.

Well, that's not how I saw it going in my head, he thought, but I'll take it. Pain scorched through his shoulder as he reached for the chain that once held him captive. When he turned to face his enemy, strange lettering appeared on the iron links.

"*Álfheimr*," Alex spoke softly, rubbing his thumb across the word. His chest warmed instantly, and his pendant began to glow beneath his shirt. The strange writing was somehow familiar. His pendant grew hotter, and when he removed it from his shirt, its light flooded the clearing in a blinding pulse. The forest shook in a single wave, and Alex was knocked to the ground.

When the last leaf had settled and the pendant had cooled, Alex rubbed his throbbing head and looked again at the chain. The word had vanished, but that wasn't all. The once heavy and stout chain hadn't only thinned, but had grown in length. Strangely, with all of its size, it had little weight.

"Soooo, *that* happened," Alex quipped. He turned the chain over. Nothing. Momentarily preoccupied at the mystery of it all, he'd almost forgotten about the danger that sulked only a few feet from him until a sharp odor snapped at his nose. Alex jerked up in response.

"You're still here? I was kind of hoping you'd be, uh, well, dead by now," he said, shaking his head.

The beast, however, wasn't dead, but it was noticeably shaken. The blast was far more than either had expected. The wolf's matted fur was smoldering, apparently singed from the intense heat, causing it great discomfort and producing the foul odor.

It reminded Alex of the day the Captain tried to color his hair in some desperate attempt to regain his youth. The cabin of the Mermaid was small, and it didn't take long for the fumes from the coloring agent to quickly fill the space. When they reached the flickering light of the kerosene lamp on the table, well, let's just say the Captain no longer worried about the color of his hair.

Alex pushed himself up from the ground, chain in hand, and made for the wolf. His heart beat faster with every step. The beast leapt.

There wasn't time to think. Instinct took over, and Alex executed what was fast becoming his signature move, his only move. He slid below the belly of the beast like a ball player, catching the wolf around the back of its neck with the chain, pulling down hard as he went.

At the end of his slide, he stood, and in a single motion tugged at both ends of the chain with all of his might. The beast tumbled from its own momentum, scrambling wildly to right itself. When it finally stood, its neck was wrapped with the chain.

Alex felt a sudden rush of pride at what he'd just done, so he took a bow. "Thank you. Thank you very much," he said in his best Elvis impersonation. His gloating was short-lived when the wolf jerked his head, sending Alex, who was still holding fast to the chain, through the air like a missile.

He landed head-first just past the tree line, and for an instant he thought of running. That idea quickly faded when he realized that the chain was now wrapped around his wrist. His face went pale as he struggled to get it off. He knew what was coming next. The wolf howled and the chain went tight. Alex was pulled back through the trees.

His long legs caught one, and he was spun horizontally through the air, landing spread-eagle on his back at the far side of the clearing.

The wolf was crazed with anger at being chained. He thrashed about violently, seemingly more focused on the chain than the boy at the end of it. Alex could barely concentrate with so much pain, but he needed to fight back. He didn't want to die, not now, not before seeing his grandmother again. Pushing to his knees, he crawled to the nearest tree, dragging his battered legs behind. He wanted to yell, to scream from all of the pain, but couldn't.

Somewhere a twig broke. It was just enough, and the wolf stopped. Alex froze on his hands and knees. The wolf sniffed into the air, found the scent he was searching for, then charged.

"Craaaaaaap!" Alex yelled. It was too painful to stand, so he crawled as fast as he could, away from the charging beast. The wolf was on him in seconds. Alex didn't dare look back; he rolled sideways sensing the creature approaching, narrowly missing its snapping jaw. This angered the beast even more. They were in the thick of the woods now, making it difficult for both to maneuver.

The beast turned, letting out a roar, then sprang. Alex moved between two smaller trees and turned back toward the clearing. The wolf skidded in the loose leaves, turned, and charged again.

The pain made him weak, and Alex fell to the forest floor. The wolf advanced as Alex rolled onto his back to face the attack. They were close now, and Alex could smell the pungent odor of the wolf's breath. A thick layer of froth gathered on its bottom jaw and hung beneath, its lungs expelling warmed breath in the form of mist from its nose and mouth.

Alex retreated with each advancing step from the wolf, sliding on his back. Suddenly the creature stopped. Its eyes swelled as it stretched for its prey, but it wasn't moving closer. Something had stopped it. The chain, of course, Alex thought. It had reached its limit. The wolf tugged and pulled, but with each effort forward, each struggle, the chain tightened, squeezing around its neck. It was the wolf's turn to gasp for air.

Remembering the blinding pulse of light from his necklace earlier, Alex reached beneath his shirt once again. No longer would it be a riddle, a mystery holding some out-of-reach answers. This time he'd give it purpose. With the chain dangling from one hand, Alex held the pendant high above his head in the other, closed his eyes, and slammed it to the ground where the end of the chain lay.

"Now!" he yelled. Everything went quiet. Alex slowly opened his eyes, peering through his thick hair. Nothing had happened.

"Hunh? Pretty sure I did it right," Alex muttered, ignoring for a moment what was waiting for him on the other end of the chain.

"Let's see," he continued, "chain around neck. Check. Look cool. Check. Pendant in the air. Did that. Yell, *now.*" Alex looked down at the ground again, hoping he was wrong. He wasn't.

In the midst of Alex's confusion, the enormous beast gave a final sharp tug on the chain. The force was so great that the chain sliced through the trees, sending Alex, who was still holding onto the end, sailing across the sky. He landed in a heap at the far edge of the clearing. The wolf charged, the chain around its neck dangling behind.

Dazed, a word flashed into his mind. Gnip-Gnop. Wait, that's not it. What was it again? Adrenaline began coursing through his veins, replacing fear and pushing pain from his mind as he stood. He quickly pulled out the journal from his back pocket and began running from the rushing beast, screaming the whole time.

It wasn't easy, but Alex's wiry frame and years of experience running from things, people mostly, an occasional Sphinx now and again, he recalled, allowed him to stay a few steps ahead of the wolf. The wolf's large size made it difficult to execute the tight turns. This gave Alex the advantage. As he ran, he flipped frantically through the pages of his journal.

"Where is it?" he asked desperately. "There. No, go back. There," he shouted.

Tired of the chase, the wolf lunged one last time, landing ahead of Alex, cutting him off. He was trapped. A low growl uttered in its throat as saliva hung from its mouth. For an instant, Alex thought he heard it laugh. The beast looked hungry, but not for food; for killing.

The end of the chain had landed between them, and there was only one chance. He stood on one leg, arms flapping in the air like his favorite martial arts movie, and the wolf stared. In that moment,

Alex dove for the chain, pendant held high once again, and yelled, "*Gleipnir!*" A flash of light, a yelp, and Alex blacked out.

Morning had arrived when Alex next stirred. A little dazed, he saw no movement at first, yet for some reason all of his senses were still on edge. The morning was cool and brought with it a damp fog that rested heavily on the forest floor, working its way through the trees and bushes, filling the clearing where he sat.

The sound was soft at first, but it was there. It was the wolf, still alive, breathing. As he stood, Alex made out movement, a push of the mist, but no real form. The rest of the forest remained eerily quiet. A mourning dove haunted in the distance, and Alex turned toward her.

Suddenly, out of the mist, the wolf appeared, its enormous black head breaking through, snapping its fangs only inches from Alex's face. He froze, his eyelids closed tightly in fear of the attack; but the attack never came. Slowly he opened his eyes and saw the wolf struggling to reach him, tearing at him. Something was holding it back. The chain! It worked, Alex thought.

He watched carefully as the wolf stretched at him. Each time it moved, lashed out, the chain flashed and tightened around its massive neck. This only made the beast angrier, however, causing it to thrash about even harder, but the chain was unforgiving in return and continued to squeeze with each move, choking the monster into submission.

With the wolf bound tightly, Alex seized the opportunity. He dropped to his hands and knees beneath the cover of the fog and crawled out to the narrow footpath, leaving the clearing and everything in it behind him.

The fog's thickness slowly gave way to the sun's persistence piercing through every available opening, giving rise to warm air and the feeling of relief. Something tells me I'm not out of the woods yet, he thought, looking up at the tall trees ahead. He chuckled and kept moving.

Some time had passed since he heard the last maddening howl of the wolf, so he slowed his pace. Alex took comfort on a fallen tree and sat upon it, thankful for the respite it afforded. When he finally settled in, the remaining glow from the sun had dropped behind the trees. Instinctively he reached for his necklace; it had become second nature to read by its light.

Things were pretty quiet now. He had time. After wrestling the leather-bound journal from his back pocket, Alex cracked open its pages. A flutter of wind swirled up from the ground and disappeared as suddenly as it arrived.

"Going to be a cold one tonight," Alex said, pulling up his shirt collar and embracing every ounce of heat he could muster. The journal had been with him for some time, or at least that's how it felt. Truthfully, he wasn't exactly sure how much time had passed since he'd been home. He'd seen several nights come and go, traveled many miles, and fought too many battles, but time appeared to almost be absent.

Still, the journal held no answers, none that he could decipher anyway. Sure, it had pretty pictures, but what did they mean? He flipped past the pages on Egypt.

"Been there, done that," he said.

With the exception of a few moments back in Egypt, Alex never had the opportunity to spend a lot of time decoding the journal. He'd been pretty busy just running for his life. Man, being a teenager stinks. Who gets chased by dead demon dogs and beat up by ticked off gods nowadays? I do, that's who.

These pictures were so random, but still, he couldn't help but think, to hope even, that they had meaning, purpose. It all seemed like a great mystery begging to be solved.

He realized long ago that although his current interest in the yellowed paper held within stemmed from his overwhelming desire to get back home, the real mystery was the journal itself; the journal, and the pendant he wore around his neck.

He never admitted it to anyone, but Alex knew deep inside that this little book not only held clues, but answers to his questions, and well, maybe everything. It was like a key to a puzzle, a roadmap to what's happened or perhaps going to happen. But why me? he wondered. Why do I have it? It has to be a mistake.

So there he sat, journal in one hand, lazily stroking the pendant with the other. Boy, it sure would be nice to have some help, though. The one person I've always relied on in the past, he thought, is several billion light years away and probably not even on the same planet. Heck, I may not even be born yet; but if that's in the past, *my* past, then how couldn't I be born yet? he considered.

"Ow, ow, owww! My head hurts," he said. His mind slipped back to a recent visit with the Captain. It was a lazy morning, just two men chewing the fat, talking about guy stuff, sitting on the deck of the Mermaid. Somewhere between the *2012 Watermelon Seed Spitting Olympics* and learning how to whittle, the Captain was showing Alex one of his prized possessions, Chinese finger cuffs.

It had quickly become apparent that the Captain had only learned half of the lesson himself. Somehow he'd gotten both forefingers stuck in the cuffs when explaining to Alex how it was done. Watching the Captain getting upset was a lot like watching Donald Duck on Saturday mornings, horrific and hilarious; then it hit him.

"Of course!" he said loudly enough to cause concern that he may have given away his hiding place. He stretched his neck back and forth several times until he was certain he was still alone. His focus returned to the journal. What if I stop fighting it, like the Chinese finger cuffs? What if I just relax and work with the journal? I don't even know what that means, but hey, why not?

Alex slowly started thumbing through the pages before him. Shapes began jumping off the paper at him while he searched for any sign of a connection. He'd seen many of the pictures before, including a snake. A slow chill ran the length of his spine and he shuddered.

"Had plenty of them in my day; too many, in fact. Next please," he said, flipping forward. The first couple of sheets revealed the earlier events from Egypt. Each played out like a scene from a familiar movie. The characters in the journal, the many forms and figures took on a whole new meaning to Alex now. He recognized them, even knew them by name; heck, he *was* them.

He paused for quite some time on one particularly rough sketch. He hadn't noticed it until now. Must've missed it, he surmised. His hand brushed over the picture. A long snout, teeth bared, and a big hook in its claw.

"I sure do miss the big hairball," Alex spoke tenderly. It's no Picasso. Well, *maybe* Picasso, he thought, as he turned the journal upside-down. Wait. Actually, it kind of looks like something *I'd* draw. Hey, wait a minute. It *is* something I'd draw. I don't remember drawing this.

Surrounding the shaded figure, scrawled all over the page in what was obviously the scratchings of a demented inmate from an asylum, were words. Alex didn't understand it immediately, but continued to study it.

"That looks like *taro*. No, *tar*. Yeah, that's it," he said. "This one says *franken*-something." His eyes jumped out of his head. He needed to be sure. Frantically he searched for it, that single word to confirm his hunch. There.

"Natron!

"That's my list!" he yelled. "I must've written this. I don't remember writing this at all! What's going on?" he wondered.

"When did I do this?" he asked, then it dawned on him. His eyes grew even wider. "What if?" he dared question. Alex feverishly whipped through the pages. "No way. Yes, here, too," he said, turning each leaf. "Are you kidding me? This one, too? Yes. So many." He turned pale with the sudden realization that it was him. He was responsible. *He* drew the pictures in the journal, all of them.

Alex was sure of it now. This journal was his, or rather it had always been his, even before it was, well, his. Wait, did that make sense? Great, now I sound like Anubis, he thought. The lunkhead must've rubbed off on me. Regardless of the confusion, Alex needed this. It was the first real connection he discovered with the journal, and it was his.

This was huge, and he wasn't quite sure how to handle it. He sat, just thinking, almost motionless. His breathing became calm as he stared down at the journal. Its uneven pages and worn leather showed its age, but how old was it? How old was *he*? Alex was feeling lightheaded. Not now, he thought. This is too important. I need to focus, he thought, and turned the page.

His fingers landed on a single word at the top of the page; *Hel*.

"Well, so much for spelling," he said. His laughter was cut short when his eyes fixed on a second word midway down the page. They widened with fright. At some point in time he underlined this word so hard that the pen tore through the page; *Death*.

"Crud. Again?" he asked. He became so focused on this word that he barely noticed the drawings at the bottom of the page.

Alex glanced down with an air of disgust at the soft worn leather journal in his hand. Frustrated, he tossed it against a rotted stump. *Why not? It hasn't given me any answers, and it's certainly not helping me get back home. In fact, just the opposite; I'm pretty sure it's why I'm here.*

"*The deed unraveled,*" Alex spoke aloud, sneering in the direction of the journal. This was all the incentive he needed, and he was off talking to himself again. In the past he always stopped himself from doing this; too many strange looks and far too many whispers; but then, in the past, he cared. Things were different now.

He finally conceded that he was indeed the original owner of the journal. The words, as poorly as they were written, were in his handwriting. The pictures were drawn by his hand as well, despite having never known that the journal even existed. When Ms. Trudie had given it to him, it was a complete surprise. The real question was, how did his writings end up in there before he'd even seen it?

So far, everything that happened in Egypt had already been written between those pages. *A minor little detail that, if I'd known sooner, would've helped me out greatly,* he thought sarcastically.

He could only assume that the remainder of what was written was also about to happen, as if it already happened. *How? That makes no sense,* he thought. *My head hurts just thinking about it; but if that's the case, then it holds my future? And my future is, at times, in my past. That's not only bananas, it's a bit unfair, too,* he thought.

Despite this, Alex knew that the journal may still be his only chance of getting home. Picking it up, he returned to his spot on the tree, sighed deeply, and opened it with a renewed perspective.

"Hold on a minute," he told himself. "Are these *bottles?*" Several rough pictures were scratched out in series and labeled. They appeared to be jars, rounded containers of some sort. His mind flashed to Egypt. He'd seen jars like these in the marketplace. There was something else, something more. He wasn't quite sure what it was, but the thought tugged at his brain, teasing him, just out of reach. He knew he'd seen these jars somewhere else, but where? he wondered.

There were five in all. Four were numbered, just as each of those four also had a label of sorts just under it. Each label had a color and an odor describing it. The fifth one, located second from the left, had been crossed out.

"Two parts of this, three drops of that," he repeated from the words. Pictures were drawn, his pictures, seemingly random across the page. It made no sense.

"Great. It's not my destiny; it's a flipping cookbook," he whispered. Alex returned to the page and read the details. Why the heck would I put a recipe in here?

Once again he quickly turned the page, hoping for more. The words, *Turn back, you idiot* were written here.

"Really? Are you flipping serious? Turn back. That's all you got? *Sheesh,*" Alex ranted. "I'd love to turn back, you moron, but how? *Man,* who's the comedian who wrote this stuff? Oh yeah, right. Forget I asked."

A lone cricket chirped in the distance, then stopped. Alex's neck snapped up from the journal. He held his breath, listening to the woods around him. It was still. The hairs on his arms stood straight up. Was it the wolf again? he wondered. Rustling from the canopy above broke through the silence. A tussle of leaves floated softly to the ground next to him. His heart jumped. Just as he was about to stand ready for battle, a squirrel chattered down at him from above, cursing at him.

"You again? Shoo," Alex said. He waved his hand above his head trying to rid himself of the interruption. The squirrel paced back and forth on his limb, then darted up the tree.

"Where was I?" Alex asked. "Oh yeah, jars." If there's one thing he learned so far, random or not, they had a meaning. There was a reason for drawing them here.

"Everything's connected," he whispered again. Alex's stomach began to roll and lurch. I haven't felt this way since gramma made me dust the kitchen shelves, he recalled. Those jars; that's it.

These drawings look just like the jars in my gramma's kitchen, the same jars that always make me sick, just like now.

He felt an upwelling of acid in his throat. "That's not funny," he muttered. As if on cue, laughter filled the air. Startled, Alex fell backward from his resting place.

"*Seriously?* Who else does this happen to?" Alex yelled. Silence was his only response.

"Only two good things came out of all of this; Tad and that flea-bitten tail chaser," he said to himself, patting at his tearing eyes. He missed his grandmother . . . *a lot.* He missed Tad, of course, but there's another, one whom he'd gotten close to, not expecting it. How could he? Anubis was, *well,* quite *un*-expected. Still, Alex reflected, he'd become friends with what's undoubtedly the strangest of characters.

"And I didn't even get any frequent flyer miles," he finished. Alex had finally calmed down enough to redirect his emotion. "Real men don't cry," the Captain's raspy voice rang in his head. This wasn't the first time that the Captain's sage advice had brought him back to reality with a cold smack to the brain.

With the laughter gone and his emotions in check, he was now curious. Should he go forward, into the dense woods and the unknown; or back toward the wolf, more danger, even death. Tough choice, he thought.

"Not," he said loudly. He tucked his journal into his pocket as he'd done so many other times and edged his way forward, down the path, ducking branches and climbing over fallen trees, listening every step of the way.

The trees towered over him, making him feel anxious as he walked. The forest seemed to awaken with false movement all around him, a trick of the mind.

"Get it together, Chronos," he said, feeling uneasy. He was so focused on looking up at the trees that he didn't realize the path had ended abruptly.

He suddenly found himself standing at the edge of another clearing, much larger than the last. The sun now dappled down through the canopy and lit the moss on the ground. As serene as it appeared, the scene before him felt odd, wrong, and even dangerous. His frayed nerves were on full alert. His eyes searched the area, but found nothing. He desperately wanted to curl up on the soft ground and close his eyes, but somehow knew that it wouldn't last long. He was right.

No sooner did he complete his thought when the laughter was back, creepier than before. It filled the space in front of him. Alex's head was spinning once again, only this time from the inside. He watched as a thin trail of mist slithered out from the woods across the ground. It billowed and grew heavy in the center of the clearing where it finally lifted and disappeared. He saw movement where there'd been none before.

Zach was now sitting hunched over in the center of the clearing, his back toward him. Something definitely wasn't right. Alex took a single step and it began.

The boy slowly stood and turned to face him, his eyes glowing red hot as before. Flames rose around him, and he was lifted, rotating high above the ground. As he did, the once-boy grew from his filth-ridden form, tearing out of his skin. Bone pierced through flesh, stretching to its fullest. Alex cringed at the painful sight.

His lower jaw broke free to accommodate his enormous face. He jerked about, slashing at both cloth and tissue as he screamed in agonizing pain. It was still of human form and structure, but far larger, easily four times his previous size, and when it was all over, Alex stood trembling in fear at what he'd seen.

Zach's clothing had since peeled off to the ground, replaced by a long fur coat that grew from his shoulders and hung to his feet. The mud and filth were gone. His hair, as red as the fire that encircled him, flickered against a small leather and gold crown that sat tightly upon his head. Shortened horns pierced the leather at the front, made of bone.

"Hey, I thought only vampires twinkled nowadays? You're not a vampire, are you?" Alex asked, half sincere. No response.

"You know, one of those pasty dudes with a cape and fangs. Any recent cravings for depressed teenage girls from Seattle?" Alex asked, holding back his laughter. Laughter was all he could muster; being scared right now wasn't an option. Again, no response.

"No? Okay, let's play word association. My gramma and I used to play this all the time. You'll love it. When I say a word, you say the first thing that pops into your mind. Okay? Ready? I say *Count*, you say . . ." Alex continued. Still engulfed in flames, the shrill voice spoke.

"I am Loki."

"Uh, I was looking for *Dracula*," Alex joked. "What the heck's a Loki?" he asked brazenly.

"I'm a god."

"Jeez. I have to say, buddy, I saw that one coming a mile away," Alex responded as he rolled his eyes.

"The next time I'm traveling alone in some far off distant universe and happen to cross paths with a mud-covered pain in the butt, please remind me not to pick up any hitchhikers," Alex said aloud. He looked around, half expecting the creepy old hag to appear with some new riddle for him. Save for Loki, he was alone.

The flames surrounding Loki grew intense, yet Alex felt no heat. They pushed outward in every direction, and he ducked in response. At their farthest, they then retreated inward in a snap. A loud crack filled the sky, and Alex was knocked over from the blast.

The force had thrown him clear to the other side of a large tree and had apparently caused the sun to disappear. His head still pounding, he brushed himself off and rose to face Loki.

"Hunh, I don't remember that tree being there," Alex said. He took a step around it, but the tree shifted into his path. My head must still be spinning, he thought, and tried once more. The tree moved with him. Alex froze. Last time I checked, trees don't move, he realized, and slowly lifted his eyes upward. The tree shifted a third time and the sun reappeared.

Alex gasped at what he saw. He could hear Loki's laughter echoing through the forest.

There, standing over Alex, twice the size of Loki, wasn't a tree, but a figure so unexpectedly enormous and gruesome that Alex couldn't help but gasp a second time. The creature's skin was greyed and scarred, likely from battle, and what little hair it had protruding from its scalp and ears was silver.

103

Alex believed at once that this was the older of its species, whatever species it may be, but he knew that older didn't necessarily mean weaker or slower, so he had to be prepared. Ha, he thought, how the heck do I prepare for this?

He'd only read about these creatures in fairy tales. They were of myths and legends, fiction; but then, much of what he'd seen lately had been of myths and legends. Even still, the stories did these creatures no justice. Boy, I've seen some weird things in my time, he thought.

Just when I thought it was safe to go walking in the woods alone, out pops a flipping, well, a flipping . . .

"*Giant!*" Alex yelled, pointing up at the creature.

The beast was massive in form, with layers of dense fat and flesh covering what was clearly powerful muscle developed from years of eating things like houses and fire trucks, Alex thought.

It wore heavy fur on its feet as boots and leather, crudely fashioned into battle gear adorning its shoulders, chest, and strapping around its waist. It pushed a warm foulness from its lungs every time it breathed and caused the cold air around its face to mist on its lips and chin.

Much as always, Alex felt compelled to say something.

"Look, I just got out of a long-term relationship with a Valkyrie and I'm feeling a little vulnerable right now." The giant bent down and roared angrily, saliva dripping from the corner of its mouth. In a fearful, knee-jerk reaction, Alex slapped him across the nose, catching it off-guard. The sting from his slap must've caused a tickle deep inside the giant; he took two large breaths and sneezed, covering Alex with a thick layer of mucus.

"Awww, dude. Really? First it's doggy drool, then it's giant boogies. Come on, can't a guy catch a break?"

The great beast reared up, its massive hand clenched high above its head. Alex dropped to his knees. He knew this would be his last breath. It let out a mighty roar that cracked the air, pushing molecule against molecule, and swung its fist downward like an anvil for the final blow. As he did, something familiar beat on Alex's eardrum.

"Hey, I know that roar," Alex yelled. Time seemed to slow as the clearing pulsed in a blue light.

In a single movement, a large figure dressed in gleaming gold appeared from the light, teeth bared, announcing his arrival with a ferocious battle cry.

"Anubis!" Alex yelled tearfully.

SIX

It *was* Anubis, and he was ready to fight. He caught the crushing blow of the giant with his crook just in time. Man, that thing's strong, Alex thought, and so is Anubis. Without hesitation, the Egyptian god immediately slid the shaft of the crook along the beast's forearm and hooked it with the end, swinging upward to its waist. A split second later he was on the stunned giant's shoulder and swung the shaft around its neck, pulling back with all of his might and giving a second triumphant roar.

The giant tried desperately to free itself from Anubis' chokehold. The crook was crushing its throat, cutting off its air supply. It was gasping and heaving, uneasy on its feet. It took two steps forward, then stumbled backward and fell crashing to the ground next to Alex, dead. Anubis had jumped free just in time and was now standing in all of his glory, seething.

Alex fell back, sitting, jaw open and speechless. Tears began to flow down his cheeks. It felt like ages since he'd seen a familiar face, a friend. He'd grown close to Anubis, having fought by his side, defeating the evil god Set; an unlikely duo, to be sure, but an unbreakable bond had grown between the two.

He ran to the behemoth, throwing his long arms wildly around Anubis' waist. Realizing what he'd just done wasn't the manliest of moves, Alex quickly pulled his arms back. Trying to gain his composure, he wiped at his tears. Anger fell over him.

"Are you kidding me? *Now* you show up?" Alex yelled. "Guess you were a little too busy to help out with that man-eating wolf or those howling she-monkeys, weren't you?"

Anubis stood, his hulking chest pushing for more air, sharpened claws extended and sniffing into the wind. He was ready for the attack. Alex knew that Anubis preferred being the attacker; it was in his blood. Before him stood a brutal warrior with the full experience of death on his side. He knew how to fight and he welcomed it, yearned for it.

"Hey, I'm talking to you, you mangy mongrel," Alex said.

"SILENCE," Anubis responded.

"*What?* Did you just tell me to shut up? Look, for all I know it's been over a thousand years since I've seen you, and the first thing you say to me is SILENCE?" Alex finished with his best Anubis-like voice.

"HE WATCHES," Anubis replied without even the slightest acknowledgement of Alex.

"Oh yeah, right. I forgot about him. We'll finish this little discussion later," Alex warned. Looking up at Anubis, he understood why this fierce creature struck terror into men. Feeling slightly inferior standing in his shadow, Alex shifted and pushed out his boney chest, making a poor attempt to mimic his large friend. It made no difference.

"Let's do this," Alex said.

"HMMFT," Anubis agreed.

The two fell seamlessly into place, side by side, like the battle-worn allies they had become. They were poised, ready for anything that Loki could throw at them, or so they thought.

"Hey, about this dead thing. We need to talk . . . soon," Alex said to Anubis.

There was no sudden movement, no blind attack to fend off. Light simply filtered unassuming, through the leaves above, as the two friends digested the impossibility of the moment.

Loki's eyes rolled to the back of his head and his eyelids closed as he rose above the flames, slowly turning; his arms were widespread. The fire danced beneath him when next he opened his eyes. This time they showed bright white, and he began chanting. Alex didn't recognize the words, but he knew it couldn't be good, not for him anyway. It never is, he thought. As the chanting grew louder, Alex's head began to hurt.

Loki's words felt like they were tugging on Alex's brain, trying to pull something out. The pain was excruciating, and Alex fought hard, but in the end it proved to be too much and he gave in. A wisp of air flowed from his ear and he dropped to his knees, grabbing at it desperately.

Loki spoke louder as the wisp swirled around them and settled several feet in front of them. Anubis, stoic as ever, stood, watching intently. Alex, still on his knees, had difficulty believing what happened next. The air, this incantation of Loki's, began to shimmer and pulse. Color came to its formless presence. Shape forced its way in. A colossal figure now stood before them.

"Another one?" Alex asked.

A second giant appeared from the air, snarling upon arrival. It apparently knew why it was here and so did Alex. These creatures appeared battle bred, likely over centuries.

It was slightly smaller than the first, but noticeably younger and stronger. The giant bared its few yellowed teeth and gave a loud bellowing roar that shook the trees.

"You got this or is it my turn?" Alex quipped.

"HMMFT," Anubis responded, sounding bored. Without hesitation, he quickly jumped to the goliath's knee, reached out a long sharpened claw, and grabbed the giant around the throat, causing him to choke mid-hiss. Alex watched the blood vessels in its eyes redden.

In a panic, it began shaking and thrashing about, trying to frantically rid itself of the annoyance that hung from its neck, strangling him. Gasping for air, he swung wildly at Anubis with his other arm. The keen senses of a thousand centuries of battle were more than a match for the giant.

Still hanging on, claws sunk deep into his enemy's throat and squeezing, Anubis caught the other arm with his dangling legs, putting it in a scissors-lock. Before it could move again, Anubis twisted his legs and snapped the beast's arm at the joint. The beast tried to howl, but Anubis' grip was too tight.

He shoved his other hand deep into the monster's chest cavity and squeezed. A frightened look washed over the already pale creature. When Anubis pulled back his bloodied claw, a small piece of its spine came with it. He discarded it as if it were simply a nuisance. The giant dropped in a heap onto the ground. In a final pulse of light, it vanished.

"Is that the best you've got?" Alex taunted Loki, as if he had a hand in its defeat.

"You dare mock me, boy?" Loki questioned incredulously.

"Yeah, I sort of have a knack for ticking people off, don't I?" he said, turning toward Anubis.

"HHUMMMPHTT," Anubis agreed.

"Glad to see you, too, Chuckles," Alex said as he smiled up at his large friend.

Loki became enraged. The wind picked up, drawing inward. The surrounding trees bent and swayed in anger, matching Loki's own. This anger seemed to fuel him, and he started to grow, pushing his current form outward. The fire that once was, rose and twisted, itself growing.

Now on the same scale as the giants who just attacked them,

Loki easily towered over Anubis, who stood engulfed in his shadow. Alex swallowed hard at the transformation in front of him and couldn't help but wonder if Loki's powers had also increased to match his size.

"Can you do that?" Alex whispered to Anubis out of the corner of his mouth. There was no mistaking his friend's response this time.

"NO," Anubis replied impatiently.

The wind dropped as quickly as it started. Everything was still. Alex believed this to be the calm before the storm. All else up to this point was child's play, a game to Loki, he thought. We're his puppets. He lured us to this place so he could attack us on his own terms. Alex looked up at his friend. Anubis stood quietly waiting for the Norse god to strike.

All of this silence, the suspense, was killing Alex. The impatience that comes with being a teenager was prodding him, poking at him, daring him to break through the quiet. It was its own source of pain to him. Too much, going to burst, he thought. Until he did burst, much the way he always did, with sarcasm.

"I get it. You're Loki. You're a schmuck, but you're Loki. Personally, I think you need to try yoga or something. Oh wait, now I *do* get it. *Low-keyed.* Those two dolts back at the inn. They knew about you," Alex said as he recalled the two younger men who had kept much to themselves that evening, whispering.

"*Sheesh*, Chronos, you have to pay closer attention," he scolded.

"Okay. So you're Loki, some sort of god. Big deal. He's a god." Alex pointed up at Anubis. "And you don't see him whining." Anubis stood, unwavering. Alex took a second look at the warrior next to him.

"Actually, you don't see him doing much of anything right now,"

Alex said quietly as he raised his fingers and snapped them twice in front of Anubis' face. "But trust me, he's a god," Alex assured Loki.

"Hey, you awake up there?" he whispered to Anubis. Anubis gave a quiet growl, deep in his chest. Yep, Alex thought. He turned back to Loki and said, "But who are you, *really?*"

"I've already told you, boy. I'm descended from the ancient ones," Loki responded as if annoyed.

"Yeah, you did, but what's that mean? What do you want?" Alex asked, not sure if he wanted to hear the answer.

"The gods shall kneel before me, much as you do before them, insect," Loki screamed.

"*Hey*, watch who you're calling names. Just because you've had a growth spurt doesn't mean you're still not a dork," Alex blasted back.

"I won't waste my time any longer with you, pest. By day's end, my children shall finish you," Loki shrieked. He was overcome with rage, and Alex knew it, so he pressed further.

"Children? You have children?" Alex was shocked.

"I have many children. Fenrisúlfr is fierce. You're but a mere morsel to the wolf who shall feast upon Odin's innards," Loki said.

"*The wolf? That's* your son?" Alex laughed. "You're kidding me? I thought he was someone's pet? Dude, that isn't right. You do know I put a collar on him and housebroke his hairy butt, right? Where'd you get him, *the pound?*" Alex mocked.

"Hel shall drink your very soul," Loki continued.

"*Hel?* Hey, wait a minute, how do you spell that?" Alex asked, remembering the note in his journal.

"Don't speak to me, boy," Loki demanded.

"Just asking," Alex muttered in response.

"Jormungandr shall squeeze the life from your lungs," Loki

screeched as he clinched his fists, and the fire surrounding him erupted.

"Settle down, Skippy. Let's recap. Your *children*, uh, what were their names? Frère Jacques, Hello Kitty, and Jar-Jar Binx? Yeah, I'd like to buy a vowel please."

"Enough!" Loki screamed.

"*Enough* is right," Alex yelled back, his voice shaking slightly. "Then tell me, why'd you help me? Why'd you stop the Valkyries . . . *twice?*" he asked desperately.

"I couldn't risk having you reach those hallowed halls. It doesn't meet with my plans. Once Odin's Valkyries arrived, I knew then I had to destroy you," Loki answered with a grin.

"Oh great, an overachiever," Alex said as he turned toward his friend. Anubis stood in quiet resolution. Alex took this as a response.

"Look, I don't think you fully appreciate my rawesomeness," Alex said to his large friend.

"CLEARLY," Anubis finally acknowledged. Alex smiled, not fully sensing the sarcasm in the response, then he watched as Anubis' snout wrinkled and contorted and simply said, "YOU REEK OF DUNG."

"Forget it," Alex said, frustrated.

Loki, floating high above the two friends, spread his arms wide. This simple motion created such an enormous vacuum of air surging past that Alex's ears popped. Much like a swimmer, he started hopping on one leg, tilting his head and smacking his ear to bring the pressure back to normal.

It no sooner equalized when Loki brought his hands together in a thunderous clap, the force of which sent both Alex and Anubis tumbling backward like ragdolls. When it was all over and the dust had settled, Alex turned to Anubis and said, "That's a neat trick. I'm guessing you can't do that either?"

"HMMMPHT," Anubis replied. Still dazed from the force, they looked up in unison and Loki was gone. All that remained was a shrinking black void where he once hovered. The two sat and watched curiously; and at its smallest, the negative space released a second more powerful blast that rendered them unconscious.

As he lay, Alex's mind drifted lazily in and out of different scenes, much like watching live theatre. He soared high above a strange and beautiful place, covered in heavy foliage, floating in the clouds. Water cascaded down tall mountains only to be channeled and diverted into ponds teaming with fish. Other wildlife moved through the scene. He heard laughing and saw children playing.

The scene suddenly turned dark, and he was in the water. The sea was thrashing, and he was miles from shore. Choking the water out of his lungs, he watched as a ball of fire shot straight up in the distance and the shoreline disappeared. Ash filled the horizon. He heard someone screaming. He was tired and sank beneath the water. Darkness swallowed him.

There was now hardness beneath him, and he was standing in the dark. He wasn't alone. Reddened eyes behind him roared to life and a shadowy figure lunged at him. It was he who screamed this time.

"Unnnghh." It was hours before Alex stirred. He felt like someone had been using his head to crack coconuts. At first, all he could do was stare up at the unfamiliar sky. Millions of dots flickered across the heavens in concert. Night had fallen. What just happened? he wondered.

As he rose from where he lay, Alex sensed the sticky wetness running from the corner of his mouth. He knew what it was. For as long as he could remember, Alex had always been a drooler.

Inhaling, the fluid stretched to an almost infinite length before it gave way and snapped back into his mouth. The rest was wiped clean with a simple dab of a shirt sleeve. He was indeed a professional.

"Good thing Anubis didn't see any of that," he said.

A sudden sense of fear shot through his veins as he searched for signs of Loki. He saw nothing, heard nothing. His hand brushed over the softness of leather as he stood. At least he hadn't lost his journal, he thought. He returned to his investigation.

It was now or never. He was going to get some answers, even if it killed him. Actually, it just might, he thought; but for now, at least, there were no gods shooting fire out of their butts at him, no dog-breathed demon mutts trying to take a bite from his hide, and fortunately, for the moment, no stinking skull-fanged females trying to sieve him with pointy objects. He had some time.

It was a clear, cool night full of light dancing off the stars. The moon wasn't quite full, but provided ample brightness for the task at hand. He pulled his legs together and crossed them. Unfolding the journal before him, he took a long sigh and settled in.

"Well, here goes nothing."

So there he sat, deciphering what's likely his own existence. A lot to swallow, he thought. Most people have the luxury of actually living their life, but not me; I have to read about it.

The journal, his writings, had become far more detailed than in the beginning. They still didn't make any sense to him, or to anyone else who could read for that matter, but more detailed nonetheless.

For some time now, the greatest mysteries of his journal weren't the pictures of animals or the half-sentences written in chaotic rhyme or verse, not the writings of death or danger; it was the figures, always one man and one woman, drawn together, each one different, but each together. A definite connection, he thought.

There were several couples drawn in all, each like a separate chapter in his journal and likely marking something great in history. Alex was quick to remind himself that the term *great* doesn't necessarily imply good.

He was certain of their importance, but he read little detail about them until now. There, in the middle of the journal, seemingly on some random page, was a magnificent account of two people bound to each other through love and duty, for all of eternity.

"Now we're getting somewhere," he said softly to himself. He hardly noticed the dark line he'd drawn around the entire edge of the paper, highlighting its significance at some time.

As he read, he became engrossed in a tale of great love and compassion. It reminded him of the story Anubis told of Osiris and Isis. Their love transcended all boundaries. Their rule was great and kind. It spoke of a peaceful land, tranquil and vast, rich with knowledge and resources, surrounded by the sea; a land green and lush, vibrant in its beauty. They lived from the land and gave back to it. It sounded perfect.

He read about the two strange figures and their great reign over thousands of centuries, but how can that be? Let's face it, he thought, the journal's been pretty accurate so far; not the best timing, but accurate, he chided. If it were true, those were some pretty old dudes; even older than Anubis. He needed more.

Alex turned the page and his jaw dropped. What he saw was unbelievable. He grabbed at his pendant, practically ripping it from under his shirt. They were identical, right down to the last detail. This was important, he thought. How come I've never seen this page before? he wondered. It's like these stinking things write themselves when I'm not looking.

The man stood strong and proud, facing the woman. There was no snake between them as on his pendant, but it was them. She was the most beautiful woman he'd ever laid eyes on. There was something warm and loving about her; motherly and kind. He felt connected to her, as if he knew her. He stared at her as time slipped by.

It wasn't until his eyes started drifting that he realized it was dawn already and he'd been reading the entire night. Breaking his senses, Alex stood and stretched. It was time to go.

"Hey, Cupcake. You ready?" Alex shouted at Anubis. The god had been vigilant all night. Sleep came difficult to the one called Anubis. The two walked side-by-side into the morning sun.

"I feel like we should chest-bump, don't you?" Alex asked. "No?" Anubis ignored him and the two moved in silence. Silence, in all of its mystery, was one of the few forces that could be molded and shaped, but only with extreme caution; too much, and time stands still; too little, and it becomes insignificant, trivial, awkward, but their silence spoke volumes and brought with it a new chapter in their adventure, and this chapter had a castle.

As they pressed on, the sun lifted higher into the sky, casting its rays downward, dancing off the silver roof of the castle and nearly blinding the two travelers. The closer they drew, it became apparent that the structure was actually made of wood. Huge timber, larger than any force of man could move, was placed seamlessly atop the next, forming what was likely near-impenetrable barricades.

It was quite clear that this was no ordinary castle for the wealthy to reside. No, not this; it was more fortress than residence, and those within were born of battle.

116

Now standing at the far end of the bridge, Alex could see that this, too, wasn't as he expected. It was shimmering, almost transparent in structure, and he wasn't quite sure that it was even a bridge. Certainly not solid, he thought.

Apprehensive, he reached forward with one of his long legs, gently placing his foot on what he saw. As the tip of his shoe touched, a ripple of colored light pulsed the entire length. As it reached the far end and the gate beyond, the bridge turned solid.

"Hah, I've seen stranger," Alex said jokingly, as he looked up at Anubis.

High above, the wind began to swirl and a familiar sound filled the air. Slowly the two raised their heads. Hundreds of small black dots dropped from the sky.

"Maybe not. Valkyries!" Alex screamed. He turned to gauge Anubis' reaction, expecting his warrior friend to already be on the attack. What he saw instead surprised him. His giant companion had fallen to one knee and quietly lowered his head.

"What?" Alex yelled in in disbelief. Of all the things he witnessed since that fateful night back home, that same night he was given the mysterious pendant that now hung around his neck; of all the monsters, the gods, the battles, this was indeed the strangest.

"Get up, you ungrateful moron. They're attacking!" Alex shouted.

"THEY DO NOT ATTACK," Anubis responded.

The Valkyries arrived in force, bladed and fierce. They dropped low and fast, encircling the two friends. They brought with them the familiar cold mist and the scent of fresh blood, as if returning from a great battle, not yet cleansed from the death. The smell made Alex a bit queasy.

"What do you mean, they're not attacking? It sure feels like an attack to me," Alex said, narrowly ducking the point of a gilded spearhead.

"JUDGE THESE CREATURES NOT. ONLY MANKIND ATTACKS THAT WHICH THEY DO NOT UNDERSTAND. ALWAYS." Anubis spoke solemnly, as if from experience. There was a look in his eyes, distant and lonely. Alex somehow knew that he shouldn't press the issue.

"THEY SEEK ONLY THE GREATEST WARRIORS," Anubis clarified.

"*Duuuhhhh*. That's what I've been saying. They're after me, numbskull," Alex explained.

"INDEED," Anubis replied. Alex didn't have time to interpret Anubis' meaning; he was a bit busy at the moment trying not to be afraid, and most definitely trying *not* to be dead. The last thing he needed now was for Anubis to see him scared. He'd never hear the end of it. Now *dead,* on the other hand, that's another story when dealing with Anubis, he thought.

The wind whipped and bolts of lightning cracked across the sky. Darkness blanketed the scene. Within moments, it was pitch black and Alex was having trouble seeing. The howls intensified as sharpened steel sang through the air. Although he could see nothing, his other senses were on overload; sound, smell, taste.

Wait, smell? Taste? At that moment, three distinct sounds echoed through the darkness like the beating of a drum, hollowed and deep.

The howls suddenly retreated into the distance and the darkness began to lift. Alex looked toward the sky and saw the last of the Valkyries disappear into the light. Silence surrounded them once again.

"Aww. Leaving so soon? And I didn't get you any parting gifts,"

Alex yelled toward the sky. He stood, confused at what just happened, when a faint odor drifted around him and found its way up his nose, slowly filling his head with the delights of food. He couldn't help but inhale deeply. With this aroma, all thoughts of the Valkyries had disappeared.

"What's that magnificent smell?" he asked aloud, sniffing at the air again. He turned toward the source, so startled at what he saw next that he nearly stumbled backward. Somehow during the attack they had traveled the entire length of the bridge and were now standing at the entrance of the great wooden castle. Two enormous hand-carved doors towered above them.

"Hey, did those whirling witches put some sort of whammy on us?" Alex questioned.

"WE ARE HERE," Anubis said. Alex rolled his eyes.

"Yeah, you're a genius. And where the heck is *here?*" he asked as something caught his eye. "*Hunh?*"

SEVEN

There, upon each massive door, was a familiar symbol. Standing on the tips of his toes, Alex ran the ends of his fingers over the carving, barely able to reach the bottom. He'd seen this before. There were three interwoven triangles, cut deep into each of the wooden doors.

"*Valknot,*" he said out loud.

Anubis dropped his head and shook it from side to side, as if somehow embarrassed.

"What?" Alex asked. "Do I have a boogie or something? Don't roll your eyes at me. Hey, I'm talking to you."

It was the same symbol he'd seen in the Hall of Records, of that Alex was certain. It seemed so long ago, the adventure that took him across the hot, dry desert of Egypt; so long ago that he thumbed through the sacred records of the great cultures of far off lands.

According to legend, an ancient race had built the Hall far beneath the mighty Sphinx. Anubis called them the Ancient Ones. It was older than the nearby pyramids; even older than the Sphinx that guarded its secrets. Everything was connected somehow.

He remembered this symbol particularly. He found it with the drawings of a great warrior ship. It had been written on a slip of paper that had fallen out of an old book, tucked away with stacks of scrolls.

He quickly pulled out his journal and, without hesitation, jotted down the single word. It was the first time he'd written anything in it. He'd spent so much of his time reading it and trying to unlock its mysteries. Might better put this thing to good use, he thought.

A sudden realization overcame him. When he first saw this word back in Egypt, it was buried down deep in the Hall, secretly hidden beneath the Sphinx. That was a different time, a different place.

How? Why here? Why now? He wasn't entirely sure of the connection between Egypt and this place. More truthfully, he just wasn't ready to accept it. Undoubtedly, his trip through the Hall of Records had given him more than he bargained for.

One thing was for sure, though; thanks to what he found in that gleaming white chamber beneath the hot desert sands, he now knew where he was. The old hag mentioned the gods of this land. They were here, behind this great door, Alex thought in amazement as he unknowingly caressed the symbol.

Here he was, standing on the other side, about to enter the hall of the great Norse gods. This carving *was* the Valknot, the symbol of their leader; and this was their hall, *this* was Valhalla.

Alex pressed his ear against the door. He could hear them. How could he *not* hear them? None of the gods he knew were exactly soft-spoken.

"*Wow*," he said, "that sounded strange, even in my head."

Well, Chronos, it's now or never, he thought. Giving it all of his might, Alex pushed the heavy doors apart and burst into the chaotic scene.

"Honey, *I'm home!*"

All manner of movement inside the great hall stopped instantly. The looming figures sat still, all eyes focused on this interloper. Silence smothered the room. Alex cleared his throat and was about to speak when he was stopped cold.

The largest, most imposing figure sitting at the far end had risen from an enormous wood-carved chair and landed the end of his staff hard against the plank board flooring three distinct times. The sound echoed through the hall and shook Alex's bones. Every individual in the massive hall stood in unison and turned toward the great warrior, heads facing the floor. Alex wondered if it was out of respect or fear. He'd find out soon enough.

"Hey, I know that dude," Alex whispered under his breath to his old friend.

"DUDE?" Anubis questioned.

"Yeah, *dude*. Seriously? We went over all of this before, remember? I swear you have *sometimer's disease,*" Alex said as he shot him a look of disbelief.

"HMMMFT. MANY YEARS AND MANY WORLDS HAVE PASSED SINCE THAT TIME," Anubis replied.

"*What?* Do you actually listen to yourself when you speak?" Alex yelped at the one towering next to him.

Three more times the staff met the floor. The commanding figure at the end of the hall spoke.

"Silence!" he thundered, staff in hand. Alex looked across the great expansion of space. Anubis can do better, he thought.

"Look," Alex whispered again, "you and I need to sit down and talk. It's bad enough you walk around on your hind legs like some sort of circus sideshow freak and, and well, you know . . . you're a *dog;* but when you start talking gibberish, I have to get some answers."

"HMMPTT," responded Anubis.

"Don't start that spitting again. *Comprende, amigo?*" Alex pressed, poking at him with his finger.

"YOU BORE ME. THEY APPROACH," Anubis said, lifting his long, sharp forefinger and pointing. Two of the figures were making their way down the long hall from the other end. The closer they got, the more distinct their features became.

122

One, the one who spoke before, was leading, but not by much. He was far older than the others, with silver hair flowing well past his shoulders and his most defining feature, a single distinct scar that ran diagonally across his face where one of his eyes should've been. He relied heavily upon his staff to walk; not from failing health as it would seem, but rather as if from some unforeseen burden.

The second figure acted anxious, almost uncontrollable, and Alex could tell this wore heavily on the first one.

He looked around one last time. The room was indeed enormous, made of wood; its roof was that of dreams. Thousands of hammered battle shields served that purpose and shimmered silver, reflecting the clear light of the fires set around the room. These fires gave both light and warmth to such a vast space and flamed upward, each from a circular stone structure. There were dozens in all.

At first glance, the table was set for a feast, covered in all manner of cooked beasts, breads, and other assorted treats. Alex's mouth began to water; but upon closer inspection, he noticed that most of the food had been devoured, as if a pack of hungry wolves had settled in for a long winter. Both food and drink were spilled along the table, flowing to the floor. Several dogs were below, snapping at each other over the scraps.

Alex wasn't quite sure he was hungry anymore.

"Come, you're welcome here. We've been expecting you," the imposing figure said with a smile. As he neared the two friends, he reached out his hand in friendship. Alex quickly became aware of how large these gods actually were. He hesitantly reached out with his own hand and it was engulfed immediately.

"I'm known as the All-Father, but you may call me . . ." the great god began.

123

"Uh, I know who you are, sir. You're Odin," Alex said meekly. He wasn't scared, just slightly intimidated. To him, Odin seemed nice enough, but something about him made Alex think he was one dude he just didn't want to mess with.

"Hello again, my friend," Odin said, looking at Anubis. Alex looked up at his large companion in confusion.

"*Again?* You two know each other? Dude, if you don't start telling me what's going on, I swear I'm going to shave your butt," he threatened. Anubis was preoccupied at the moment with the second figure. He sniffed at the air. Alex saw something large in the other's hand. It looked heavy, like some sort of weapon. Anubis noticed it, too.

They faced off, warrior to warrior, each sensing the other's power, feeding off it. They were preparing for combat. Alex knew he needed to do something or blood would be spilled.

"And the air was filled with testosterone," Alex commented out loud, trying his best to break through the tension.

"Is this what passes for a god where you come from?" the other questioned mockingly.

Anubis let out a low growl; his claws were clenched. Alex had seen this before.

"Thor, your arrogance has brought embarrassment to my house in front of our guests," Odin said angrily. Thor ignored his father, his eyes never leaving Anubis. They were of equal height, with the Viking god being of thicker form with a mass of unkempt red hair on his head and face.

"Thor, hunh?" Alex interrupted. "I pictured you as a blond, and taller; much taller."

"Thor, your skills are needed elsewhere," Odin spoke again.

"Yeah, Red, didn't you hear your daddy?" Alex taunted.

"Insolent child. Do you think mere words will protect you?" Thor questioned as he turned toward Alex. Anubis was there to meet him.

"No, but he will," Alex responded, motioning with his thumb toward his large friend. Anubis was seething for battle. His chest pushed out his cold breath as saliva began to form along his mouth. His sharpened claws extended; he was ready.

"I said now!" Odin bellowed and slammed his staff to the ground. In the echo of the moment, Thor was gone. He disappeared in a flick of light.

"You must be hungry," Odin said calmly and turned toward the table. The half-eaten food from before, the masticated morsels and bits left behind for the animals, had been replaced by new fare, hot and steaming. Mouthwatering and hypnotizing aromas filled the air.

Alex looked up at Anubis and said, "Dude reads minds, too. Can you do that?"

"HMMFF," Anubis responded.

"Didn't think so," Alex continued. They followed Odin back toward the far end of the table. As they walked, Alex noticed a young maiden of similar size and age as he on the other side, serving hot beverages to those who still stood. Something drew his eyes toward her as he watched her top off every glass in the room. Her pitcher never went dry.

Must be magic, he thought, and dismissed it for nothing more. Strangeness, it seems, was becoming familiar to him, normal even. Besides, he was far more intrigued by her familiarity than her waitressing abilities. There's something about her, he thought. I know her from somewhere.

Her features were soft and smooth, and she wore her thick blonde hair up in a tightly braided bun. A thin white veil covered the top of her head. She danced around the table with the greatest of ease, humming loudly. She seemed genuinely happy, oblivious to everyone around her. Alex smiled. It had been some time since he'd seen that kind of joy. Something familiar about her, he thought again.

Lost deep in thought, trying to solve this latest puzzle of the merry maiden, Alex barely noticed when Odin gave a slight nod to yet another stranger, a man who, when brushing past Alex, placed a small piece of paper into his hand, winked, and smiled. Then Odin spoke.

"Safe travels, Gerry."

"*Gerry?* You mean *Egypt* Gerry? *Tad* Gerry?" Alex grilled the elder god. Startled, he looked down into his hand. His eyes widened, his mouth agape. By the time he looked up, the stranger was already passing through the door. As he left the room, Alex heard him say, "By the way, Alex, how's that journal working out for you?"

Alex first learned of Gerry in Egypt from Tad. The mysterious man had been there too. He visited her, taught her to speak his language. She *knew* him. But he was here? Now? How could that be? Alex wondered. He was only a name until now.

Just as he was about to run after him, Alex heard something else that pulled him back, something so amazing, so incredibly unbelievable that it stopped him flat. He searched frantically. He needed to be sure. His heart was already racing when he heard it again; singing.

"Two paths that cross, forever bind, as you travel through space and time. And when you do, one deed becomes two. Many a deed comes undone, but in the end, two destinies become one."

"Gramma?" Alex's head snapped back toward the source. It had to be. Nobody else could sing that poorly, he thought. Only it wasn't his grandmother he saw; it was the young maiden. She was twirling and spinning, completely oblivious to everyone and everything around her, so much that, as she passed through yet another door, she actually said, "Excuse me," as she bumped into the jamb. The girl. It *is* her!

He was torn; chase the one person who could answer his questions, all of his questions, or run after his grandmother, throw his arms around her, and never let her go. He missed her so. His heart ached just thinking about her, and now she's here, finally here, in the next room. He hesitated. What are you doing, Chronos? he wondered. Go after her. Go after her now, idiot.

Deep inside, he knew what to do. He'd see her again someday, but there was something bigger, more important. He turned and ran after the stranger. When he reached the large entrance doors, he was met with a flash of blue light. The hall was empty. Gerry was gone.

Alex knew he had one last chance for happiness. He turned and ran back into the hall, back toward the girl. He didn't have time to take the long way around, so he hood-slid across the table like his favorite television characters, knocking food and fare everywhere. It was rude, but for some reason he feared he might lose her, too. He'd never forgive himself if he did.

Sliding off the table and onto the far bench, Alex took a single step and landed, skidding on what appeared to be some sort of pudding. When he finally stopped, he was at the door, and she was gone, too. He stood there staring, trying to process what he'd seen. Tears filled the bottoms of his eyes, overflowed, and found their way down his cheeks. He wiped at them when he felt a heavy hand upon his shoulder. It was Anubis.

"It's not fair," Alex muttered, fighting back more tears. He gave one last turn toward the door as they walked away together.

"NO, IT IS DESTINY," Anubis said.

"Really, dude? That's all you got?" Alex yelled at him. "You seriously have to work on your bedside manner. You know, it comes from spending way too much time playing with dead things," Alex said laughingly.

He wasn't sure, but he thought he saw Anubis smile as well. Well, it was kind of a smile, he thought. There were teeth, definitely teeth. Another time and Alex would've believed it to be indigestion rather than a smile, but they hadn't eaten in some time. Like most teenagers', Alex's thoughts eventually ended up in one place; food.

They followed Odin to his high seat at the end of the table and sat beside him. Alex was quiet for once. His head hung toward the table. The cry of a bird echoed through the hall and he looked up. Two ravens were circling above. Remembering how excited the pigeons became back in the tavern, he shifted uneasily, pulled up his collar, and covered his head with one hand. Odin laughed as if he could hear Alex's thoughts.

The ravens landed, one on each of the All-Father's shoulders. Alex looked on as Odin leaned into one and whispered. This guy's wacky just like Crunch, he thought. In fact, put some chocolates in front of him and it would be difficult to tell them apart.

Alex always thought fondly of his principal, Mr. Crunch. Most people knew him as a stout man with many quirks, two pet birds, an insatiable love for chocolate, and a messy office at the end of the hall. Alex, however, knew him as a kind fellow who had always been nice to his grandmother, and, in Alex's mind, that made him alright.

"Loki has more in store for us, for you, my friend," Odin spoke.

"Did the birds tell you that?" Alex joked.

"Why, yes, they did," Odin replied calmly. Alex now had his proof. This guy was certifiable.

"So tell me, my son, how have you found our land thus far?" Odin asked. There was something about when he spoke. Perhaps years of experience had brought him wisdom, or maybe it was the fact that every other being within earshot of the All-Father stopped what they were doing each time he opened his mouth. Regardless, Alex suspected he was called the All-Father for good reason.

"Well, when E.F. Hutton talks, people listen," Alex replied jokingly. If there was one thing Alex liked more than watching old movies with the Captain, it was watching classic television commercials. The room stared at him silently; confused.

"Wow. Tough crowd," he mumbled as he looked around, then turned to Odin and responded, "I like it fine enough, if it weren't for everybody trying to kill me." Alex mentioned this last part for the effect more than anything else. The room stood silent and gave up no response, no reaction. Alex was disappointed.

"*I said*, everybody's been trying to kill me," he repeated himself.

"Is life not a battle itself?" Odin broke through the silence. A wave of nods washed down the table.

"Oh, so *now* you respond," Alex said to the others surrounding the table.

"Tell us of yours," Odin invited. Alex knew he may never get another chance like this. He had the table.

"Well, first, there were the stinking fireballs you guys were sending my way when I got here. Then, as if that weren't enough, a whole bunch of long haired, wind-surfing screaming pixies in battle armor started poking at me with sharp things. I found it particularly nice when they uh, well, *leveled an entire village!*" he finished loudly.

Odin merely smiled and said, "Go on."

"Are you flipping kidding me? Wasn't that enough?" Alex asked incredulously. Odin calmly waited in silence.

129

"Okaaayy," Alex continued. "How about the stinking hell-hound the size of a motor home? Will that work for you?" The entire hall erupted in a frenzy of nervous chatter.

"Now that got their hackles up, didn't it?" Alex whispered to Anubis, who'd been sitting quietly this entire time. He looked down at Alex with narrowed eyes. "Oops, sorry about the hackle comment. Was I barking up the wrong tree? Ha, get it? But seriously, these dudes were dogging me, though. Oh, snap. Dog gone it, I just can't let it go," Alex said.

Odin raised his staff as earlier and sent three shock waves through the hall when he landed it to the floor. The room fell silent.

"Tell us of this beast," Odin asked.

"Yeah, Loki called him *Fahrvergnügen* or something like that. Which doesn't make sense, because the mutt was much bigger than a Volkswagen," Alex began.

"I believe you mean *Fenrisúlfr*. We know of him," Odin corrected him. He seemed unusually calm to Alex.

"Yeah, that's him. Anyway, Fido tried to jump me blindside, but I laid a full blown WWE smack down on him. Let's just say that pooch isn't doing any butt-sniffing in the near future. Am I right?" Alex finished with a wide smile and raised his hand high to Anubis, who in turn ignored him.

"Dude, don't leave me hanging," Alex pleaded.

"Please continue," Odin interrupted. Alex glared at Anubis, trying desperately to burn a hole into his skull with his mind. It didn't work.

"Well, as I was saying, Boris the bouncing beagle came at me with everything he had. In the end, there was this magic chain I, uh, acquired," he continued. He felt a bit silly at first mentioning such things as magic in front of others, but then looked around and realized that he was surrounded by gods. He was the only human in the place, so he shrugged and thought, why not?

"So I roped the little doggie, no pun intended, with this magic chain and jump started it with my pendant. Alex one, wolf zero," he finished. Alex looked around to gauge everyone's reaction to his story. Having just retold it, it sounded unreal, even to him. He was surprised to see little reaction from the room, so he continued.

"Then this Apache helicopter swooped down out of the clouds, guns a-blazing and . . ."

"ENOUGH," Anubis finally spoke.

"Too much?" Alex asked. Odin rubbed at the scar across his eye. He seemed to be thinking of something distant. Alex gave him his moment, which allowed him to further test the capacity of the human stomach by shoving even more food into his mouth. A part of him believed that it would disappear as quickly as it appeared. Let's face it, Alex thought; here, it's a likely possibility.

"Fenrisúlfr grows too fast and cannot be controlled. It seems the prophecies of Gleipnir have been woven into your own. To bind the wolf was the only way. Still, I fear we haven't seen the last of the filthy beast. Prophecies, after all, are destined to be fulfilled," Odin said.

"Dude, I have prophecies," Alex said, looking up at Anubis with a hint of conceit. Anubis gave no response.

"That's just cold," Alex said to his friend.

"You have many," Odin interrupted, giving a deliberate nod toward Alex's pendant. "Not all have come to pass."

"Aww man, you, too? Why does everyone speak in riddles?" Alex asked desperately.

"And what led you here to this sacred place?" Odin asked. Alex suspected the All-Father already knew the answers to the questions

131

he asked, including this one, but he answered anyway.

"Well, after those ghostly groupies herded us over that funky looking bridge like sheep . . ." Alex continued.

"And do you know where you are now?" the All-Father questioned.

"Yeah, we sort of realized where we were once we saw the Valknot," Alex replied.

The expansive hall erupted in laughter. Plates shook on the table, whole glasses of ale fell to the floor. It was so loud that Alex instinctively ducked, fearing more blasts were heading his way.

"*Uh*, was it something I said?" he asked quietly.

"A simple mistake, my son. The great symbol carved upon the door, the one you called Valknot, well, is not," Odin explained.

"Is not what?" Alex asked.

"Is not, *knot*," Odin clarified.

"It's not, *not* what?" Alex asked again, wiping at the corner of his mouth as tiny morsels of food fell to the table.

"Not not, *knot*," Odin simplified. "The knot is not knot; it's knut," he continued.

"Nut what?" Alex was getting confused.

"Not nut, knut," Odin corrected him.

"What nut?" Alex pleaded in frustration.

"The knot. The knot is knut," Odin explained. Alex eyed him narrowly from behind a regenerating pile of pork.

"Are you doing this on purpose?" he asked. Odin simply waited calmly. Several moments passed when a look of embarrassment shot across Alex's face. He realized what he'd said.

"Oh, I get it now," he said softly, his face turning warm. "You mean it isn't Val*knot*, it's Val*knut*." He slumped down where he sat, trying desperately to hide.

"Precisely," Odin said, somewhat exhausted himself. Alex's head was starting to pound. He hadn't thought this hard since the last time he and his grandmother did the Sunday morning crossword puzzle.

"Glad we cleared that up," Alex said to Anubis as he rolled his eyes and rubbed his head. Anubis sat staring back at him with what appeared to be a puzzled look.

"*What?* Oh, like you understood," Alex said. When he turned back, he was startled to see Odin had a knife in his hand. Not certain what this old man with one eye was up to, Alex kept his distance. His teenage imagination quickly got the better of him. His nerves frayed when Odin, for no apparent reason, began scratching at the table with the knife, like a demented killer from a late night horror movie.

"What do you see, my son?" Odin asked, referring to what he just carved into the table. Alex felt a sudden rush of relief once he realized what Odin had done.

"Three triangles," Alex replied with obvious conviction.

"And what of their meaning?" Odin asked. "Think hard." Alex stared at the symbol for some time.

"Think of it as a map," Odin encouraged. Alex cocked his head and squinted his eyes. He didn't see it.

"I'm sorry, sir, but if I followed this map, I'd end up back at the beginning," he said.

"Precisely," Odin said. "Most humans believe it's the symbol of Odin and my connection with life and death, and they'd be right; but it's so much more than that. The truth is, it represents our journey here to this land and how everything around us is connected. How we're connected. In short, our beginning and our end, our origin and our destiny. You'll hear of this again, before

133

long," Odin explained. "The fact that they're interconnected implies our rebirth, our rise from the ashes, so to speak. As you put it, back at the beginning."

If Alex ever pictured a wise person, it would've been eerily similar to the figure in front of him. Silver hair flowed from his head representing life's many experiences, the scar on his face showed the sacrifices made, and his wrinkles mapped the hardships endured. This was someone who deserved respect.

"I think I understand, but what's all that have to do with me? Why am I here?" Alex asked.

"You must have patience, my son," Odin said.

"Patience? I'm a teenager with overactive adrenal glands. Patience, he says. *Hah,*" Alex responded. He recognized the look in Odin's eye. It was identical to the look his grandmother would give him in moments like these. As a mature man all of thirteen, he found it somehow both frustrating and quieting at the same time.

"Uh, forgive me for asking, but what happened to your eye?" he asked, stuffing yet another piece of pork into his already packed cheeks. He was eager to change the subject, and this was an obvious choice to him.

"Gain doesn't come without sacrifice, but I suspect you've already learned that lesson; and if you haven't, you soon will," Odin explained with a smile as he motioned toward the door where Alex had last seen his grandmother.

"Yeah, I'd say. Will I ever see her again?" Alex asked, grabbing another slice of warm bread. Odin simply smiled. Not the answer I was hoping for, but still, I'll take it, Alex thought. Dude's a bit like talking to a Magic Eight Ball.

"So what's the deal with the chain? Was it *real* magic? Like David Copperfield magic or more like magically-delicious magic? I saw this dude once, sawed a lady right in two. Oh, it's real, I know it is."

"Gleipnir was forged in the fires of Álfheimr by the elves of that land. They've provided us with many tools with which to defeat our enemies."

"*Elves?* You have elves, too? Dude, that's *Rawesome!* So much better than the giants we saw," Alex blurted out.

"So you're familiar with the *Jotunn?*" Odin asked curiously.

"Yeah, them we've met. Loki's minions, I'm guessing," Alex said regretfully.

"Indeed," Odin said.

"So, these elves; are they the kind that make shoes in the middle of the night? Because I have to tell you, I could use a fresh pair of kicks," Alex said as he raised his foot high above the table at which he sat. It was a rather awkward pose, even for him.

"Yes, their skills are legendary. We even entrusted them to craft the same ropes that support that, how did you say it, funky looking bridge," Odin said. Alex smiled.

"Got a lot, do you?" Alex asked. "Enemies, that is, not elves."

"I fear we do. A burden we gods must bear," Odin replied solemnly.

"I feel you, brother." Alex shook his head.

The night ran long and, aside from the evening's earlier events, Alex was rather enjoying himself. For once, there was plenty of food. For every bite he took, three would replace it on the table. Alex quickly realized this place, or at least the food, was enchanted. At the moment all he cared about was the food; sweet, delicious food.

The gods surrounding the table laughed heartily and drank, then drank some more. Much like the food he ate, their glasses never seemed to empty. Occasionally he glanced around the hall, searching

135

for either of them, but he knew they were gone.

His thoughts brought him back home to the worn chair in front of the fireplace. They'd sit for hours; his grandmother with her knitting, him helping and laughing. Oh, they could laugh. She had her moments of clarity and seemed to save them just for him.

He also knew, much like Egypt, there was a deed. A deed unraveled, he thought, and he was stuck here in this strange place until it was fixed. Until he fixed it; a series of all too familiar questions flooded his mind. But why me? he wondered. What do I have to do with all of this? What's my connection to everything?

It had been some time since Alex had slept, and he was starting to feel the effects of a long night of eating. His eyes were heavy and started to droop. He let out a yawn, but it wasn't until he returned the last piece of pork to the table that he realized he was tired.

Odin was amused by Alex, and although frequently called him son, Alex suspected the All-Father's interest in him was slightly less paternal. He gave Alex a telling glance.

"Come. I've something to show you," Odin said, and the two rose from the table in unison. All others followed.

"Silly gods. You don't have to stand for little old me," Alex said jokingly. "Please sit." He looked up at the All-Father.

"Hey, do that staff thing again," he said. Odin let out a chuckle that made the dust from the rafters above settle down to the table. As requested, he raised his staff high above his head, his eye never leaving Alex, and landed his staff to the floor. The others sat in unison.

"It's been some time since I've had a young one at my side. I rather like it," Odin admitted, still smiling.

"Yeah, hanging out with me has its perks, doesn't it?" Alex said, looking over at Anubis rather smugly.

136

"HMMFT," Anubis responded. He stood and unfolded himself slowly, rising to his full height. Even next to these gods, next to Odin, Anubis was a sight to behold. Dressed in full gleaming battle armor and a being the likes of which had never been seen in this land before. Or has it? Alex wondered.

"You're not very talkative this trip, and that's saying a lot. What's the matter, cat got your tongue?" Alex laughed. "*Ha,* even tired, I still got it. Get it? Cat. And you're a dog. You know, cats and dogs hate . . ." Anubis stared blankly back at him.

"Never mind," Alex finished, shaking his head in disbelief. Odin raised his staff one more time.

"It's okay. You don't have to . . ." Before Alex could finish, Odin's staff found its place once again, and the great hall vanished before them in a swirl of mist.

All three were now standing, much as they were in the hall, outside the entrance to another room. Alex looked down the long corridor. It seemed endless, with door after door running as far as he could see in either direction.

Without a word, Odin pushed the closest one with the end of his staff and it creaked open. He stepped blindly into the darkness, quickly followed by the other two.

The room was vast and long, far larger than Alex expected hidden behind the small, modest door. He felt the importance of this room immediately, much like that of the great chamber that gleamed white, buried beneath the sands of Egypt. This room, however, was different in its presentation. The space was expansive, but dark and unassuming, almost thick. Alex could practically smell the history in the room.

Made entirely of wood, the room appeared to have been

hollowed out from a single tree, where no seams between floor, wall, and ceiling existed. There were, however, several thick posts carved ornately into dragon-like creatures, spiraling upward to support everything above. The carvings seemed out of place, foreign even. In truth, Alex had seen pictures of dragons like these in his History book, but recalled finding them detailed under Asian Culture, not Norse.

A single lantern was lit in the center of the room, hung by iron links from above. There were no tables as there had been in Egypt, no chairs upon which to sit. Rather, much like the tavern back in town, there were logs, split lengthwise and fashioned into benches.

These benches ran the entire perimeter of the space, hundreds of feet in all, each placed about four feet from the wall. Alex assumed this was to allow people to sit and watch events unfold in the middle of the room. Aside from the benches and the center posts, the room appeared to be empty.

"Uh, god-dude. I mean, Mr. Odin All-Father person. I hate to be the one to point out the obvious, but I think you've been robbed!" Alex cried.

Odin laughed and patted him on the shoulder, unintentionally buckling him to his knees. It was apparent that he realized his mistake, when he lifted Alex by his shirt collar and set him upright.

"No, my son, no thief would dare enter this sacred place," Odin said boldly.

"But there's nothing here. The place is empty," Alex said incredulously.

"Ah, but there are times that what we can't see is just as precious, just as valuable and important, as what we can," Odin explained.

"Uh, no offense, but *you* can't see anything. You only have one

138

eye, and I'm pretty sure the other one drifts a little. Just saying," Alex remarked. Odin laughed.

As Alex walked through the space, he felt a strange sense of connection here. He felt this way only one other time in his life, in the Hall of Records in Egypt. It was a pull, something tugging at him from the inside. It felt comfortable to him, like being home.

Reaching the midpoint of the room, Alex sat, almost in a daze. Odin and Anubis stood watching him closely.

"This isn't right," Alex said, looking up at Odin. He paused for a moment, deeply contemplating, then spun around, facing the wall behind him. Odin smiled. The dim light from the lantern cast vague shadows on the walls. Alex's head began to spin. The walls jumped to life, pushing reliefs outward from its wood. Sounds and colors were all around him as scenes became vivid on the walls; moving, shaping a story, several stories.

Alex watched as a single being battled magnificent odds, fighting monstrous creatures, while others looked on from above. A great tree blew in the wind. Alex shuddered. A snake wove its way into the story, followed by an intense feeling of pain. The scene vanished as quickly as it appeared, leaving no signs of what he'd seen.

"Who's that poor sap?" Alex asked as he turned toward Odin.

"Why, that's you," Odin responded.

"What? You've had too much happy sauce." Alex shot him a look like he was crazy.

He stood and moved closer to where the scene had unraveled and gently touched the wall, his curiosity growing.

"How could that possibly have been me? I just got here." He scratched his head.

"Oh no, my child, you've been here before. Many times," Odin explained with a smile.

"Are you kidding? Wait; are there cameras on me right now?" With great animation, Alex walked over to one of the massive dragon-carved posts, pressed his face to it close, and said, "Hello, anybody in there?" and knocked on the structure for dramatic effect.

"That's the thing about history, lad; it can always be changed." Odin slapped him hard on the back and gave a hearty laugh. Alex stumbled. "The real question is, are you going to change history, or do you intend on making it? Both are journeys set before men, but only one can be achieved by the gods."

"Let's just say for a moment that I believe you, or even understand you, and for the record, I don't. I most certainly haven't fought any giant snakes or any of those other nasty dudes before. I think I'd remember. Now dogs, yeah, I've had my share," he said, shooting a knowing glance at Anubis. "But I didn't see any of those mangy mongrels, now did I?"

"Things are never as they seem. That's one of Loki's many weaknesses. He only sees what rests before him. He doesn't see that which stirs within," Odin explained.

For as long as Alex had been a teenager, he had a response for everything; but as he stood there trying to understand what Odin said, his mouth open, he was uncharacteristically silent. After several long moments he spoke.

"Nope. I got nothing," he said finally.

"HMMFT," Anubis responded.

"Oh, you're funny. Funny looking, that is," Alex shot back.

Odin continued, "Our many lands are in an uproar over Loki's insolence, his measure against them. His tricks have turned dangerous and his head is full of anger toward the gods. He wishes to rule, so he plots against us, me. His anger has maddened him beyond reason. I'm told he recruits his brethren, the *Jotunn*, and his

140

own vile children."

"Yeah, giants; he has plenty. Well, actually, thanks to us, he has a few less now," Alex said proudly. He stood, staring at Odin wide-eyed, much the same as when he was younger sitting through storytime at the library. Only this was real, he thought. Wait, what am I thinking? Is it real? Is any of this real? Alex wondered. He'd soon have his answer.

Odin must've recognized Alex's look and continued, "Loki's vision is narrowed. Far more has gone into the making of this story." He raised his staff once more, and the room filled with dense fog. As it lifted and enveloped him completely, Alex felt the floor beneath his feet start to spin. Surprisingly, he felt calm and, when the fog finally thinned, the large room had been swept away.

EIGHT

They were now standing just inside what appeared to be an oversized sleeping chamber. A large bed, too large for any human, was positioned to the right, near the opening to a balcony. To the left, a fire raged in the basin similar to those from the hall.

"Well, beats taking the stairs, I guess," Alex remarked. "How come when you do it, my stomach turns inside out?" he asked Anubis sarcastically. For an instant, Alex swore he saw Anubis smirk. As they walked across the room, Odin spoke again.

"The First Ones traveled here from a far off place. The edge of the world. The beginning," he began. Alex's thoughts immediately went to Egypt. He'd seen something there, something completely amazing and, in fact, utterly unbelievable. He remembered the hidden chamber and its gleaming white marble. The ancient records had been archived there for an eternity, but for what? For whom? *By* whom? he wondered.

Then it flashed through his mind; that picture. His heart raced. *Atlantis;* dare he dream it was real? He always hoped, like most misguided souls. They're crackpots, loons, he thought; but someone had put it there, centuries before they stumbled upon it, centuries before the pyramids themselves were built above. Perhaps this was what Odin's talking about.

"They brought with them the power and knowledge to create our Nine Worlds," Odin continued. "Among them, Asgaard, Ālfheimr, and your world, Midgard." Odin seemed to sense that Alex was lost in thought.

"You see, my son, all stories, all legends, all magic and power and knowledge are connected. It comes from a single source; an ancient,

142

lost source. It's both your origin and your destiny," Odin attempted to explain.

"Everything's connected," Alex muttered to himself.

"We've seen our story played out over the millennium. It's already been written. Loki wishes to change that, make it his to control, like puppets. He knows not the danger that comes with wielding such power. Only one does," Odin said with finality.

Alex looked up at the All-Father. Odin was smiling down at him. He didn't want to ask the question, but he knew he had to.

"Who's that?" he asked quietly.

Odin laughed heartily. "Why, you already know the answer, my boy."

Alex turned pale with anxiety as the All-Father left the room. He stood, unable to move, frozen by what Odin had said. So many thoughts ran through his mind, he couldn't pinpoint just one. It felt like he was going insane. They were uncontrollable, too many. For an instant, he wondered if this was what it was like inside his grandmother's head sometimes.

His grandmother; she was here, he'd seen her, or so he thought. It certainly sounded like her. Odin didn't say it was, but he didn't exactly say it wasn't either. It had to be her. He needed it to be her. Familiar tears filled his eyes; but if it was, what was she doing here?

Wait. It couldn't be her, he thought. He must've imagined it. He'd seen a young girl, not somebody's grandmother. How could it be? he wondered. The last time he'd seen her, she was in the upstairs window of their house. So long ago, he reflected. I need to get back. I need to see her again.

A feeling of renewed conviction filled him. He was going to see her again, even if it killed him. Around here, likely, he thought. People, even gods, talk about destiny an awful lot. He wasn't sure what his destiny was, but he did know one thing; if he was ever going to get home, he needed to get out of here first.

He was pretty certain he was here for a reason. Somebody or something brought him here. If, as he thought earlier, this *was* like Egypt and there *was* a deed, then he needed to be prepared. Not just to mend it, but for far more.

"I just realized something. I'm the universe's flipping TV repairman," Alex joked. Too bad they don't make tools for that, he joked as he looked back at Anubis and smiled.

"Tools, check." After all, what better tool than Anubis? he thought.

I'm betting this particular deed has something to do with that Loki dude, Alex thought. He pulled at his shirt tail, bringing it up to his eyes, wiping at them. This is no time for tears, he told himself, and gave a big sniff. Anubis had been watching closely for some time and sensed Alex's sadness.

"COME," Anubis beckoned Alex.

"Hey, is this about that tool comment?" Alex asked nervously.

It was quiet and dark. The fire that blazed from the far side of the room surprisingly gave little warmth. Its light clashed with the darkness entering the room through the open balcony, greyed by the overcast evening sky. It brought with it cold and dampness.

Alex didn't much care for being cold, but it was a heck of a lot better than being broiled on the desert sand, he thought. He let out a shiver. He wasn't quite sure if it was because he was cold or if it had something to do with what was about to happen.

Anubis sat cross-legged on the floor, his crook placed in front of him. As he raised his arms and drew his hands over the crook, it began to glow softly. Alex felt the familiar warmth close to his chest that only came with a similar light from his own pendant. He

144

removed it from its hiding place and it lit up the room.

The two objects seemed to have a connection. As one would grow in intensity, so did the other. They soon began to pulse in harmony. The cold suddenly withdrew from the room in response. Their shadows danced off the walls, larger than life.

Alex watched as Anubis' eyes turned ghostly white. He desperately wanted to yell, but couldn't. His throat tightened with every attempt. The room began to spin and his head throbbed. In a final burst, the glow was gone.

Alex found himself in an infinite space, void of time and matter. All that he saw was of mist and blackness. There existed nothing solid that he could see as distance, too, seemed to escape this place. He fumbled around to feel his way, but felt nothing, saw nothing. Even his friend was gone. This last part frightened him most. Sure, there were plenty of times when Anubis wasn't around, but his companion had always been there when he needed him.

Alex felt his throat loosen, and he immediately took full advantage of it. Calling out for Anubis, he received no response. Why couldn't he see him, hear him? Where was he? In the midst of his growing fear, Alex suddenly felt calmed when a sound far in the distance drifted lazily into the space. No, not a sound; a voice. Anubis! Alex was relieved. Wait, not Anubis; someone else.

Alex struggled to push his senses deeper into the darkness, around the sound, hoping to hear the words or even recognize the voice. Was it Odin again? Had he returned? It sure didn't sound like him. His brain was telling him he should be scared, but he was at peace. No good ever came from a mysterious voice, he thought; at least not to me.

"Alex."

Did it just say my name? he wondered.

"Alex," the voice repeated.

"Who's there?" Alex asked into the black.

A softness entered the space, and the feeling of happiness filled him. He hadn't felt this way in a long time, not since the marketplace, not since Tad. He didn't know why, but he couldn't help but smile. The thought of her always had this impact on him.

The softness was followed by a gentle light as the smell of Jasmine filled the space around him. He felt like he was floating, lifeless. The light seemed to be moving toward him, and he watched as a single shape came into focus. He recognized it instantly. It was her!

He couldn't believe his eyes. Instinctively, he wiped at them, still not quite believing what he saw.

"Is it you? Is it *really* you?" Alex cried out in hopeful joy.

"It is," Tad replied with a gentle smile. His heart jumped to his throat. He instantly became a teenage boy again. So many thoughts raced through his head. He knew that whatever he said next had to be perfect. Many things, perhaps even his future, their future together, rode on what's said next. They would likely be the most important words he'd ever utter. He took a deep breath.

"So, I've been working out," Alex blurted. He cringed from embarrassment. *Seriously?* I sound like Jackson, he thought.

Tad looked stunned and confused. Oh no, she thinks I'm an idiot, he thought. Heck, even I think I'm an idiot. She reached out and softly touched his hand as if she could sense his feelings. Alex immediately went numb. His face turned hot and red.

A fleeting memory of something the Captain once told him flashed across his mind.

"A man chases a woman until she catches him," the Captain said. "Heard it from a song, I did. Must be true."

146

Well, true or not, Alex liked it. Trying desperately to regain his sense of dignity, he puffed out his chest again, cleared his throat, and asked, "Are you real or a dream?"

"Can you not feel me? Do you not think of me often?" Tad replied softly. Alex blushed as he looked down at his feet. He had his answer. She was real, as long as he held her in his heart.

"But how's this possible? How can you be here?" he asked.

"You aren't the only one with a destiny, and it seems ours are connected," she explained.

"Is this another Gerry thing?" Alex questioned.

"No. It was you who brought me here," she told him.

"*Me?* How?" he quickly asked.

"We're connected. Everything is connected," she added. Alex's eyes widened.

"Can you stay?" he asked.

"I cannot," she replied solemnly.

"Why not? Will I see you again?" he asked desperately.

"We'll be together again. *That* is our final deed."

"How can you be sure?" Alex begged.

"Each of us has a destiny, and this is mine," Tad responded with a quiet smile, and with that she began to fade into the light. Alex reached out for her. He could feel her slipping away. He only wanted, no needed, more time with her. He had so many questions, so many things left to say.

Before completely disappearing, Tad leaned in close, and Alex was certain he felt a small kiss on his lips. His eyes lit up. She was gone.

As the void lifted and the room came into focus, Alex jumped up, threw his hands into the air, and began to wave them about. Although intended as a dance of pure joy, it wasn't even close, but pure joy was most definitely involved. If it weren't for the unending smile that split across his face and the occasional, *"Woot! Woot!"* it would've appeared more like he was in extreme pain.

It was a nervous jerk, followed by the bouncing of his head, all the while his arms were high above, moving back and forth. He didn't care what he looked like; it was the first time he'd been this happy in a long time.

His flailing legs shot out from under his long thin body with little control and knocked into a table, sending him tripping over Anubis, who still sat cross-legged on the floor. When all was over, Alex was looking up at Anubis, cradled like a baby in his lap.

With a smile from ear to ear, he reached up with his arms and wrapped them around Anubis' head, leaned in, and kissed him square on the snout.

"DUDE," Anubis barked.

"See, you do remember," Alex said, rolling off his friend's hairy lap.

"ARE YOU DONE?"

"Boy, you sure are a wet blanket. Still, don't tell anybody about what just happened or I'll call the vet on you. Got it?" Alex said earnestly.

"YOU TASTE LIKE CAMEL."

"Yeah, well, you're not exactly wearing cherry lip gloss yourself, but still, you have a point. I need a bath," Alex conceded as he turned his nose toward his armpit and gave a short sniff.

"Wow," was all he said as he left the room coughing. The evening was lingering, and when Alex returned to the chamber washed, he jumped onto the bed, tired from a long day. Sleep wasn't in his future anytime soon, though. As he pulled his journal out from his pocket, he noticed Anubis on the balcony.

Better to leave him be, Alex thought, as he opened the journal. Besides, too much to do. He rested on his stomach and dove in. Flipping past Egypt once again, he went straight for the pages he hadn't read yet. The unfamiliar writings were different and appeared more detailed. Still, none of it was any clearer to him.

It wasn't a total loss, though. Egypt had taught him one thing; as odd as it sounded, the journal was a single source where both history and future collide, each becoming the other, creating something new. More important to Alex, it foretold of his future.

With the confirmation that Egypt, his journey, was somehow chronicled here between these tattered pages, he focused his efforts on what came next. It was here that he made out the word *Álfheimr*. The chain, he thought; but how? He next pulled the familiar torn paper from the journal. Raising it to the gentle light of his pendant, he could read the word. They laughed at him before. His face turned red from embarrassment.

"Not Valk*not*, Valk*nut*. Duh, I get it now. Chronos, you idiot. No wonder they laughed," he spoke louder.

So, then what's this one mean? he wondered as he stared blankly down at the next page. On it were several notes about water; separate thoughts, seemingly random.

One was a comment about mixing water with clay. The word *MUD* was scrawled in all caps next to it. *Duh*. A second was the symbol of three wavy lines which he now recognized. Yet a third mentioned something about rivers of tears setting him free. Odd, to be sure, but tears *are* made of water, he thought. Stranger still, was a rather crude drawing of a bull with large horns sketched next to it. No clue, he thought, and continued on.

It was the last passage, however, that sat heaviest on his chest. A short piece of writing had been scrawled out, referring to rising

149

waters and falling walls, of destruction and chaos, of life lost. Beneath this was written a rather ominous inscription.

Mom, Dad, it can't end like this!

He stared, motionless. This was the first time, the only time, he'd ever seen anything about his parents. He didn't remember, couldn't remember them. He'd sit and try for hours when he was younger, but always drew a blank. The house where he lived had no pictures of them, no trinkets or keepsakes staged about the place. His grandmother never spoke of them. It was as if they never existed.

Except for two things; *he* was living proof they were real, and now, this. But what's it mean? he wondered. He couldn't help but read it over and over again. How he missed them so. He often thought it was strange to miss someone he'd never seen; but then, *would* he see them one day? Had he seen them already?

Alex became lightheaded and couldn't focus. The thought of seeing his parents, the chance they may actually be alive, was unimaginable to him. It was bad enough being on some multi-dimensional road trip to save the universe from itself, and his best friend was an Egyptian god, but this was too much. For as long as he could remember, he wanted it, but he just couldn't handle it right now. He suddenly felt clammy and his palms began to sweat.

The walls of the room began to close in on him. The ceiling inched closer. Was he imagining? Time appeared to be speeding up. In the past, when things went wonky on him, mostly because of something Anubis did, he thought, time seemed to slow down; but not now, not here, and it most definitely wasn't a welcomed experience.

Flashes, pieces of forgotten memory, or perhaps some unknown future, warped into view. His stomach twisted in pain, causing him to curl up. Alex closed his eyes. All he could do was sit and wait.

* * *

When he finally had the courage to open his eyes again, thoughts of his parents had left him and the room had vanished.

He was standing high atop a jagged mountain, Anubis at his side, and he was cold. It was a barren and desolate place, allowing the wind to cut sharply across the land. The sky was dreary and lifeless, as if the sun had never blessed this place with its warm kiss. The harsh landscape was full of cracks and crevices, making it difficult to move and capable of tearing a gash in a person's side as easily as Anubis' claws. Steam lifted from the depths and billowed along the ground.

A soft rumbling was growing all around them. Alex looked and saw nothing. The noise became so intense it vibrated the ground beneath their feet. He felt like he was standing next to a jack hammer.

"Do you hear that?" Alex asked. "That vibration; can you feel it, too?" Alex turned and looked up at his enormous friend. Anubis' chest was heaving, pushing out cold air from deep within his lungs. His muscles were drawn tight like the string of a bow, ready to release its energy. Alex realized instantly what was happening.

"Not this again," Alex said, worried. "Look, have you thought of trying needlepoint? All this anger is going to get you killed. Actually, it's going to get us both killed, and uh, I rather like the whole living thing. Although with you, I can never tell if I am; *living*, that is." Alex gave Anubis a sharp look.

Froth was building at Anubis' mouth; his claws were clenched tightly, as if preparing for battle. Alex was worried. The last time he'd seen this reaction, it was only seconds before they'd become embroiled in a fight to the death with Set.

"Anubis, what's wrong?" Alex whispered desperately. He soon

151

had his answer. From out of the rising steam, a dark figure appeared. It floated in the distance, seemingly unaware of the two.

"Now look, you. Don't go chasing people we've just met. It's impolite." Too late; Anubis let out an earth-shattering roar and took off after the figure, springing from the tips of the sharp stones without hesitation.

"Well, that's just grand. Here we go again. If I didn't know any better, I'd say you enjoy this stuff, you flipping hairball," Alex shouted after him. He followed quite slowly and not without great effort, as he didn't quite possess the same skill as that of a warrior god.

"Oof. Oww. Hey, wait up," he yelled. Anubis was moving fast, and the gap between them was growing. Alex watched as his friend disappeared into the mist.

"Nooo! Wait!" he screamed helplessly. The harder Alex tried to keep up, the more he lost his footing. Every movement, every step, slipped, causing his pants to tear across the serrated rock. It wasn't long before they were colored red from his blood. He was reminded of the stinging pain each time the cloth brushed across the open wounds, but he had to bear it; he needed to find Anubis.

When he reached the mist, it shrouded him in moisture. He no longer felt the wind blowing, only the cold. He was tired of being cold. It's true, Alex thought; it was a far cry from the searing heat of the desert, but not exactly what I had in mind.

"Anubis, where are you?" Alex yelled. The space was void of all sound, and he was forced to feel his way through it. He sensed something move behind him.

"Anubis? Is that you?" he whispered when he turned around. Unfortunately for him, it wasn't. The dark figure stood towering above him. It caught him off-guard, and he stumbled back, onto the sharp stone, cutting the palms of his hands when he tried to stop his fall.

"*Ahhh, sheesh,*" he yelled in pain. When he looked up from his bloodied hands, the figure was gone. Fear mounted, building from deep inside, making him even more anxious than before. An overwhelming sense of pressure consumed him. He had no idea where his friend was.

Anubis was always there for him, protecting him. Alex constantly teased him, but somehow he believed Anubis knew how he felt. They'd become close, more than friends; but now his friend was gone.

Fear was all around him, filling him with doubt. His heart beat hard and he grabbed at it, trying to keep it from jumping out of his chest. His mind drifted to Tuat. *Pure* is what Anubis had said. His heart needed to be pure. He passed the test, but that was Egypt, this was something else.

Where's Anubis? he wondered. The fear caused his heart to swell, sending tears to his eyes. He needed him more than ever. Everyone had left him; his parents, his grandmother, Tad. Now even his greatest friend, now even Anubis. He was alone, always alone. The tears were heavy now, and his body convulsed with each breath. He forced his eyelids closed, but it didn't work. They kept coming.

"Alex." He heard his name drift into his ears. "Alex." It became louder. His senses were returning. Clarity forced its way into his mind.

"ALEX," the voice boomed. It was Anubis. He was calling out for him. Alex lifted his eyes and wiped at them. When they cleared, he found he was sitting in the entrance of a dark cave. He could hear dripping from within. Anubis stood beside him.

153

"Dude, where'd you go? You can't leave me like that," Alex said.

"I HAVE REMAINED AT YOUR SIDE THE ENTIRE TIME," Anubis explained, looking down at Alex with confusion. Alex wasn't certain, though; in fact, he wasn't certain of anything anymore.

"Are you real?" he asked, reaching out and pinching Anubis' side.

"ARE YOU FINISHED?" Anubis asked loudly. The walls of the cave shook in response. The last time the two of them were in a cave, things looked pretty bleak, Alex recalled. They'd both been captured and thrown away, left for dead. In the end, it was death that saved them. Not much good comes from dark caves, he thought. Bats, no thanks; and, oh yeah, stinking demons. That's what comes from caves. I'm guessing this is no different.

Alex stood and looked up at his companion.

"You ready?" he asked.

"HMMFT," Anubis confirmed.

"Let's see what kind of trouble you can get us into this time. *Sheesh,* I'm always cleaning up your mess," Alex said as they entered the darkness.

Together they ventured deeper into the cave, Anubis leading the way. They traveled downward for what seemed like miles, blindly feeling and groping their way through every twist and turn. The walls were sharp and dangerous. Alex had learned from above to stay away from them. The last thing he wanted was to bleed more.

The cold wind that left him above now shot through the narrow winding corridor howling like a wolf, leaving Alex chilled. Great, just what I need, another poodle in my life, he nervously thought.

Before long, the sharpness of the walls gave way to subtle grooves, worn smooth with age. Alex could barely make out the transition in the midst of the blackness. The wind cried lonely and filled the passage with its wails. It sounded eerily familiar to him, like shrieks of pain. His thoughts wandered to the great trench in Egypt where he'd seen too much suffering, too much death.

He placed his still bleeding hand on the wall, pausing to rid his mind of that place. When he pulled it away, he watched the bloodied print soak into the walls of stone, but it was what he saw next that drew his breath cold. The grooves suddenly bent and moved; they were shifting before his eyes. He looked closer, trying to force out every ounce of available light from the darkness. There, on the walls, he was certain he saw movement.

The once smooth lines began to take shape and form, change into something else, something more. Whole figures rose up and out of the stone, as if breaking free from the ancient ties that had bound them for centuries. The cold wind blew stiff and loud. The walls vibrated to life. Alex now realized it wasn't the wind shrieking.

He struggled to bring focus to his sight, and when it came, he soon wished it hadn't. The shapes formed into faces, faces that in turn pushed forth with expression. My blood must've awakened them, gave them life, he thought. No, not alive; dead was more like it, undead. They reached and clawed, coming at him from every angle. He was surrounded and trapped, cut off from the one who could help.

"Zombies!" Alex blurted out. The word echoed through the corridor carried by the wind, settling in the unevenness of the stone, only to be spit out and sent back toward them.

The dead were closing in, pulling at him. They pressed and pushed, smothering him with their reaching hands. Everywhere he turned, he was met by death. There were so many, Alex couldn't see. A sharp claw landed on his shoulder and he fought it off, only to have it return again, stronger. It grabbed at him from the mass of walking dead. Alex knew he needed to fight, but he couldn't move; he could barely breathe.

The last thing he saw was the grey of their lifeless faces. Pain shot from his shoulder down the entire length of his arm as the claw squeezed. It was pulling him downward. He tried to call out one last desperate time, but couldn't. He felt a quick jerking motion and was suddenly dragged through the crowd by the relentless claw across the floor of the passage, away from the dead. *Away* from the dead?

It was Anubis! He'd returned. Alex found himself choking back tears once again. Get it together, Chronos, he thought. The dead turned on them, searching blindly. They were coming.

As Anubis lifted Alex from the ground by his shoulder, he let out a threatening warning to any who dared follow. Alex covered his ears; he knew what to expect. The deafening cry rattled the walls and shook the ceiling, loosening heavy stone from above. The roof collapsed as they ran, leaving the dead behind them, closing off the passage and their escape.

"Nice one," Alex yelled. He was truly grateful, but this wasn't the time to be showing any sign of weakness. Anubis looked down at him from the corner of his eye, much like a parent does to a child when scolding him.

"Dude, I had it under control," Alex explained.

"FORGIVE ME. IT WILL NOT HAPPEN AGAIN," Anubis said.

"You mean the whole shoulder thing, right? Not the lifesaving bit, *correct?*" Alex tried clarifying. Anubis was silent. With his silence, the two moved on, through the dampness of the passage.

Although they were miles under the earth, light seemed to find its way the deeper they went, dancing off small metallic flecks in the walls and casting unwanted shadows in all of the wrong places. After what had just happened, shadows made Alex nervous and edgy. He wondered where the light was coming from. It wasn't until they rounded the corner that he'd have his answer.

Unexpectedly, the narrow passage opened into a large cave. The roughness of the stone had returned to this space, with large stalactites growing downward from the ceiling, reaching for their mate on the ground. The dripping he heard earlier had turned to a steady flow as several small rivers ran through the cave, dissecting the ground. Alex thought it strange that this space was actually warm, and not cold and damp as he would've expected deep underground.

Movement from across the vast space caught his eye. It was the figure they'd seen from above, the one Anubis chased earlier. He watched as it slowly flowed across the uneven ground, unhindered. It moved, hunched over, appearing heavily burdened by some immense weight, yet was wispy and light in its efforts.

"Good. We're in the clear. It hasn't seen . . . *Hey,* where'd you go?" Alex asked, quickly whipping his head from side to side, surveying the area for his large friend. He spied Anubis down on all fours at the river's edge, lapping up the coldness.

"*Seriously? Now* is when you go all canine on me?" Alex asked incredulously as he approached. The lighted cave flickered. Alex hesitated. Something wasn't right.

"Anubis?" he said tentatively. The great warrior beast growled in response and continued drinking. Alex moved closer to his friend. Anubis turned on him, gave a ferocious snarl, and snapped his sharp fangs at him wildly.

"*Whoa!* Easy boy," Alex yelled as he pulled back. Anubis stood slowly and faced him. A savage look was in his eyes, and he was still

157

growling. His teeth were bared and saliva found its way to their tips. Alex glanced down at the clear water and watched as it turned a murky red. The water, he thought; it must've changed him somehow.

A worried smile broke across his face. He knew this wasn't Anubis; at least, not anymore. He also knew this was a delicate situation requiring an even more delicate touch.

"You, growling at me?" Alex asked in his best Al Pacino impersonation. He was nervous. If imitation was the best form of flattery, then Alex was certainly no flatterer.

"I said, *you*, growling at me? Heh. Get it?" Alex asked nervously. He was out of jokes.

"You've tasted the blood of my father," a shrill voice cut through the cave and startled Alex. When he turned, the dark figure was standing close behind him.

"*Waaaaa*," Alex shrieked, nearly jumping out of his skin. All of his senses went on high alert. A chill ran up his back, causing the hairs on his neck to stand up.

"It now courses through your veins," the figure continued, "growing stronger, choking you from the inside. Soon, you'll be his." Anubis' eyes glazed over in a thin white film.

The figure stood only inches from him, its head held low, as if purposely hidden. Slowly, cautiously, Alex careened and stretched, not certain he wanted to see, but something inside was driving him. What he saw was beauty. She was exceptional, not quite on the same level as Ma'at, but more earthly, yet unrealized.

She turned away in response, as if ashamed, and this made the teenage boy in him even more curious. He pressed forward, forgetting Anubis' growls, if only for a moment.

Shadowed by her hooded veil, Alex could barely see the paleness of her skin and the soft lines that graced her cheeks. The flickering light within the cavern caressed her. Alex was intrigued, captured and drawn in by her beauty. He raised his hand toward her face.

When she turned to meet his hand, all evidence of beauty had disappeared. While her right side remained stunning, her left was without skin and muscle. Only bone remained. Her hair was long and raven, flowing softly down on one side of her face, while ghostly-white and sparse on the other.

The black shroud that covered her head dropped long to the floor. Only her face and hands were exposed; fleshy and pink on the right, skeletal and bleached to the left. He could only assume the rest of her body was similar. Her pupil was green and widened, likely from being underground for so long.

Alex jerked his hand back in response. At least the Valkyries had the decency to be one or the other, he thought, but not both, and certainly not at the same time. Still, even in the face of danger, Alex knew to always be a gentleman. He recalled the first time he learned that valuable lesson.

It was Mr. Nichol's class, and in walked Margaret Stimpson, head cheerleader and girlfriend to none other than his arch nemesis, Jackson. She was dressed for homecoming in her uniform and smiling from head to toe, trying desperately to draw attention toward anything other than the tip of her nose.

Being head cheerleader didn't come without sacrifice, and Margaret had been preparing all week for homecoming. All of that preparation made her a walking time bomb of stress. Teenagers and stress meant one thing.

In what could only be classified as F5 on the AC scale and residing at the tip of her nose was a pimple; but it wasn't just any pimple; it was a pimple of epic proportions.

Now Alex, being of scientific mind, had long ago created a scale upon which to classify his schoolmates' stress-related misfortunes. Witness the birth of the Acne-Chronos scale, or AC scale for short. When Alex saw Margaret's pimple in all of its swollen glory, he just couldn't stop himself.

"Auntie Em, it's a twister!" he shouted. It was one of the few times in his life that most of the other kids in the class had laughed with him and not at him. *Most*, that was; not all. There was one who didn't.

It was late in the afternoon, and Alex had almost forgotten about the morning's grand event, when he caught the blunt side of Jackson's fist as he rounded the corner, heading toward his locker.

"Who's seeing twisters now, Chronos?" Margaret said, standing over him laughing. Jackson stood next to her, cracking his knuckles and smiling. It was then that Alex learned a second, even more valuable lesson. Boys will be boys . . . and sometimes, so will girls.

Margaret leaned in close to Alex, still sprawled out on the hard floor, raised her hands to her nose, and pinched hard, jettisoning white pus all over Alex's face.

Always be a gentleman, Alex reminded himself. He cleared his throat and looked pitiably at the figure that now stood before him.

"Look, I'm sorry, but I'm just not into Goth chicks. I like my ladies to have, well, life. You know, like a heartbeat, maybe a pulse or something. Skin would be nice." Okay, so being a gentleman wasn't as easy as I'd thought, but still, I think my gramma would've been proud, he thought with a smile.

"Besides, that look went out of style a couple of years ago. I hear Steam Punk is the latest craze. I'm pretty sure they did a study," Alex cracked.

She seemed to be ignoring him, staring intently at Anubis. She

160

began chanting in a strange tongue. Alex's head began to swim. He tried backing away, but the ground beneath him seemed to be moving, heaving and rolling, much like the fun house at a carnival. Every step he took was lost with each drop of the floor. He kept his arms spread wide, trying hard to steady himself. There were few things Alex could make sense of anymore.

First and foremost, Anubis hungered. Second, and quite likely, she was doing this to him, controlling him, or at least making him believe something was happening. Then Alex heard it, that all too familiar sound; the sound that shook everything around him. Earth, stone, even the water in the rivers vibrated in fear. Alex instinctively covered his ears to ease the intensity. It didn't work.

RRAAARRRGGHH!

Alex knew what came next. Anubis would attack. Only this time it would be him. He had to move fast. He'd seen an attack by Anubis and desperately didn't want to be on the receiving end.

Sidestepping to his right and rolling back around Anubis, who was charging fast, Alex barely missed the first deadly swipe of the warrior god's powerful claw. Anubis let out another roar.

Great, Chronos, tick him off some more, Alex thought. Anubis' massive chest was filling with anger and pushing out hatred with every breath. He was maddened, and froth seeped from his mouth and fell to the ground; his teeth were bared. He turned and lunged again. Alex tucked into a somersault on the run, just below Anubis' crushing grasp, again narrowly escaping. He knew his luck wouldn't last.

"Hey, easy, boy. It's me, Alex," he yelled over his shoulder as he ran. Anubis returned to all fours and ran after him, bounding from one stone to the next. Alex was reminded of Egypt, being chased by the hounds of Set. It was in the outer chamber that he first fully realized their strength. It was life and death then. This was no different.

Anubis sank his claws into the stone, pulling himself upward along the hardened walls to the ceiling high above. Alex had nowhere to hide, no cover from which to seek protection. How could someone protect themselves from that? he thought as he watched Anubis chasing overhead, crushing the stone beneath his every step.

Alex barely noticed when the cloaked figure glided away into the far reaches of the cavern. He didn't have time to worry about her now, not with a 10-foot tall battle-hardened razor blade chasing him.

He watched helplessly as Anubis dropped from the ceiling, crook in hand, and landed in front of him, stopping him in his tracks. This was it, Alex thought, as he looked into his friend's eyes. For a moment, he saw sadness; but sadness quickly turned to anger, and anger turned to madness.

He tried to move, but this time he wasn't fast enough. Anubis caught him on the side of his head, splitting it wide open behind his ear and sending Alex across the cavern floor. He stopped hard against a stone table that rose solidly from the floor. He was dazed and bleeding heavily.

RRAAARRRGGHH! Anubis thundered, announcing his intent. Alex was tired and losing blood fast. He was becoming weak, making it difficult to concentrate. He knew he had to move, to rise. Anubis was coming, he could sense it.

He pushed up from the floor, only to fall back. His head pounded, and with each beat, forced pain and blood through the open wound on the side of his skull; but there was another problem. Alex could taste blood. The iron was sharp on his tongue. This could only mean one thing, Alex thought. His head wasn't the only thing bleeding.

His body ached with pain as he drifted in and out of consciousness. He had to stay awake. Death was coming. Everything was black again. He closed his eyes, but something deep down was forcing its way up. It pushed at him from the inside, telling him to fight back, to breathe, to live again. Familiar warmth blanketed his chest, only this time it wasn't his pendant; it was life itself.

He summoned all the strength within to slowly pull himself against the stone table. Still woozy and unsteady on his feet, Alex leaned on it for support. The blood from his head ran freely down his face to his shirt, now wet and stained red.

It was there on top of the table that he saw them. So intense was his pain that he wasn't quite sure if he was imagining it. He reached out, struggling to touch them. So weak, so much pain, Alex thought, grabbing at his head. If he could just touch them, he'd know they were real. They looked just like those from his grandmother's kitchen, vibrant colors, each one; but they couldn't be the same, he thought.

There, scattered across the cold stone table, were five glass jars filled with all manner of colored liquid. They sat, much like those from home, preserving their vile contents. His stomach lurched and he grabbed at it. It twisted and lurched again.

He began vomiting uncontrollably. His head seared with pain as his body jerked wildly with each convulsion. The more Alex convulsed, the greater the pain in his head. The more intense the pain, the more he vomited. He wasn't certain if he was vomiting because of the pain or because of the jars.

He was wiping at his mouth when he heard it. Something was

behind him. A second noise sang out through the air, slicing it. The crook, Alex instantly thought, and he moved just in time to see it come down hard on the table. It cut cleanly through the solid stone where he'd been leaning only seconds before, sending the corner sliding to the floor.

"*Aaiieeee,*" Alex screamed as he ran away stumbling and clutching both his head and his stomach. I'm so tired, need to stop, rest, Alex thought, as he fought to keep his eyes open. His body slowed with every weakened beat of his heart. He was getting more and more weary, his pulse was slowing and he knew it.

He began to worry, not about himself, but rather about his friend. This wasn't him, not the Anubis he knew and loved. She did this to him. She was responsible. I need to change him back, make him stop, make him remember. I need to save him. I'd gladly die here today if it meant saving him.

Tears found their way through the pain. He let them flow. Anubis was close; Alex could hear his chest expelling the rotten air inhaled from the cavern. He turned to look, stumbled and fell, his energy depleted. He stopped moving. Anubis stood above him, victorious.

It wasn't enough for the warrior god. Anubis lowered his crook, hooked Alex's ankle, and swung hard. Alex was lifted high over Anubis' head and flung against the far cavern wall. The impact buckled the stone wall and Alex fell, slumped to the ground, near the river. Anubis approached again, relentless in his task.

"*No, please stop,*" Alex begged weakly. Anubis either didn't hear him or didn't care. He lifted Alex's limp body above his head, let out a tremendous roar that echoed off the walls of the cavern, and slammed him down hard onto the stone table. Alex's back broke. He stopped breathing.

"HHMMFT," Anubis said with finality. Save for Anubis' heavy breathing, silence filled the cavern.

NINE

Anubis turned and walked toward his new mistress. She was in control now, and he obeyed. He stood by her side, ever stoic, ready for her next command.

Suddenly, light flooded the cavern, growing in its intensity, pushing its glow into the darkness, peeking into every crack and fracture. Anubis turned to see Alex's body rise, surrounded by light. Alex hung, limp and quiet, above the cold stone slab.

Seemingly from nowhere, a rush of fresh air forced its way through the space and found him, as if summoned from a great distance. It enveloped him, mixing and turning with the brightness as it worked its way into his nose, searching for his lungs, filling them. His body snapped rigid.

The intensity of the light dulled and Alex drifted gently to the stone beneath him. A warmth came over him in the chilled air of the cave and the sting of oxygen burned his insides. He was alive.

He remembered exactly two things; his back was broken, and Anubis was still in the cave. Fear returned, and an odd numbness moved along the center of his spine causing his body to twitch and jerk. I can move? he asked. My back's not broken? Alex would've normally jumped for joy, but there was another problem. The female simply lifted her long skeletal finger and pointed in Alex's direction without a word.

Anubis became angered and snarled at what he saw. His task wasn't complete. His muscles tightened as he leapt into a full charge, gleaming gold crook out in front. His movements were swift and left wreckage behind in the form of shattered and broken stone. He moved fast and nothing stood in his way. He was getting closer.

166

Alex sat on the edge of the table, shaking off the grogginess of his wounds. Sore and achy, he had no idea at first what happened or why he was sitting on the table, but he saw Anubis charging. That was all he needed to know. The past few moments flooded into his throbbing head. He remembered.

He quickly jumped off the table, his heart racing once again. It felt good to be alive, he thought, even if it was only for a moment. Anubis let out his battle cry.

"RRAAARRRGGHH!"

Alex returned with his own battle cry.

"Crrraaaaaapppp!" he yelled as he ran. He was still weak, but knew he couldn't stop moving. To stop would mean certain death, and well, death just wasn't on his schedule today. He needed a plan, if for nothing else, to buy some time so he could come up with a better plan. Think, Chronos, think. If he were running from Jackson, he always had a trick or two he learned from watching old movies with the Captain or reading one of his old books.

Of course, if it were Jackson, I'd at least have a fighting chance. Here, not so much, he thought. Here, I'm a chew toy. A moment of clarity flashed through his mind. Books, wait; that's it!

"Why didn't I think of it before?" he yelled, causing his head to pound. The blood had stopped flowing, but the pain was still unbearable. "Not books . . . *journal*." Alex reached around to his pocket as he tried to run, pulling out the worn leather volume. He began fumbling through the pages, miserably trying to stay upright. His tired eyes were having difficulty focusing on the words blurred across the pages. Something Alex had read earlier in his journal held the answer to helping Anubis, but he was having trouble remembering.

"It was in here. I know it," he said aloud, running side to side, trying to throw Anubis off. Anubis stayed his course, growling and snapping close behind. Let me think; was it before Egypt and after Valknut or after Egypt and before Valknut? Alex wondered as he flipped furiously.

What? "Heed the Waters of Naxos," he read. The mystery of the journal had always been too strong of a pull for him, even at the most inopportune times. This was no different. Despite running for his life, being chased by arguably history's most fearsome warrior, his mind reeled with the possibilities of what this latest writing meant. He'd never seen it before, yet an entire page had been dedicated to it.

"The Waters of *Who?* What's a Naxos?" he asked. "Sounds like cough medicine. Warning, Naxos may cause drowsiness and in some extreme cases, even death. Do not operate heavy machinery or ride a demon horse with a Valkyrie. Consult your doctor before taking Naxos."

Anubis was closing fast, and Alex's momentary distraction was sharply interrupted when a set of razor sharp teeth snapped only inches behind him.

"Right," Alex said as a bead of sweat rolled down his brow. "I'll have to come back to that one." Anubis was at full speed and about to take another swing at him when Alex suddenly sidestepped and stopped dead in his tracks, just before the river's edge.

Anubis, caught by surprise, was moving too fast to stop. He slid past Alex, wildly trying to tear at the stone floor. He was able to spin around and dig his nails in, but his momentum carried him into the river, leaving deep scratches etched into the stone.

"Sorry, dude," Alex shouted after him. This infuriated Anubis, and when he broke the surface of the flowing river, he let out a vicious roar. He dug his claws into the hardened bank of the river and pulled himself up, ready to go again. Alex just shook his head in disbelief, turned, and took off running once again. Only this time he wasn't fast enough.

Anubis was on him in three steps and caught his ankle with a swipe of his claw. Alex was sent sprawling along the ground. The journal flew from his hand and landed several yards away, on the table.

He clamored and crawled, scrambling on all fours to retrieve it. Anubis was toying with him, savoring what was to come. Alex reached the table and pulled himself up as Anubis paced back and forth behind him, deciding his next move.

Alex's eyes lit up. Although the journal was turned around, he was able to make out the opened page. On it were drawn five jars, just like on the table. This was the page he was searching for.

He didn't want to bring unnecessary attention to his plan, so he left it, straining to read its words upside-down and backwards. He held his breath. Everything counted on this. Anubis was getting anxious, so he needed to work fast.

Alex leaned in and grabbed the first of the jars. He already determined that this particular jar, located second from the left and crossed out in his journal, was of no use to him. What he needed was a distraction to buy more time, he decided, so he slowly picked it up, trying greatly to hold down what was left in his stomach while looking at its contents.

Memories of long summer days in his yard eased into his thoughts. He'd spend all day practicing his slider under the warm sun. Again, window . . . not my fault. I'll say it until my dying days, he thought. Alex gripped the open jar in his hand and let it fly with the accuracy of a professional ball player.

No sooner had he thrown it, droplets of its rancid contents

trickling down his hand and arm, when a horrific thought shot through his mind. Was it the second from the left or second from the right, upside-down?

"Crud!" he shouted and immediately turned back to the journal. His heart pounded. His distraction had worked for the moment, but what good was it if he'd thrown away the wrong jar? As his eyes narrowed and focused on the yellowed paper, his worst fear was realized.

Looking nervously over his shoulder, his mind raced. Anubis was still preoccupied with the sound of the breaking glass, but wouldn't be for long. Alex frantically searched the table and floor surrounding it. Nothing; only four jars remained. Sweat continued to bead across his forehead and he wiped at it. It felt odd to him, too wet for sweat and too foul an odor, even for him.

Alex looked at his hand. It was still wet with liquid from the jar. He quickly snatched up the empty jar on the table and placed his hand against its opening. Three small drops fell into the jar. Was it enough? he worried. It had to be, he told himself. Now, what the heck do the numbers mean?

Alex spun the journal around. He wasn't about to make another mistake. He read the numbers in order from left to right, placing the once empty bottle on the table between the others. Four, one, five, and three. Well now, that makes complete sense . . . *not*, he thought. But wait; the colors were all wrong, too. Alex anxiously reached for the first jar and brought it to his nose. Maybe the smell would help. It proved to be a bad decision.

"*Auuggghhh.* That's awful," he said as he pulled the jar away. "Man, why's this have to be so hard?" he asked. "Even if I can mix it correctly, how am I going to get lunkhead to drink it?"

He lifted another and inhaled deeply. The odor was so pungent

170

that it tickled the far reaches of his throat and he began coughing. He quickly put it down. A wisp of smoke lifted from the opening.

"Seriously? I think I just burned my spleen," he said between coughs. Well, I threw away the other one, so that's it for the bottles, he thought. Guess it's time to dust off my rawesome culinary skills. After all, nobody can cook like me. Well, I can make a mean toast; so he began.

Three drops of which? Number five, he read. No, first it's two drops of number four, then three drops of five. Okay, now it's one drop of glass number one, right?

He scratched his head. It has to be right. When he finished, there was a single bottle with a pale blue liquid inside. Not quite the weapon, or color, of choice when fending off a god, he thought, but still, if they're anything like gramma's jars, maybe he'll at least blow chunks. That ought to slow him down a bit. Well, he thought, one way or another it's about to get messy up in here.

A faint noise from behind entered his thoughts and broke his concentration. He turned to see Anubis standing tall on his hind legs, staring at him, breathing heavy. Alex froze.

They stood, each facing the other, waiting for their move. Fate showed her hand at that moment when a single strand of hair fell from Alex's head and landed across the tip of his nose. His eyes widened. He knew what was next. It played out in his mind to the finest of details.

His nose twitched. Alex slowly crinkled it to relieve the sensation. Unbearable, he thought, but he didn't dare move. Great, death by hair, just what I need. He cracked his mouth and blew quietly upward at the hair, trying to dislodge it from its resting place.

The effort had his desired effect, almost. The hair gently lifted and vibrated, then slid downward along his nostril.

"Ahh-CHOO!" Alex sneezed, turning when he did and grabbing the strange concoction he just brewed. It had to work. It's now or never, he thought. As he turned back, Anubis was upon him, bending him backwards, pinning his upper body to the table.

The warrior's claws sank into his shoulders, and Alex cried out in pain. Anubis lowered his head slowly, moving in closer. Saliva hung from his lips just above Alex's face. A low gurgle came from deep inside the beast.

Despite the pain, Alex held tight to the bottle, waiting. Anubis took a deep breath, his massive chest inflating, and let out a final death-cry. He went in for the kill. Now! Alex thought.

He lifted the glass and flicked it into Anubis' open mouth. The jar sailed deep into his throat as intended, causing Anubis to choke. The great warrior pulled back in surprise, releasing Alex's shoulders and grabbing at his own throat.

"Nailed it," Alex said and rolled off the table to his knees, clutching his bleeding shoulders; but it wasn't over. He looked up, watching Anubis closely for any sign of familiarity. Anubis, his back toward Alex, hunched over and dropped to all fours. Something was happening.

Alex began to worry. Was it the right mixture? Is he choking? Did I just kill my best friend? That last question resonated in his head. He could do nothing now but wait.

It may have been the strange and mystical being that lured them here, or perhaps even what little light existed deep within this cave that played tricks on the mind. Either way, Alex watched helplessly as shadowy figures slid down from the walls and surrounded Anubis, dancing and swelling around him. They blanketed him, restricting his movements. Dark and formless, they reached and stretched around him, tightening their grip.

Anubis, hunched over and appearing burdened by the deathly shapes, began to breathe heavily once again. A welling of strength seemed to grow uncontrollably inside him. He bellowed a mighty roar and shrugged death from his shoulders at once. Anubis turned to face Alex. His whitened eyes changed slowly to black. Alex saw the familiarity he was searching for. It was over.

"I don't remember everything that happened," Alex said softly.

"I DO," Anubis said sharply. Alex noticed he seemed far angrier than he ever remembered, maddened even. He'd only seen that look on his friend's face once before; Set.

Perhaps he was angry at this unnatural creature for using him, playing him like a fool. No, that would be beneath Anubis, Alex thought. It was more than that. It was as if Anubis angered for being forced to attack the one he protected, the one he loved.

He turned toward the retreating figure and stretched his arms wide, golden armor glistening in the dim light, and released a ferocious battle cry.

RRAAARRRGGHH! The earth beneath them trembled in response as the ceiling vibrated, sending stalactites crashing to the ground. He was on her in four strides. Launching himself upon her back, Anubis wrapped his powerful arms around her torso and sank deep his extended claws, one into her chest and one at her stomach. She wailed in pain.

In a single movement, Anubis drove his canines deep into her neck and clamped down hard. As she fell, he pulled his claws apart, shredding her, biting as he went. The large cavern filled with the echo of her dying shriek. Anubis stood, her pink flesh still hanging from his teeth, and he hungered no more.

"You good?" Alex asked hesitantly.

"HMMPHT," Anubis responded upon his return. The wildness

had left his eyes, replaced by what looked like deep sorrow or regret. Alex stretched up on the tips of his toes and placed a forgiving hand upon Anubis' shoulder.

He always felt a connection to the beast before him, a friendship that transcended most natural boundaries, but it wasn't until this moment that he realized how deeply Anubis cared for him in return.

A warm sensation filled his heart, rising from deep inside. His body began to tingle. *Man,* he thought; better not let Anubis know how I feel. I'd never hear the end of it. The warmth spread through him like a wildfire. It became almost uncomfortable.

He looked down, his pendant was glowing. Great, here we go again, he thought. A flash of light pulsed through the cave, and in an instant, they were gone.

When Alex next opened his eyes, they were back in Odin's chamber. The fire still flickered; all else was silent. He reached down and grabbed his pendant.

"Man, it's like this thing has a mind of its own lately," he said as he cradled it in his hand. "Too bad there's no off button," he said, shaking it. "What's next?" he asked, looking over at his large friend. Anubis seemed unaffected.

The two, comfortable in the room's silence, went their separate ways, Alex to the softness that called out to him from the bed, Anubis to the balcony to wait. Alex sank into the covers and closed his eyes, waiting for sleep to come.

It was at the moment when the black blanket of sleep entered a person's mind and covered their thoughts, turning them into dreams, when the chamber suddenly flooded with light. Motion had filled the room. The All-Father had entered.

Upon Odin's entrance, Alex jolted upright, feeling as if he'd been

174

caught. Odin, however, paid no attention to the matter. It was obvious to Alex that there were more pressing issues to discuss.

"I've spoken to my son, Thor. He apologizes for his behavior earlier. He'll take you to the great sea," Odin said.

"Uh, why?" Alex asked hesitantly, eager to draw the focus away.

"You'll need his strength," Odin explained simply, as if Alex should understand. As usual, he didn't.

"Look, I can't speak for tall, dark, and gruesome over there," Alex said, motioning to Anubis who was standing on the balcony overlooking the horizon. "Well, actually, even Anubis can't really speak for Anubis," Alex explained, "but I'm pretty sure we won't need Thor's help just to go to the beach. I mean, have you seen these guns?" Alex asked as he raised his arms and flexed his thin biceps. Odin simply smiled in return, which made Alex feel a bit uneasy.

"Not the beach, my son; the sea. It's where Jormungandr the great sea snake lives. He must be destroyed," Odin explained.

"A great what? Are you flipping insane? Yeah, I haven't mentioned this yet, but we don't do snakes. Uh, Anubis has this uh, *thing*, with snakes. You need to call our agent. Why on earth, uh, I mean why on *Midgard* would we want to see a snake? Let alone a *great* snake." Alex paused to catch his breath. "By the way, what's so great about him?" he questioned. The words no sooner left his mouth when he began regretting them.

"His size," Odin responded simply.

Alex slumped over where he sat. He felt defeated once again. If there were some sort of plan to all of this, some destiny he needed to fulfill, then this *must* be a part of it. Awesome, Alex thought sarcastically. Just when a guy goes and gets comfortable, some one-eyed dude goes and throws a snake in the mix.

"Hey, Chuckles, you hear that? We're going fishing. Or is it snaking? I don't know, but I guess we're going."

"I AM PREPARED," Anubis boomed.

"Of course you are," Alex mumbled. The word settled on him, gnawing at him. *Prepared; I've heard that before.*

"Wait, what? Prepared? Like Tuat *prepared*, or something else?" Alex questioned feverishly.

"HMMPFT," Anubis responded simply.

"Look, if you know something about all of this, I'm going to . . . well, I don't know yet, but it'll be bad, really bad," Alex threatened. He turned and Odin was gone.

"What's up with people around here? You look away for a second, and poof, they disappear," Alex ranted. "Hey, you must've scared him off. What'd you do this time?"

Dark clouds billowed in the distance as thunder rolled up over the mountains and down toward them. Louder and louder, the room began to shake. *Something tells me this isn't ordinary thunder,* Alex thought, as he raced onto the balcony.

A wall of clouds several stories tall, pushing at them, building in its intensity, stopped just outside their room. It rolled back onto itself, then through and over again. Lightning flashed deep inside.

"What's it waiting for?" Alex shouted over the noise. The storm sat a few feet in front of them. It reminded him of a beating heart the way it moved. The two friends stood, poised for the attack. They'd been in this situation before and neither was letting his guard down.

As if in reply to his question, a large figure rose from its depths, shooting upward above the storm, and hovered. The clouds dropped in a sheet of rain to the ground, thunder and lightning remained.

176

"We must go," a booming voice said from above. The large figure slowly lowered itself on to the balcony next to the friends. Alex cocked his fist back, ready to land, then hesitated. It was Thor, and he was smiling. "Today we shall be victorious on the battlefield, and by the grace of Odin, we shall die there, too."

"*What?*" Alex shouted. "*We* aren't doing any such thing. There was nothing said about dying," Alex ranted. "I think I'd remember something like that." Thor laughed from behind his curly red hair.

"My father has told me of your many great feats to come, and I'd consider it an honor to battle at your side," Thor said. Alex could tell that humility wasn't Thor's strong suit.

"You know I understand about half of what you goddies say," Alex remarked sarcastically. He knew there was no use arguing, that there was something bigger out there than his own needs right now. Only this time it was a stinking snake, he thought.

"Come, little one," Thor said as he rubbed Alex's hair. "Let's see what you can teach this old warrior."

"How about checkers?" Alex quipped. "I can teach you that." With that, the unlikely trio walked out of the room and silently into the unknown.

As Thor led the two friends back over the mystical bridge, Alex turned his head, taking in one last glimpse of a quiet and peaceful time. He wanted to remember it, hold onto it, and hold onto her. Warm thoughts of Tad drifted through his mind. A knowing smile broke across his face, and his eyes filled with tears. I'll see her again, Alex thought. She said it was our destiny.

"HOLD," Anubis cautioned in a tone that vibrated through the air.

Alex took a deep breath, wiped his eyes, and in quiet resolution, turned toward Anubis. He knew it wasn't long before they'd face battle. It seemed this was also his destiny; so many battles.

He hadn't noticed the water before. It flowed heavily under the bridge, deep, black and cold. Where'd that come from? Alex wondered. He quickly looked up at Anubis, who stood gazing over the bridge into the water. His chest was heaving. Alex heard a familiar sound build from deep inside his warrior friend. Anubis sensed something, something dangerous.

"*Sheesh*, we've barely left the place and you have to go and tick somebody off," Alex yelled.

"NOT SOMEBODY. SOMETHING," Anubis corrected him.

"*Aww, man*. It's not another giant, is it?" Alex asked desperately.

"It's not a giant," Thor said with a great smile. His thick muscles tightened in excited anticipation.

"Seriously, dude, you're *smiling?*" Alex snapped in disbelief. "Is your helmet made of tinfoil?"

"We long for battle," Thor said boastfully.

"*We?*" Alex asked.

"Mjölnir and me," Thor responded.

"Mojo who?" Alex asked as he looked around for somebody else. It was just the three of them.

Thor raised his hammer in response. Alex rolled his eyes and turned back to Anubis.

"*Great*. Dude named his hammer. I've said it before; too many Valkyries to the head can cause brain damage. Living proof, he is," Alex said, pointing his thumb back at Thor.

"SILENCE," Anubis boomed.

All at once, the skies darkened and filled thick with black clouds. Thunder rolled up in the distance as lightning cracked down from the clouds. Alex didn't like storms much. He never got used to them whenever they moved up the coast and found their way into his sleepy little harbor. What he did like, however, was that Mittens, his grandmother's cat, liked them even less. She'd dart across the room at the first hint of a rumble. Alex smiled. His smile didn't last long.

A lightning bolt struck behind them, sending Alex ducking for cover behind Anubis. He looked around, nervously waiting for the next blast. There's always a next blast, Alex thought.

Anubis turned and looked down at him. Alex felt the awkwardness beaming from his eyes and suddenly realized his manhood was in question. He needed a story, an excuse, and fast. Fighting monstrous beasts and demon dogs was one thing, but having someone, even a 10-foot tall drooling fur ball, question your manhood, well that's something else entirely.

"*What?* You had a flea on your back, that's all. You're getting a bath when we get out of this. You're welcome, by the way," Alex snapped.

"Have no fear, child. We'll not die here today. Odin has other plans," Thor yelled through the growing wind, his hammer raised toward the sky. Alex noticed that despite being pelted in the face by the now driving rain, Thor was smiling.

"Are you having a good time there, Ms. Trimpet?" Alex yelled. "Maybe I should send out for tea and biscuits?"

He saw the look on Thor's face change from elation to borderline psychotic. With a drop of his massive arm, Thor sent a lightning bolt deep into the blackness below. The raging waters opened in response, and Alex watched helplessly as something from the depths swam upward, growing in its enormity. Instinctively, he rolled away from the edge of the bridge as it broke the surface of the water. When he finally looked up, Alex froze in fear.

Arched high above him was a creature so enormous in size, so grotesquely terrifying that merely calling it a snake was gravely laughable. This is no snake, Alex thought; it's a flipping locomotive. A locomotive pulling about nine *gazillion* box cars, he continued.

It flexed and throbbed as a single massive muscle, while its tongue darted and searched, smelling for its foe. It was only seconds before it caught Alex's scent in the raging storm, and when it did, its pale green eyes narrowed.

Alex couldn't help but notice that just one of its scales was easily the size of the mainsail on the Mermaid. How he wished he were there right now, sitting in the comfort of the ship's cabin. This beast was far bigger than any creature they'd ever encountered. How are we ever going to beat this? Alex wondered. His body began shivering uncontrollably, and for an instant, he couldn't tell if it was from the icy rain soaking into his bones or his deep fear of all things slithery.

The air suddenly filled with a wondrous roar. Anubis was attacking. Alex searched for his friend, but couldn't see him. The rain was too heavy, the wind too strong. There was one thing he could see, though, and it was coming straight down at him, all forty stories.

As the colossal reptile dove, it landed across the bridge, crushing it in its descent. The cabled ropes, of which Odin once spoke, whipped violently as they sparked and snapped, sending debris to the waters below. The resulting force threw a towering wall of spray upward into the sky.

Alex was still on his back and slipping fast, when his survival instincts took over, and he began clamoring and clawing his way, grabbing at anything that would hold. It was too late; the bridge was no more. There was nothing.

Alex was pulled under, into the black icy waters below, sinking. The wreckage of the bridge surrounded him, sinking with him. He could hear the sound of the bridge creaking and moaning under the pressure as it twisted, amplified in the frigid depths. He desperately tried swimming to the surface, but as the heavy debris sank downward, the waters pulled at him like a vacuum.

In the midst of the darkness, Alex saw something spark brightly above. A long shadow wound its way toward him. Alex feared the worst, but he was wrong. It wasn't the snake. Being wrong, however, didn't help. A second flash of light revealed a large frayed bridge cable closing in fast. Elves, Alex thought for a moment.

He kicked and pulled, but when the rope wrapped its way around his leg, it was no use. More cable followed, covering him; he was tangled, caught like a fish in a net. Deeper and deeper he went.

No air, pressure; can't breathe. He could feel his lungs burning, filling with the bitter cold waters. Something brushed at his hand, out from the darkness. Was this the snake? Alex wondered. There it is again. His heart raced to life as his eyes searched. It was Anubis.

Anubis reached again, grabbing his hand, pulling hard. It was no use. Both were sinking now. Alex could feel his body relaxing. His mind screamed out to fight, but his body had accepted his fate, his death. He knew it wouldn't be long before his mind followed. For a moment, he felt at peace. Everything was silent. His eyes closed.

TEN

Wait, I'm not dead?

"NO," Anubis responded.

Hunh? How did he hear me? Alex thought. We're under water. It was in my head.

"HE IS NEAR," Anubis boomed. Although Anubis' snout didn't move, Alex could feel the water push past his face when he spoke.

Wait, can you hear me? Alex wondered.

"IS THAT IMPORTANT NOW?" Anubis asked.

Uh, I rather think so, Alex thought. How long? he questioned.

"HE IS HERE," Anubis thundered angrily, and the two turned to see a glimpse of the great sea snake's tail as it slithered past them, sending them both tumbling through the water.

When they finally stopped and Jormungandr was nowhere to be seen, Anubis gripped the cables that bound Alex, gave a tremendous roar, and pulled with the strength of the god he was.

How *long*? Alex demanded.

"ALWAYS," Anubis answered.

Watch out! Alex's head throbbed. As if in response, Anubis turned just in time to see the giant serpent dislocate its lower jaw, much like other snakes do right before they feed. As the monster bared its sharpened fangs, preparing to feast, a sudden look of intense pain unexpectedly shot across its face.

From out of nowhere Thor appeared, catching the side of the beast's head with a massive blow from the blunted edge of Mjölnir, sending it rolling back into the darkness. He paused for a moment as if to relish in the fact that he just saved the two friends, then took off after the serpent. The two were gone from sight.

Alex watched helplessly as the battle-hardened muscles in Anubis' arms stretched to their capacity, his teeth bared, chest heaving. Another mighty roar and Alex felt the cables tug at him, but they didn't give way. Try as he did, Anubis couldn't break free the ropes.

For as long as Alex had known Anubis, and there was a chance it was a long time, he'd never seen him fail at anything. Based on the expression upon Anubis' face, Alex guessed failing came as a surprise to the warrior god as well.

It's no use, Alex thought desperately. Odin said they're made by the same elves, the same magic, that forged the weapons of the gods. With that single thought, Anubis reached for his crook. It began to glow as he lowered it gently to the ropes. A bright blue flash of light surrounded them and lit up the water. Alex felt a pulse and everything went black.

When Alex next awoke, he was still in the water, floating. His head was pounding.

Would you please warn a guy first before you go all crook-magic on his butt? Alex wondered, secretly hoping that Anubis would read this particular thought; but Anubis was nowhere to be found. Alex was completely alone, surrounded only by the dark waters.

A glimmer of light flashed in the far distance. It had to be them, he thought. Alex gave one last look around and kicked off, swimming toward the unknown. Living on the coast in a harbor town, Alex was an exceptional swimmer. In fact, hardly a day went by during the summer that he wasn't in the shallow waters of the harbor swimming. Unlike his running or his dancing, his swimming was near perfect; at least that's what his grandmother would say.

His arms and legs were long, perfect for a swimmer. His feet, the same oversized pedestals that he frequently tripped over, were like flippers in the water and cut through it with great ease.

It was strange, he thought, that he couldn't remember learning how to swim. It just seemed to come naturally, like he was born to it. He always assumed that, like most kids, his parents had taught him, but still, like the memories of his parents, it seemed just out of reach somehow.

He was close now, the glow was getting brighter. Sounds began to echo all around him. Movement in the darkness was lit up brightly in bursts and flashes of light. Alex was all too familiar with this scene; he'd seen it before. He knew that a battle of epic proportions was being played out in front of him, two mighty warrior gods working together, trying to fall an even mightier foe.

Uh, they got this, Alex thought. No sooner did Alex think it when the great snake stopped thrashing about and turned toward him.

Oh, snap.

The monster flexed its enormous body in a single movement and took off, undulating at breakneck speed toward Alex, the two gods in pursuit. It was moving too fast, and Alex knew he had little time to react. Besides, he thought, I have nothing to fight him with. Plan B, Alex thought.

He turned and began kicking for his life, swimming faster than ever. He understood water, how it reacted with movement, shaped itself around and into everything. He also knew how to move with it, use it for his advantage.

He could feel the serpent behind him as the force of water from the snake's head pushed at him. It was close. He didn't dare turn around for fear of losing his lead, regardless of how small it was.

184

Loki's Wrath

A faint thought, a thought too impossible to be possible, fleeted through his mind. Instinctively, Alex gave a single hard kick with both feet in unison, arched his back, and spread the flat of his hands as he went. This single fluid motion, combined with the force of water pushing him forward, sent him upward at just the right moment, allowing the snake to barrel past, inches beneath him.

There was little time to enjoy his narrow victory when the tip of the snake's tail whisked past and snapped toward his floating body. It caught him behind his legs, sending him spiraling through the water. His legs were broken.

Alex screamed out, grabbing at the backside of his legs. The pain was excruciating. He wriggled and writhed in agony, which, in turn, caused him even greater torture. He became nauseous. He had to stop. All he could do was float and endure. His breathing became heavy and slow. If it weren't for the icy waters numbing his legs, he would've passed out.

He watched helplessly as the massive reptile twisted in the distance, turned, and began speeding back toward him. A surge of adrenaline flowed through his blood. His body told him he shouldn't move, couldn't move, while his brain sent signals telling him he had no choice.

With every desperate attempt, the nerves in his legs shot out piercing pain, causing him to buckle over, grabbing at the source. In the end, he knew it was useless. If he couldn't move, he couldn't fight. His friends were too far away yet to help. There must be something, he thought desperately.

Even without movement, the agony from his broken legs radiated through his body, shooting waves of tingling warmth up into his head. The cold waters were no longer helping to numb the pain, yet there was still a growing warmth. His chest began to burn.

185

My necklace! Alex thought. He pulled out the mysterious pendant and light suddenly beamed outward from it, striking at the dark. The frigid water around him began to warm and bubble. His pendant burned hotter than he ever remembered. The waters became turbulent from the heat.

The approaching snake reared back in fear, its head now weaving side to side through the water high above Alex. Its tongue flicked and fluttered, trying to determine its next move. It wasn't much, Alex thought, but it stopped the advancing threat long enough to give his friends time to arrive. Arrive they did.

Anubis, in full armor and seething for battle, his crook raised and spinning, announced himself with such savagery that it startled the mammoth sea creature. The crook sang out in anticipation as Anubis moved through the water toward the beast with a singular intent.

Alex watched as Thor also moved swiftly, his hammer propelling him through the water, searching for its target. They advanced, each on opposite sides of the giant beast. Fearing both the impending attack and losing its window of opportunity, the serpent recoiled, then lunged forward at Alex for the final death strike. As Alex shrank away, the beast widened its mouth, exposing its long poisoned fangs.

As the great monster bore down on Alex in its moment of desperation, Anubis appeared over the top of the beast's large head, hooking its nostril with his crook. The downward force was great, dragging hard at him, but in a final pull of focused strength, Anubis sent himself over its nose, removing the crook as he went and placing himself between it and Alex.

Slowing through the water, Anubis turned, facing the battle as he preferred. The charging beast hissed in anger. As it did, Anubis

186

grabbed at its fleshy tongue and was pulled into its mouth. Alex watched feebly as Anubis wedged one end of his crook into the roof of the snake's snapping mouth, the other through its searching tongue. The snake flailed about angrily.

When the giant serpent jerked upward in painful reaction, Thor was there to meet it with the mighty Mjölnir, slamming the beast's snout downward with a crushing blow, cracking its skull. The move succeeded in driving the crook farther into its lower jaw, forcing its gargantuan mouth open.

Appearing desperate and sensing its end, Jormungandr raced toward the surface of the black water. As it broke into the parting skies, Thor grabbed at its tail, holding it firmly, sending it falling back to the sea. The sheer size of the serpent caused a small tidal wave rolling into the rocky seaside cliffs along the shore. It sank lifelessly into the icy depths, its body filling with death.

The scene below was serene, peaceful even, but it was far different above. Violent waves crashed about, sending spray upward and pounding everything else downward. The full force of the sea had been beckoned, and she came.

Caught unaware by Thor's actions, both Anubis and Alex were sent uncontrollably toward those same dangerous cliffs. Tossing and tumbling in the frigid sea, they reached out for anything, for each other, for air. The cold black water pulled at them both. Alex had lost sight of Anubis. He sank farther, his body stiff, his muscles screaming from the cold, his mind failing him.

Taking his last breath of sea water, Alex felt something brush faintly against his hand. His mind jumped alive. He didn't know what it was, he couldn't see, but he grabbed at it desperately, and as he did, his pendant glowed brightly and lit the blackness with a burning white light.

* * *

When Alex woke, they were on the shore, dangling upside-down from Thor's massive fists, violently choking out stale water from their lungs. Thor was laughing.

Surprisingly, they were dry and already warming in the afternoon sun. Something was different. It took Alex only a moment before he realized there was no pain.

"Crud! My legs," he said, quickly patting each one down, reassuring himself that they were still attached. Confused, he began muttering to himself as he tried to make sense of everything. "They were both broken. How? What the heck is going on? Okay, first, a sea monster. Yeah, you don't see that every day, but hey, it's me. Why not?" he asked out loud.

"But then," he continued, as he scratched his head, "breathing under water? Come on. Who does that? Flipping mermaids, that's who. Had to be a dream. Broken legs; now that was most definitely *not* a dream. Pain. But now? Man, my head hurts."

When he finally stopped to catch his breath, Alex felt an odd sensation, like he was being watched. He turned hesitantly, dreading what he'd see. His worst teenage fears were confirmed; both Thor and Anubis were staring at him. His face reddened.

"HMMFT," Anubis sputtered.

"Yeah, I might mumble, but at least I don't smell like a wet dog," Alex snapped. Anubis lowered his snout to his side and sniffed. His reaction spoke volumes.

"Hey, cretin, let me down," Alex yelled. Thor readily obliged and dropped them both. Alex landed face-first to the ground.

"Oof," he uttered as the air left his lungs. He coughed and sputtered, trying to breathe. Anubis was far more graceful in his landing, twisting in midair and landing solidly on both hind legs.

"Show off," Alex said between coughs. "And you," he said, turning toward Thor, "gently next time, gently." Thor simply laughed.

Alex stood and brushed himself off. "I suppose you want me to thank you for saving my life?" he asked Anubis. "Well, let me tell you, it's not happening. Once again, I did all of the work while you played twister with an overgrown worm's tongue."

Thor interrupted, "You're an odd little warrior, aren't you?"

"Hey, where do you get off calling me odd? I'm not the one who talks to his hammer," Alex responded angrily. Still, he rather liked being called a warrior.

"My apologies," Thor said as he desperately tried to keep from smiling. It seemed that watching Alex made him want to laugh. "It wasn't your friend who saved you, but rather it was you who saved him," Thor explained.

"Uh, I think your hair got in your eyes, Curly," Alex responded while coughing up the last of the water from his lungs.

"You know not who you are, little one," Thor said.

"What kind of question is that?" Alex asked.

"It wasn't a question," Thor replied, glancing down at Alex's chest.

Alex looked down and saw that his pendant was exposed. He quickly snatched it and returned it to its familiar place, hidden under his shirt. Trying to avoid Thor's obvious point, he said, "Great, now you're starting to sound like him." When Alex looked up, Thor was gone.

"Of course," he said quietly. Alex was exhausted, but there was no time for rest.

"THE ONE CALLED FATHER SUMMONS US," Anubis bellowed.

"I don't hear anything," Alex responded.

"WE MUST GO," Anubis shouted and lifted his crook high into the air.

"Hey, no, wait!" Alex shouted. It was too late. "Oh crud, not this again." Before he could utter another word his stomach lurched. It felt like someone was pulling his insides out. Alex clutched at his stomach. It was Egypt all over again. Everything went fuzzy. Anubis had moved them.

When next they appeared, the space in front of them shimmered into clarity. Alex was buckled over on his knees. He recognized the room between convulses, but was too busy trying to keep down the remainder of undigested pork he'd eaten earlier. His attempts proved to be unsuccessful, and he let loose all over Anubis' massive hind feet.

Much better, he thought, as he wiped at his mouth with his shirt tail. Anubis shot him a look as if to say, *You realize I'm a god, don't you?*

"My bad," Alex said, feeling the full weight of Anubis' stare upon him, "but in fairness, I did tell you to warn me next time," he snapped, still holding his stomach. Without a word, Anubis placed his large claw on Alex's head and he began to feel better. When his stomach had finally stopped doing backflips, he looked around. They arrived back at Odin's sleeping chamber.

Despite having just lost his last meal, a smile came over Alex's face. There were times, believe it or not, when some things are more coveted by a teenage boy than food; the comfort of a soft bed, for instance.

Alex ran to the end and dove, yelling, "Dog pile!" while executing a perfect mid-air twist and landed on the oversized bed.

190

The pillow was even softer than his back home.

"DOG? WHERE?" Anubis shouted, his head snapping back and forth scanning the room. His hackle rose, and he began sniffing the air for intruders. He raised his crook, ready for the attack.

"Whoa, slow down, my brother from another mother. There's no dog. Sorry," Alex said. "I forgot. No dogs. It's just a saying. It means . . ." Alex stopped, figuring any human explanation would get lost somewhere in the translation. Besides, Anubis was now too preoccupied policing the dark corners of the chamber, looking for hounds. He lives for this stuff, Alex thought, and left him to it.

"Ahhhh. A guy could get used to this. That's assuming nothing creepy or god-like drags us off to la-la land," he clarified. Suddenly the door burst open and light from the hall flooded the chamber.

"*Waaaaa!*" Alex screamed and sat up, straight as a board. Terrified, he nearly fell out of bed. A large shadow cast across the floor. Anubis rushed from the darkness and was at his side, sniffing toward the door.

Alex was puzzled. Anubis didn't attack. He wasn't even growling. Still, Alex didn't dare move for fear of this latest unknown.

"SOMETHING IS WRONG," Anubis said.

"Ya think?" Alex replied sarcastically. "Now go sic 'em, you overgrown hairball," Alex demanded, pointing nervously toward the shadow.

"SILENCE," Anubis shouted.

"My apologies for intruding," a familiar voice broke through the conversation. It was Odin. As he approached, Alex, too, could sense there was something wrong. He appeared distraught.

Odin looked at Anubis and simply said, "I'm sorry, my friend, but it's time." Anubis nodded in understanding. Alex was even more baffled.

191

"Time? Time for what?" he asked.

Quietly, Odin moved toward the bed and sat down. From his look, Alex could tell it was bad news. It was a familiar look. His grandmother used it on several occasions. The first was when he was old enough to start asking questions about his parents. He did that only once.

Alex waited patiently for Odin to speak. It was one of the longest moments of his life. Odin started slowly.

"Many years ago, I gave my eye," Odin began, pointing to his scar, "for infinite wisdom and knowledge. At the time it seemed such a small price to pay, but, as I've said, gain doesn't come without a sacrifice."

"Yeah, I know; your eye," Alex quietly interrupted.

"Ahhh, no, my child, the price wasn't my eye. The real price was the very knowledge I sought," Odin corrected him. "The ability to foresee coming events has been my burden."

"What events? What's happened?" Alex pleaded.

"It's been written of a great battle. A battle between the gods," Odin explained.

"Yeah, *Ragnarok*, I know. Loki mentioned it. Something about a battle to end all battles," Alex broke in.

"Yes. It seems Loki's been testing you from the beginning. I believe he fears you," Odin said. "It's also been written of certain events leading up to *Ragnarok*. Signs, if you will."

"And these signs; has anyone seen them yet?" Alex asked tentatively.

"Yes. The first tells of strangers to our land." Odin made a point of looking at each of the two friends. "The second, the binding of the great wolf. And now, my son's death." Odin trailed off, seemingly lost in thought. His eye glistened in the light of the fire.

192

"Your son?" Alex yelped. "Your son's dead?"

"Yes, my son Baldar has been taken from me. His lifeblood ended at the hands of Loki. His malice goes too far this time. He's set forth a chain of events that even he cannot undo."

"I don't understand; if you knew about these events ahead of time, why couldn't you do something to stop them?" Alex asked. "You're Odin after all."

Odin laughed quietly, his thoughts still distant. "Remember, our destinies cannot be changed. Only history can," he repeated from earlier. "Even with all my wisdom and knowledge, I'm helpless, left to mourn my loss; but there will come a time, it's also been foretold, of retribution and rebirth."

"Valknut. Can we help?" Alex asked, putting his arm around Odin. He'd seen enough death in his short life since Egypt. All were senseless killings. And for what? For power? Control? He needed to do something, anything.

"You will, my child, as you have many times before," Odin replied, nodding at the pendant around Alex's neck. "We're so grateful you've returned."

Alex quickly dismissed the All-Father's remark as the rantings of a grief-stricken parent. He's just suffered the loss of his son and wasn't making any sense, Alex concluded.

The room was quiet. Now wasn't the time for words, Alex thought. The two ravens from dinner had returned, fluttering into the room. They cawed and pecked at each other on the edge of the bed. One flew to Odin's shoulder, jolting Alex alive with thought.

He took a deep breath. Something had to be done. Unfortunately, that usually meant a lot of pain for him. He winced at the thought of having to suffer through another battle, risking life yet again; then it came to him suddenly.

"Well, let's give this thing a test drive, shall we?" Alex said to Anubis as he lifted his pendant.

"HMMFFT," Anubis agreed. A peculiar look came over Alex's face. He was trying to concentrate, but it looked rather like he was constipated more than anything else. Nonetheless, the pendant began to spin and, with it, Alex could feel the warmth. He beamed with excitement.

"Stand back, ladies and gentlemen. Please keep your hands and feet inside the cabin at all ti . . ." The pendant sparked and fizzled out.

"You've *got* to be joking," Alex yelled, shaking the pendant. "What the heck's wrong with this thing?" he asked.

"YOU MUST PREPARE," Anubis said.

"Are we back on that again?" Alex asked. "You have anything better?"

"DO NOT FAIL," Anubis responded.

"Oh, *much* better. *Thanks,*" Alex said sarcastically.

He wrenched and twisted, contorting his face into the most unnatural of positions and stared cross-eyed at the pendant; nothing.

"ARE YOU INJURED?" Anubis thundered.

"Oh, very funny. Suddenly you're a comedian, are you? If you must know, I'm sending my full-on whammy voodoo magic deep into the soul of the pendant," Alex responded.

"DO NOT," Anubis responded sounding sarcastic.

"You have any bright ideas, Sunshine?" Alex asked. Anubis simply stared back at him. Alex shook his head, took a deep breath, and raised the pendant once again.

"Maybe if I go all Shaolin Monk on it, it'll work." Alex cleared his mind and began humming. It wasn't long before the impatient teenager inside surfaced, and he opened his eyes to see the

194

wondrous feat he performed. He was confident of his success. Unfortunately, the pendant still hung lifeless.

"ARE YOU FINISHED?" Anubis bellowed.

"You know, when you left this thing on my doorstep, and yeah, I know it was you, you lummox," Alex yelled, eyeing his hulking companion keenly, "the *least* you could've done was leave instructions."

He looked up at the All-Father apologetically and saw the sadness. Odin managed a weak smile in response, but Alex could sense the pain from the elder. Thoughts of his grandmother filled his head. What if this was her? he wondered. He choked back the feeling of rising tears, cleared his throat, and lifted his pendant once more.

His heart pounded as the pendant began to turn. Faster and faster it spun, creating a whirring noise as it went. The sound grew in its intensity, causing his ears to ache and throb. He glanced worriedly up at Anubis, who appeared unaffected.

Something was definitely happening now, he thought. The room blurred, seeming to bend and warp. His hands tingled ice cold and, when he raised one to look at it, he watched horrified when it appeared to melt toward the floor.

Alex was scared. He never felt this sensation from the pendant before. Heat, most times, was just some dumb heat, he thought. What I wouldn't give for some heat.

"Anubis?" Alex spoke.

"HMMMFT," Anubis replied. Suddenly, a burst of light filled the room and they were gone.

"And so it begins," Odin said in the silence of the room. "Again."

* * *

When the light finally faded, the two friends were standing at the base of a snow-capped mountain range. The wind was stiff and cold. Alex pulled his collar up high around his neck, hoping it would help. Anubis lifted his head and inhaled deeply.

RRAAARRRGGHH! The warrior god howled up the mountain. The echo found its way against the warming snow, and it began to slide.

"Up there?" Alex asked. "Are you absolutely positive?" Anubis didn't answer; he simply began to climb the steep incline that wound its way to the top.

"Well, just promise me no more howling. The last thing we need is a billion tons of snow coming down on our heads." Anubis quickened his pace. "Hey, are you listening to me? Do you know how much a billion tons is?" Alex yelled after him. Anubis rounded the next corner and trailed out of sight. Alex was left talking to himself. "It's like, like a whole bunch of millions. Just picture a million, but a whole lot more."

Alex could feel it. Something big was about to happen, something bad, and they were willingly heading toward it. Are we flipping crazy? Alex wondered. The Captain once told him, "There are plenty of people in life who run from a fire, but far less who run toward it."

Easy for him to say, Alex thought; he's a volunteer firefighter. Of course, his role was more ceremonial than actually fighting fires, but leading the company band in the annual parade wasn't all that bad. There was that one time, Alex remembered, when the band followed the Schusters' horse. Not pretty, he thought.

It wasn't long before Alex noticed the drop in temperature. His breathing was heavy and his legs tired. He stopped to rest, looking back. They'd made good progress so far and were approaching the snow line. There was moisture in the air, and white powder had begun to fall, settling on the cold ground.

I hate the cold, he thought, crossing his arms for warmth. His mind flashed to Egypt. As he moved further up the mountain, the snow beneath his feet began to crunch with each passing footstep. The higher they went, the colder it got. These elevations became rough and difficult to navigate. Anubis moved even faster now, leaving Alex in the far distance.

"Oh no, please, don't wait for me. I'm doing just fine," Alex muttered as he struggled over a jagged outcropping. A smile suddenly ran across his face. He had an idea.

"Riiiiiicollaaaa," he yelled. The word had the intended effect. It echoed down the hill, bouncing off the surface with every roll and back again, until it was quietly snuffed out.

Anubis stopped, waiting for Alex to catch up. It took much longer than either had expected, and upon arriving, Alex sensed his large friend's annoyance. He tried to speak, but his teeth kept chattering and his body had long ago started to shudder. Anubis seemed unaffected by the frigid temperatures and just stared.

Alex wiped at his cold nose, and a small icicle fell from its tip. Anubis reached into his pack and pulled out his cloak. It was the same one he wore in Egypt when they first met. Alex quickly wrapped it around his body and drew it up tight. It was instant warmth.

The feeling came back to his fingers in a flush of burning needles. The spot where his nose once held the icicle resumed its dripping. Blood rushed back into his legs and they started to cramp. He rubbed at them to ease the pain. In a few short minutes, all sensation had returned to his body.

197

"Are we there yet?" Alex asked, shaking off the remaining shivers. "Yeah, that's right. I said it."

"WE ARE CLOSE," Anubis responded, pointing to an opening in the frozen snow. Alex wasn't paying attention and had begun to fidget inside the cloak. It felt like something was biting him.

"What the heck's in here?" he yelped at Anubis. He twisted around, grabbing at his legs, his back, then his arm. It was biting his chest. He jerked violently, trying to make it stop. His hand brushed over something hard and round, about the size of a golf ball. He pressed down on it to keep it from moving. He'd caught it.

When he brought his arm out from under the cloak, he could feel it moving inside his closed fist. It bit at his palm. Alex shook his hand vigorously and something fell to the ground. It was a large black Scarab. He watched in disbelief as it scurried off along the trail and burrowed into the hard snow.

"Dude, seriously? I knew you needed a flea bath, but that's just ridiculous," Alex yelled. "I think I need to get a rabies shot. Feel my glands; do they feel swollen to you?" After receiving no pity from Anubis, he finally settled down.

"ARE YOU DONE?" Anubis asked.

"I'm ready now. Let's go." As he started to walk toward the ice cave, his large foot became tangled inside the long heavy cloak and he tripped.

"I'm okay," he said as he immediately jumped up and brushed off. They approached the opening with extreme caution. Both knew that this cave likely held a powerful enemy. It would undeniably be their most dangerous journey ever.

This quest wasn't of winged messengers or giants, not of man or beast. No, this would be no ordinary battle; it would be one of wit and wisdom, of mental strength as much as physical. Alex wasn't sure which frightened him more. Loki was indeed powerful, a being whose essence was born from malice and mischief, of evil with intent.

Beyond that, they knew little of this god. At least in Egypt, Anubis had been familiar with Set. They had that advantage. Here, Alex thought, Loki has the advantage. They entered the ice cave side by side, not as equals, but as something else, something more.

Once inside, there was no turning back. Alex looked up at Anubis. They were like family now and there's no one he'd rather fight alongside than him. They'd been through a lot together. It wasn't over, but Alex was thankful.

There were no catacombs in which to get lost as in Hel's cave, no dead with which to battle, but rather it opened immediately into a single small space. There was one way in, one way out. It made it easy for the occupant to see any who approached. Alex had guessed they'd already been seen from some distance, giving Loki enough time to hide or escape.

Still, Anubis needed to make sure. He lifted his head and sniffed in all directions.

"HE IS GONE. HIS SCENT REMAINS. IT REEKS OF DEATH," Anubis thundered. Alex could smell it, too. The air was thick and hung heavy inside the cave. The cold wind funneling in through the entrance did nothing to rid the place of the odor. They ventured farther in and parted, Alex to one side, Anubis to the other.

The cave was empty except for an old wooden table and a single chair located near the center of the space. A makeshift fire pit nearby had long since gone cold. The place looked abandoned, but they knew better. One of Loki's tricks no doubt, Alex thought.

Deep inside the cave, stone jutted out from the surface. Melting

199

ice from above had dripped over the centuries, creating a depression in the stone in which icy water now collected. A ripple shot across the pool and found its way back to the center again, only to be followed by another. Something was making the water move, but Alex felt no vibration.

He glanced over at Anubis, certain it was him, only it wasn't this time. The warrior god was too busy searching the cave for any remaining signs of Loki. Alex was intrigued, so he moved in closer. Peering over the edge of the bowl, he witnessed the impossible. It was so unexpected that he pulled back instantly, shaking the cobwebs from his head. I must've imagined it, he thought.

"Uh, dude. Dude!" Alex yelled to his friend. "I think I've found Loki."

ELEVEN

In an instant, his enormous friend was there at his side. The two slowly edged over the bowl. The water stopped its movement and became placid. What they saw was an entire scene unfolding before their eyes.

It *was* Loki. His large form was crouched under a great tree at the edge of a mighty river. Alex recognized the tight leather crown atop his head and suspected the horns protruding from it were as much for intimidation as for suggestion. In the distance, a waterfall raged downward from the mountains, feeding the river. His back was to them. The two stood and watched, bewildered.

Loki was pulling something from the water. They looked on as he yanked and heaved at it with great strength. The surface of the water broke into a frenzy of movement. What's that? Alex wondered, leaning closer to the bowl. Fins? It was a fish net. Loki was fishing. Even a god has to eat, he assumed.

The large net was brimming with fish, far more than any one being could eat, even a god. Heck, Alex thought, that's more than an entire village could eat in a year. How's that possible? he wondered. Alex remembered what Odin had said about the elves of this land and of the great magic they possessed. That's it! It must be magic.

It was a lot like watching television, Alex thought, but with no antennae or wires, and a whole lot creepier. Anubis poked at it with a long claw, snarling at the one in the water.

"Down, boy," Alex said as he tried to hold back his laughter. "He can't hear you."

"Oh, but I can," Loki's voice echoed through the cave.

"Waaaaa!" Alex shrieked like a ten-year-old girl at a boy band concert. It startled him so much he grabbed at Anubis' arm and nearly scampered up his leg. Loki's response had quite a different effect on Anubis.

"RROOOAARRGHHH!" Anubis, arms spread wide in defiance, boomed so loudly the small cave shook violently. Loki's taunt had angered the battle-hungry warrior. Not a smart thing to do, Alex thought. His roar reverberated off the stone, causing a large piece from above to land hard on the table, crushing it to the ground from the impact.

"I guess dinner and a movie is out," Alex joked as he covered his ears to soften the noise. The dust soon settled, but an uneasy feeling came over Alex when the vibrations continued.

The low rumble began to build, growing louder and louder. The sound was deafening, far more than Anubis' great cry. The cave began to shake once again. Something was coming and Anubis was ready; only the attack never came.

"Avalanche!" Alex yelled. The fear of being trapped overwhelmed him. His survival instincts kicked in, and he ran for the door; too late. The rushing force from the advancing snow blew in hard through the small opening, sending Alex backward across the cave. He landed against the far wall in a slump. The opening was covered.

Alex slowly stirred, his body bruised and achy. He was clearly shaken. As his senses returned, he became panic-stricken once again. All light had left the cave. He didn't like small dark spaces. It reminded him of Egypt. The last time he was trapped like this, it was with Anubis.

Fear turned to anger. It was Anubis' fault, Alex thought. He rose, still unsteady on his feet, leaning against the cold wall and grabbing at his side.

"You! You did this, you moron. I told you not to howl like that. Now we're trapped. What now, genius?" Alex yelled.

"REMEMBER THE OLD ONE'S WORDS," Anubis said of Odin.

"Which words, numbskull?" Alex asked angrily.

"YOU CANNOT CHANGE DESTINY," Anubis responded.

"Yeah, so? How's that help us now?" Alex asked in frustration.

"THIS," Anubis said as he motioned toward the snow blocking the entrance, "IS NOT OUR DESTINY."

"Sometimes I wonder if we're even in the same conversation," Alex said sarcastically.

They moved separately in the darkness. Alex stumbled, feeling his way along the stone wall. Anubis quietly extended his crook and the end began to glow. Alex felt sheepish, but his blood still boiled.

"Don't think I'm going to suddenly thank you or something," he said spitefully. "All that means . . ." Alex pointed to the crook. "Is that you're about as useful as a, well, a flashlight."

"HMMMFT," Anubis responded, seemingly annoyed.

"And a dim one at that," Alex continued, ensuring that he gave the last word. He moved along the wall, steadying himself with his hand. The snow had pushed into the cave.

Alex knelt and began pulling at the snow with his bare hands, trying to dig out. The cold quickly stung at his fingers. He curled them into fists and blew over them, but no amount of breath could provide enough warmth. To make things worse, each movement twisted and pulled at his side, sending waves of pain across his back.

Anubis stood, indifferent and watching. It wasn't that he was heartless, more that as a god, and one associated with the Underworld, he barely understood this level of pain. It seemed strange to him, almost foreign. Only death came to him with all of

203

its suffering and anguish. For certain that in battle Anubis had seen, even caused, his fair share of pain; but in battle, pain was never his purpose.

All of that, however, didn't make Alex feel any better. Still furious with his friend, he snapped, "Can't you just do that whammy thing and transport us out of here?"

"NO," Anubis replied.

"Why not?" Alex asked. "And don't get snippy with me."

"IT DOES NOT WORK LIKE THAT," Anubis responded, as if this answered Alex's question.

Alex turned and sat in the cold snow. Defeated and exhausted, he was clearly upset and put his head in his hands. *If only I could think straight. We need to get out of here.* Often, during particularly stressful times in his life, like when being hunted by demon hounds or beaten by Valkyries, Alex would think of his grandmother. This was no different.

It was her way. She could calm him with a simple look or a loving pat on his head, but she wasn't here now and he needed her. Not to wipe any tears away; he was done with that, but rather to give him strength, courage to carry on.

He also thought of Tad. How he missed her dark brown eyes. *Her smile's enough to start wars over,* he thought. Well, if he couldn't be with either of them, then he'd at least take comfort in knowing they were safe and he'd see them one day.

"I need to do this. Not just for Odin, but for them, for me," he said. He hadn't realized he'd been speaking out loud.

Laughter filled the air around him, entering his ears and stinging sharply. Its high pitch pierced his brain like a hot poker. Alex squeezed his head in painful reaction, trying desperately to make it stop.

"Did I say something funny?" he asked sharply. Anubis looked at him with questioning eyes. Alex knew immediately that he couldn't hear it.

He jumped up, temporarily forgetting the stiffening pain in his side. He immediately regretted it. The laughter grew, and Alex became confused, disoriented. Was it real or in his head? he wondered. Stumbling toward the water in the stone, he peered over it. It was Loki; only this time he wasn't standing near the river. This time, he was staring back.

His maniacal laughter filled the cave, then found the entrance and pushed outside. Alex gripped at the edge of the stone basin for support, his eyes forced shut trying to deal with the agony and confusion.

Anubis rushed to the bowl and swiped at it in anger, casting the water across the floor.

"DEATH SHALL NOT FIND HIM THAT EASILY," Anubis bellowed. Loose stone fell from the ceiling, narrowly missing Alex.

"Hey, watch it," Alex snapped back. He thought hard for a moment on Anubis' comment.

"What do you mean, death shall not find him that easily?" Alex asked, lowering his voice to mimic Anubis'.

"DEATH IS TOO GOOD FOR HIM," Anubis responded.

"Yeah, but then what do . . ." Alex began.

"I WILL NOT ALLOW IT. IT HAS BEEN WRITTEN," Anubis continued coldly. Alex wasn't sure what he meant, but sensed there was more to this than he first believed; more than the death of Odin's son.

This time it was about far more than battle, more than death even; it was about something bigger. The old hag had mentioned the destinies of these gods; even the great Odin himself spoke of them.

It was as if Anubis intended to ensure that Loki's destiny played out as written.

"WE MUST ATTACK," he shouted. The cave was suddenly quiet. The pain in Alex's head left as quickly as it had arrived. His senses returned, one by one.

"Yes, but where? How do we get there?" Alex asked with some difficulty. Anubis paused, as if taking a moment to separate himself from the conversation. He stared back at Alex and appeared to sigh.

"IT IS TIME," he announced. Alex looked at him strangely.

"I know it's time, but how?" Alex implored.

"NO. IT IS TIME. TIME SHALL GET US THERE," Anubis bellowed as he lifted the pendant that hung around Alex's neck with the end of his crook.

"Hey! Watch it with that thing," Alex shouted angrily, pushing it out of the way. He'd seen what Anubis' crook could do and was uncomfortable being so close to the wrong end of it.

Alex understood. He clutched his pendant and took a deep breath, remembering the last time he tried this. Still not sure how it happened, he crossed his fingers and closed his eyes. A flood of warmth enveloped him almost immediately. Light penetrated through his eyelids. He felt a rush of air, then nothing.

At the precise second they arrived, even before all the light had faded, Anubis let swing his crook, bringing it down and narrowly missing Loki. Relentless, he quickly raised it again and spun it sideways, swiping at Loki and slicing at his throat. Once again, Loki had moved, matching Anubis' speed. This time he wasn't quite as quick. His neck was bleeding.

A look of shock tore across Loki's face. It seemed nobody had ever attacked him before. Likely, nobody had ever dared, Alex thought. Anubis waited for no one. He struck again. This time the crook whisked past Loki's head and sunk deep into the tree behind which Alex hid. The shock on Loki's face turned to terror, but quickly disappeared as arrogance replaced it.

"You dare strike at me? Attack *me*? You who are beneath me?" Loki shrieked.

"I AM BENEATH NONE," Anubis thundered, grabbing Loki's throat in his claw, and began to squeeze. Terror had returned.

Alex knew what came next. He stepped back, hiding behind the tree in fear; fear, not of his enemy, but of his friend. Anubis leaned in close and sniffed at Loki's neck. He caught the scent of his blood. It was like sweet nectar to him. Alex watched as the wild beast waiting just beneath the surface of his friend rose, free and uninhibited. Any ounce of humanity, of caring, was abandoned. For now, in this frenzied moment, Anubis hungered for one thing.

RRAARRGGGHHHH! It was a blood feast, brutal and unforgiving. Anubis seemed to lust for the taste of Loki's blood.

Alex knew their enemy wouldn't make another mistake. Unfortunately, he was right. Loki pulled a small dagger from his side and sunk it deep into Anubis' ribs. Anubis howled in pain, dropping the Norse god.

"You're indeed a worthy opponent," Loki said with a frightening smile, rubbing at his bleeding neck, "but I suspect what you feel isn't the bite of the blade, but rather the sting of defeat." Anubis pulled the bloodied knife from his ribs and howled once more.

The warrior god rose slowly, clutching at his side. He wasn't done. Loki's smile widened. The two charged one another, clashing with such force that the sky above split open with a crack of thunder. Loki met Anubis squarely with his fist to the jaw, sending him backward against the tree.

Anubis was down, stunned by the heavy blow. When next he stood, a portion of tree was missing where he landed. All that remained of the missing piece was a pile of splinters at his feet. It was only the second time Alex had ever seen Anubis visibly shaken.

He assumed that shaken or not, losing a battle, any battle, had never entered his warrior friend's mind. Anubis moved toward his enemy, slicing at him with his claws, but it was the Norse god who had the upper hand now. For every swing, Loki would counter with a feint. He's just toying with him, Alex thought in a panic. I need to do something.

He jumped out from behind the safety of the tree. His friend, no, his brother, needed his help. Nothing could stop him. Except maybe a giant, he thought, as he advanced.

"Giant indeed," Loki said with a devious smile. Alex stopped, stunned and apprehensive. Crud, he thought. Did that loon just read my mind? So that's the way it is, hunh? Alex placed a fingertip to each of his temples, drawing on every ounce of concentration. Okay then, ice cream sundae, he thought. Alex waited; nothing. I guess not, he consoled himself.

Suddenly, the ground began to shake. Whatever it was, it was getting close. The bright sun, high in the midday sky, was blotted out. The shaking stopped. Alex slowly turned around, wanting badly to be wrong for once, still hoping it was a giant sundae. Well, it was giant alright.

Alex looked over at his friend. He was still swinging. So much for helping Anubis, he thought.

"I've got this one. You just take care of Loki," Alex shouted.

"HMMPFT," Anubis agreed, finally shaking off the impact from hitting the tree.

An enormous hand reached downward from the sky and

slammed into the ground where Alex stood, pinning him beneath his palm. The giant pulled back his hand and opened it to see his prize. Dirt sifted through his fingers, and when it was gone, his hand was empty. He appeared confused until he spied Alex running at his feet.

Even preoccupied, Alex could hear the battle raging behind him, two gods, powerful, angry; each with the same objective--death. One wanted it, the other lived it. Never before had history seen such a sight. Never again would it, as one would die here today. Alex turned to get a glimpse. What he saw scared him.

Anubis was on his knees, Loki's hand upon his head. His great friend couldn't move. Loki raised his other hand and, with it, lifted water from the river. Hundreds of feet high, a waterspout twisted sharply from its source. Loki turned his hand and the water bent and swayed. Alex's eyes met with Loki's, and the Norse god smiled.

An endless funnel pounded Anubis, choking him where he knelt. Alex had a plan, but he needed to act quickly or Anubis would surely drown. He veered around the large tree and came up behind Loki, the giant still in pursuit. Loki was vain, if anything, and Alex could use this.

It's all mind games with him, tricks, Alex thought. If I can distract him just long enough, it might work. When he broke Loki's sightline he barely had enough time to slide under the water funnel. Loki's smile turned to worry.

Just as planned, the lumbering giant followed, so large, he ran through the streaming water, not only causing a temporary break in the flow, but a break in Loki's concentration as well. The water fell to the ground in a wet crash, flooding the area around them.

The unintended result of such an immense amount of water was that it instantly skimmed the grass beneath the giant's clumsy feet.

He slipped wildly, awkwardly trying to gain his balance before finally falling to the ground in a splattered thud. Beneath him lay Loki.

It was all Anubis needed. The warrior god grabbed his crook and was on his feet before Loki could react. The tables were turned. The giant rolled to his back and pushed himself up. Alex heard it grunt.

With Loki exposed, Anubis didn't hesitate. A flash of gold was all Alex saw, and the crook landed to Loki's chest. Alex looked up; he had his own problems right now. The giant was standing over him. At least for now, Anubis was safe.

The angered giant raised both fists into the air and brought them down, smashing them into the ground with such force that it buckled the earth beneath them. The resulting shockwave sent Alex flying through the air. He landed at the river's edge face-first and head down in the shallows of the water. He jumped up, soaked and dazed.

"FIGHT," Anubis thundered as he landed another blow to Loki's chest.

"I said, I've got this. You're welcome, by the way," Alex yelled back, his head still a little fuzzy. The giant was coming. Its thick legs carried it fast in a short distance, much like a sprinter exploding off the starting block.

Alex knew he couldn't stop it, nor could he fight it and hope to win. He needed something else, an advantage the giant didn't already have. But what? he wondered. Size was out. Strength maybe? It'd be close, he thought, looking down at his own thin arms.

Whatever it was, he needed to figure it out, and fast. The giant lunged at him with both hands. Without concern, or more to the fact, without thought, Alex charged toward the giant. Caught by surprise, the goliath slid along the ground on its belly, arms wide open, reaching for his small prey.

210

Alex ran between his large hands and at his enormous face. He took a single leap and landed on its rounded nose. Once there, he pulled himself up by the giant's thin hair, onto his head.

The creature was so startled that the feeling forced a sort of chortle from his belly. Alex stopped, balancing himself on the giant's thick back; then it started, the chortle turned into full-on laughter. Alex was tossed around like a child in a bounce house.

It took superhuman agility, but he managed to fall off the giant's back and land gracefully on his butt. This was no time to be sitting down on the job, he thought. From the corner of his eye he could see both Loki and Anubis locked in battle, clawing at each other like rabid beasts. Can't help him right now, he thought of his friend.

He got up and ran between the giant's legs, confusing the massive being even further. Putting a few more feet between them, Alex scurried up the tree and hid within the leaves. He watched patiently as the puzzled monster whipped his head back and forth, searching for him. For all of their size, he thought, they aren't very bright. Bright; that's it, he thought. That's the advantage I was looking for. He shoved his hand down into his pants pocket. They were still there.

Much like a toddler searching for his favorite plaything, the giant moved under the tree just beneath where Alex hid. Leaning from the branch, he waited for the right moment. It came soon enough when the large creature below walked beneath him a second time.

Alex chipped the two small stones together and they sparked. Nothing happened. It wasn't enough. He tried again, but with similar results. Feeling defeated, he could do nothing but look on as the giant moved away, stopping to bend over and lift a large rock. It seemed he was still looking for his lost toy; then it happened.

The smell came first. Alex watched as the giant's hair began to

211

smolder. It sensed something was wrong and stood, sniffing at the air around him. A small orange flicker pushed up a string of twisted black smoke from its head.

A second later, his head was engulfed in flames. The frantic beast tried desperately to pat out the growing inferno, but nothing was working. Pain soon followed, and the giant could no longer stand still. It began to run, bawling the entire way and trampling everything in its path.

Alex snickered at the sight. "Gee, I was just starting to like that one, too," he said jokingly.

Loki, however, wasn't as amused. He lifted his empty hand toward the sky, and Alex was suddenly jerked from the tree by some unseen force. Loki paused, savoring the moment. He smiled wickedly at him, then dropped his hand to his side. Alex fell hard to the ground. The wind left his lungs. He was gasping and couldn't breathe.

Loki wasn't done with him yet. His laughter broke through Alex's pain as he rose above the ground. Slowly drifting downward over Alex's limp body, Loki squeezed the air from his lungs with every lowering inch, crushing him.

Anubis raised his crook and the tip vibrated. Air shot from it, hitting Loki in the small of his back and knocking him to the ground. Alex was up and coughing, forcing oxygen back into his lungs.

"Dude! How come you've never used that one before? Would've come in handy a few stinking times, don't you think?" Alex shouted, much like the squirrel from the forest. Anubis had his chance. Loki was down. With the speed only a god could possess, he ran at Loki, roaring so loudly that even the river danced in fear.

Anubis suddenly stopped, mid-charge, confused. He was

surrounded. Loki had replicated himself many times over. Where there was one, now there were twelve. They moved and spoke as one, they attacked as one, but, much to Alex's surprise, Loki had made another grave error, his second thus far. He was overconfident.

It didn't seem to matter to Anubis that he was far outnumbered. One enemy, six enemies, twelve. To him, they would all suffer, all die.

For every move, every advancement that Anubis made, his opponent countered and fell just out of reach. It was like they anticipated Anubis.

Loki was a god of mischief and deceit. His weapons of choice were trickery and deception. Nothing was as it seemed with him, Alex thought. Even the first time he came to Alex he was in disguise. There must be a way we can use that to our advantage, Alex concluded.

Alex watched helplessly as his friend swiped and clawed at them, each time only to have one disappear, then reappear again. For every one that Anubis would attack, three more would pounce. They weren't real, but each blow took its toll on Anubis. For the first time, Alex saw him weakening. This time it may be too much.

Blood ran from Anubis' side as the dagger wound from earlier had split open during the onslaught. It was slowing him down and he was favoring it.

Anger surged inside Alex as he watched his friend struggle. His head became flush. He needed to do something, so he did what came naturally; he improvised. No plan, no organization as with most teenagers, Alex just charged in. It's what Anubis would do, he thought.

Singling out just one, he ran at him, leaning in just before impact and expecting to hit hard; a flicker of light, then nothing. He passed right through him. Alex's speed, however, proved too much for the task when he tripped and stumbled into Anubis. The warrior instinctively grabbed him, ready to kill, not realizing it was his friend. Alex recognized the crazed look in his eyes, the same look he'd seen in Hel's cave.

Alex only had one chance. He grabbed at his pendant, squeezed his eyelids tightly, and concentrated. A flash of blue light pulsed outward with incredible force, sending Anubis to his knees and knocking over all twelve of Loki. As the force dissipated, so did all but one who lay on his back, his hair and clothes charred. The tree behind which Alex once hid was on fire and the river boiled.

Anubis, visibly shaken, rose to meet Alex.

"I AM IN YOUR DEBT," he roared.

"Don't mention it," Alex said with a smile. "Wait; actually, go ahead and mention it. Mention it a lot," he continued as he pushed out his chest in self-adulation. Alex's eyes widened. "In fact, mention it right now," he said frantically, pointing behind Anubis. Loki was up and charging.

Anubis turned and met his enemy head-on. His movements were fluid from centuries of battles. He was far more experienced in the art of war than his opponent. His crook swung low, catching Loki's advance around his ankles and sending him upward, feet-first. Before he could land, Anubis rushed to his side, clutched his throat, and slammed him to the ground with every ounce of strength he could summon. The earth buckled.

"COWARD!" Anubis boomed. The ground shook beneath Alex's feet from the impact.

That was too easy, Alex thought, as he stepped out from behind the tree. He was right. He felt it at first, before he looked up; the rush of wind caused by the wings of a thousand birds. They chirped and cawed in thunder, flying upward at first, high above, then circling back and turning, diving straight at them.

The two friends ran, swatting at the swarm. They were being pecked and clawed. For every bird they knocked to the ground, a dozen small cuts bled. Anubis swung his crook wildly, trying to give himself enough room to maneuver, but they were too fast and too many. Alex pulled his shirt up over his head, protecting it from the sharp talons scratching at him, so they attacked the exposed skin on his back. The cuts stung to a point of numbness. It was endless.

"It's no use," Alex yelled, holding a deranged bird in each hand, then threw them like a baseball at the others. They fluttered off, only to return. "It's impossible. How can he control everything?"

"What's impossible to humans is inconsequential to a god. I don't exist upon your plane of reality," Loki proclaimed, and the swarm lifted as quickly as it arrived. He'd made his point.

"You said it, not me," replied Alex, still breathless and bleeding from dozens of small cuts to his skin. "I'm pretty sure you're just a Fig Newton of my imagination. You know, experts say . . ." Alex stopped. Something else was happening.

Loki's eyes had turned red as before. A gust of wind tussled Alex's hair. A small twist of air funneled up from the ground at Loki's feet. As it grew, its force pulled inward, drawing in anything it could. The leaves from the tree above were yanked from their stems. The stones at the river's edge began to vibrate; smaller ones lifted and siphoned in. He was a vortex, growing and twisting. He'd become the wind itself.

Alex held fast to the tree, wrapping his arms around its trunk. Anubis sank his claws deep into the ground. It was too much, even for him. The earth became loose and he began to slide.

215

Another of Loki's tricks, Alex thought. It can't be real. His mind raced. If this is to be a battle of wits, then let it, he decided. A singular thought came into focus. Alex smiled.

"Anubis," he yelled. "The knife." Anubis understood. He lifted the small dagger up in one clenched fist, struggling to hold fast to the earth slipping beneath him with the other, and slowly opened his claw. The wind did the rest. The dagger sliced through the air, blade first, at where Loki stood. Everything stopped. Debris fell to the ground, and with it, Loki.

It was the Norse god who now bled from his side. Once again, Anubis caught the scent. The beast within surfaced. Despite his weakened state, he let out a tremendous roar. Alex was certain he saw a hint of fear in Loki's eyes, but before Anubis could attack, Loki raised his hand, rendering the Egyptian god immovable.

"The raw power that surges within you; I can feel it. I fear before long you shall win this battle of strength, but survival is essential to my plan. I shall fight you on my own terms, on my own time," Loki said as he rolled over the bank of the river and into the rushing water.

Once again his laughter filled the air. Alex covered his ears. Even under water Loki's laughter caused him piercing pain. He turned to step away, trying desperately to avoid it when his oversized feet caught on something, sending him downward. He landed in Loki's fish net. He thrashed about, trying to get up, but each time he did, he became more ensnared.

"THERE IS NO TIME TO REST," Anubis shouted.

"*Rest?* Who's resting, you big ape? I need help," Alex snapped back.

"YES YOU DO," Anubis responded, reaching down and grabbing Alex by his collar. He lifted him with ease and, as Alex unfolded, hanging from Anubis' hand, the net slinked to the ground.

"See, I almost had it," Alex said. "Now put me down." Anubis dropped him. Alex crumpled into a mass of knees and elbows.

"Hey. You did that on purpose," Alex cried.

"HE ESCAPES," Anubis roared.

"Not on my watch. Here, take this," Alex said as he stood, shoving one end of the fish net into Anubis' claw. Snatching the other, he dove in after Loki. Alex knew he was no match for Loki's strength, but his speed, particularly in the water, was difficult for anyone to beat, even a god.

He swam deep, hoping to move undetected. It worked. Once past Loki, Alex arched upward and kicked like he never kicked before. The water streamed around his long frame. Certain that he reached the other side unnoticed, Alex scurried up the far bank. Once on shore, he ran to the nearest tree and wrapped the netting tight. Yanking hard, he positioned both feet against the tree.

Far on the opposite shore, Anubis dug hard into the ground. His muscles tightened; he, too, looked ready for the fight. All went according to plan, except for one small detail. Loki did notice.

Too high to jump over, the Norse god swam directly at the net, all the while his laughter penetrating Alex's head. It was like a thousand pins pushing outward from inside his skull, but he needed to hold on. Faster and faster Loki swam until he hit it.

It was a quick jerk at first. Loki had been caught. Alex's heart leapt for joy. It was over, and he loosened his grip, staring at his bloodied hands. Loki was indeed in the net, but he hadn't exactly been caught. He pushed his head against the netting and started kicking harder.

The net stretched for some distance before it reached its limit, and the two on opposite shores felt the draw. Alex pulled back hard.

217

It was wet and slipped through his hands, further cutting his palms and staining the net red.

On the other side, Anubis tugged with all of his might. It was no use; the net began to drag him as well. The dirt was building in front of his feet as he dug in hard, but he was losing his footing. With a final push, Loki sped up. Alex was whipped from around the tree while Anubis' foothold slipped again, each still holding the net.

Both were dragged into the water. Loki had the upper hand now and was heading out to sea, taking Anubis and Alex with him.

Alex tried to let go, but his hand was tangled. The weight of his body dragging against the water pulled at his shoulder and it quickly dislocated. The pain was unbearable. With every twist and turn, every thrash in the water, his shoulder throbbed, sending jolts of pain up the side of his neck and across his back.

Anubis continued to heave with everything he had. His strength was endless, but it was his will that was extraordinary. It was relentless. Loki wouldn't escape this day.

Without warning, the net went slack. There was no more pull. Alex floated in the water, trying to hold his shoulder immobile while kicking to stay afloat. It was awkward and painful, but he was able to free his hand from the tangled netting. What's going on? he wondered as he glanced over and saw Anubis bobbing in the water. Everything was quiet and still.

Suddenly the water broke upward in a spout. At its lead was Thor, net in hand and heading for the shoreline. He landed with such force that Alex felt the shock wave from the water.

As the two friends reached the shore, Thor, with his great strength, was pulling the net out of the water. He captured Loki.

"We were just about to reel him in, weren't we, Anubis?" Alex said, sputtering out water.

"HMMPFT," Anubis agreed. Both knew that without Thor's help, they'd likely have been dragged out to sea, but neither was about to admit it to Thor.

Anubis grabbed Alex's wrist with one of his massive claws and placed the other behind Alex's shoulder.

"Oh, cool. You're going to do one of your ancient Egyptian healing thingies, right? Hey, Big Red, watch this," Alex said with a trusting smile. A sudden realization came over him.

"NO," he bellowed. Anubis jerked quickly on Alex's arm and his joint snapped back into place.

"*Ahhhhhh!*" Alex screamed, grabbing at his shoulder. "What the heck are you doing?" he yelled.

"ANCIENT EGYPTIAN HEALING THING-IE," Anubis responded. Thor burst out laughing and slapped Alex on the back, snapping his head back and sending him into Anubis. Catching him, Anubis stood him back onto his feet.

"*Sheesh,* Thor. You know steroids aren't good for you, don't you?" Alex joked, still shaken. "And you," he continued, looking at Anubis, "give a guy a warning next time."

The unlikely trio stood there relishing in their heroic deed, but each knew it wasn't yet over. The final act of their story still needed to be played out. Without a word, Thor knotted the end of the netting and hoisted Loki up over his shoulder.

Ironic, Alex thought, that it was Loki who now flailed around inside the netting, much like the many fish he caught earlier that day. The fisherman had been caught by his own net. Alex chuckled a little inside at this thought.

This time it was Thor's turn to lead. He raised mighty Mjölnir above his head and the clouds parted. A low rumbling could be heard in the distance. Alex watched as Thor's eyes lit up from excitement while a grin parted his grizzly red beard. What a nut-job, Alex thought.

Lightning ripped downward from the sky, striking the great hammer, and all four disappeared in a terrific blast. All that was left was a small scorched crater, still ablaze from the strike.

TWELVE

They arrived much the same as they'd left, at the end of a lightning bolt, but they weren't alone. Standing just outside the entrance to another cave, as if they'd been waiting for their arrival, were Odin and several others, even a giant. Wait. What? Alex had to look again. This was no ordinary run-of-the-mill giant. It wasn't dressed for battle, nor did it have any weapons or show any signs of aggression. No, this one was a female; a giantess.

"Well, I'll be," Alex said aloud as he rubbed his head. The mood was solemn and quiet. Alex recognized a few of them from the feast. There was Odin's wife, uh, Mrs. Odin or is it Mrs. Father? I think he called her Frigga or something, Alex thought; but there was one more, standing away from the others, as if observing.

Who's that lovely creature over there? he wondered as his mouth hung open. She was truly beautiful, with long blonde hair falling around her shoulders and beyond. She wore a flowing gown of feathers, but it wasn't the feathers that interested Alex. Something around her neck caught his eye. It was glowing.

Odin noticed Alex staring at her longingly and smiled.

"My son, that's Freyja," Odin said. "Among other things, she's the goddess of Destiny. Befitting that she's here, yes?"

"*Word*," Alex said, looking at Loki still slung over Thor's shoulder like a sack.

"Which word?" Odin asked, looking confused. Alex looked up at him with a half-smile.

"Please, let's not start *that* again. I meant, yes, quite befitting," Alex said. No one else spoke. Even Loki, trapped and tangled as he was, dared not speak. One by one, Odin led them into the opening.

221

Alex was last to enter, and as he did, he realized the giantess had stayed behind.

Just into the darkness of the cave he turned around to see her lift a large snake from the ground and cradle it in her arms. Alex shuddered. The others had moved farther into the cave and he ran to catch up, not wanting to be anywhere near the snake. Man, I hate those things, he thought, as he gave a second full body quiver. He was still busy brushing a thousand imaginary creepy-crawlies off his body when he reached the others.

"Hey, giant lady-dude back there has a, uh, *hello?*" He stopped, suddenly taking in everything that came into focus. The others were standing quietly in the center of a large opening, not unlike Hel's cave. In the middle, Thor had set Loki down and was lifting the third of three large stones up on its end.

Alex watched as Thor then unwrapped Loki from the net and grabbed him. It was then that Loki began to speak.

"The day of your undoing is near," Loki screamed. "Take heed my warning. Brother shall fight brother. Our world will burn red with flame. The wolf comes for you, Odin, the snake for you," he said, looking into Thor's eyes, "and before it's over, the skies shall blacken and the world pulled to the sea. The old one has seen it. Death's coming, and its name is *Ragnarok!*"

Frigga handed Thor what appeared to be a coil of wet rope. Her look was that of loss and heartache. Perhaps not only of what has been, but also for what will be, Alex thought, as Loki's words echoed in his head.

When Loki saw the rope, he became incensed. It was apparent to Alex that a plan had been set in motion; the gods of this land had been busy. This time Loki had gone too far, and these gods, in their grief, had no choice but to punish him. Thor lifted him by his throat and placed him across the stones.

He then threw one end of the coiled rope over the top of Loki's body and into Alex's open hands. It landed with a splatter. Whatever it was, it was gross, Alex thought. A familiar odor wafted upward from his hands and found its way into his nostrils. It was as foul as the rotting flesh that once covered him in Egypt so long ago. The putrid smell stung at his eyes and burned the inside of his nose.

"Bind these to the stone," Thor said to Alex. Hesitantly, Alex wrapped the end tightly to the side of the stone. He didn't want to, but he gave it an extra tug for good measure. The slickened cords slipped through his hands several times, but he finally managed to tie it off. Lucky me, he thought sarcastically; only two more to go.

"*Ugh*," Alex muttered as he wiped the wet fleshy material onto his shirt. He finished all three and stepped back. A chill entered the cave and settled itself around Loki. It was an eerie sensation that reminded Alex of Tuat and his own moment of judgment. He watched as the ropes transformed into iron, twisting and tightening on their own. Magic, Alex thought.

"Skaði," Odin summoned, breaking through the silence. There was movement in the darkness from where they came. An unexpected chill ran up Alex's back. He knew immediately what caused it. Only one thing gives me the heebie-jeebies like that, he thought.

The giantess entered, carrying the large poisonous snake now wrapped around her arms. Alex pressed and flattened himself against the wall as she passed, holding his breath and squeezing his eyes tightly shut. The snake hissed, seemingly searching for its own destiny with its flicking tongue.

From half-shut eyes, Alex watched as the others stepped aside, giving way for the giantess to do her part. High above where Loki lay, she placed the snake on the stone so that its dripping poison would find its way downward onto his face.

"Oooh. Time for us to go," Alex said to Anubis, in sudden realization.

"HMMPFT," Anubis agreed. As they turned to walk out, another entered the cave and rushed to Loki's side. In her hands was a bowl. Alex could tell she'd been crying. She stroked at Loki's hair. No words were spoken between them. There didn't need to be.

This emotion was all too familiar to Alex. His mind slipped to thoughts of Tad. He'd only known her briefly, but his feelings for her spanned centuries, lifetimes, even worlds. For her, he'd do anything. He believed it was the same for these two.

"Sigyn," Odin said, nodding. The woman at Loki's side gave no acknowledgement of the All-Father's presence. She moved, positioning herself with bowl in hand at Loki's head. As the poison dripped slowly from above, she caught it. Odin lowered his head and walked out of the cave. The others followed quietly. Alex, of course, was the first to speak.

"What happens when the bowl is full?" he asked, already knowing the answer.

"Sometimes pain can move mountains," Odin answered cryptically. Alex somehow knew what he meant.

"Why do I get the feeling you're talking about something else?" Alex asked. Odin smiled. As they left behind the cave and the horror that was Loki, Alex heard a scream of pain so agonizing that the ground shook violently. A chill ran up his spine as he tried to stabilize himself.

"Was that an earthquake?" he asked as he looked back at the entrance. Anubis stared down at him knowingly.

"Oh, I get it, pain can move mountains," Alex said.

"Is that it then?" he asked, looking up at Odin.

"No," Freyja finally spoke. "There's much more to this. More than even Loki is aware. More than just a beginning or an end as he spoke. For now, Loki's been bound, evil's in its rightful place; but not for long. In the end, we all share the same . . ."

"Destiny?" Alex interrupted.

"No. We all share the same fate," she corrected him. Alex looked confused.

"I don't get it. Aren't they the same thing?" he asked.

"Far removed, I'm afraid. You see, fate is what brings us together; destiny is what separates us," Freyja explained as she wrapped her hands around her necklace.

The sun outside was now setting in the distant reaches of the land. It was under this sky that Alex found the courage to ask Freyja about the necklace she held firmly in her hands. He listened as she detailed a story of love and loss and how this necklace, she called it Brisingamen, had protected her. In the end, it had become a part of her destiny.

Deep inside, Alex quietly drew the similarities; he and his pendant, Freyja and hers. Too close for coincidence, he thought. It was only recently he grasped the concept that everything's connected; now his understanding of destiny was being tested. The difficult part was wrapping his brain around the fact that even separate destinies could somehow be intertwined.

His brain began to hurt, which, in the past, had always been his clue to stop thinking and change the channel, so to speak. This was usually followed by a big bowl of double-dipped chocolate lava ice cream to help ease his troubles. No chance of that here, Alex thought, as he looked around.

It was desolate and cold high atop the mountain. What little warmth the setting sun had given was lost moments ago when it disappeared behind the far range.

"Who's thinking what I'm thinking?" Alex said, raising his hand. "A blazing fire and some fresh pork." He turned to Odin with a large grin. "Can I get an Amen?"

Odin raised his hand and awkwardly placed it against Alex's.

"Yes. Finally," Alex said as he turned and looked at Anubis.

"HMMPFT," Anubis responded.

"Okay, Mr. Odin sir, anytime you're ready," Alex said. With that, Odin smiled and raised his staff. When he brought it down onto the stone, all Alex heard was a loud crack as the entire mountain seemed to flash brightly. The space around them warped and twisted out of shape, stretching through time while time itself seemed to speed up, then lurch to a stop, only to speed up once again.

Before arriving, Alex heard one last tormented scream from inside the cave. The mountain shook in response, reminding him of the true power of one's destiny. The scream then faded, taking the mountain with it.

They were inside Odin's hall. A fire cracked lively in its basin, sending shadows dancing against the walls. When Alex looked around, the others were gone. It was just the three of them now, Odin, Anubis, and himself.

They'd been through a lot in a short time. Alex felt older somehow. Perhaps it was his growing understanding of his role in all of this. First Egypt, now here; one thing was for certain, this couldn't be the only deed throughout history in need of mending. There must be others. Maybe dinosaurs, he thought briefly. Nah.

"Will everything be alright now?" Alex asked.

"Everything will be as it should be," Odin responded solemnly.

Alex saw the sadness in his eye and hugged him. Odin smiled quietly and gently patted his back.

"Don't fret, my son," he began.

"I know, I know. Destinies, woven, connected. I get it," Alex interrupted.

"I was going to say there's fresh pork in the other room," Odin responded.

"Oh. Yeah, right. That, too. Who's hungry?" Alex asked.

"WE MUST GO," Anubis boomed. Alex pulled away from the All-Father and looked up at his friend. Anubis was right, he thought. As strange as it was, Alex considered this towering behemoth his family. He trusted him, even loved him.

"Yeah, what he said," Alex said, pointing his thumb at Anubis. "Will we ever see you again?" he asked Odin.

"Why, you already have," Odin answered.

"Again, I got nothing," Alex said, shaking his head. Confused, he turned to Anubis and back again to Odin.

"You guys make a great pair," he said. "Can you at least tell me if I'm going home this time?"

"If the gods will it." Odin closed his eye. Alex was pretty certain it was his attempt at a wink, but with only one eye, who was to say.

"Is that a yes? Because I have to say, I've had my fill of gods lately. I mean, this one here . . ." Alex motioned to Anubis. "Follows me around so much I feel like I'm being stalked. Yep, thinking about taking out a restraining order," he said as he laughed. Anubis returned no expression.

"Oh, come on. That was funny. I'll tell you what, when we get home I'll give you a big bowl of *Doggie-O's* and a soft chew toy," Alex said. A picture of Mittens flashed through his head. I should be ashamed, he thought with a grin.

It wasn't like last time. He was so unsure then, but he'd grown since Egypt. Here, now, Alex knew he'd at least restored the *deed unraveled*. It was far from over for the gods of this land, but for him, he'd played his part. History was back on course; mended. There was still so much more to learn, but for now, he needed to move on and let destiny take over; assuming he could.

He pulled out the leather-bound volume from his back pocket and stared at it. It held so much between its covers. This little journal was likely the most important piece of documentation in the history of, well, history, Alex thought. Hard to believe I wrote it; the journal that is, not history. At least, I don't think. One thing was clear to Alex; nobody must ever know of its secrets, of its power.

It wasn't until this moment that Alex realized the importance he played in history, too; the power he alone held. I'm not a god like Anubis or Odin, but I do have mad skills, he reassured himself. Whether knowingly or not, they'd put certain events in motion, forever changing, or in most cases, preserving history.

Apparently that wasn't the only power he possessed either, he thought, as he grabbed at his pendant. With this, I can travel through space and time on my own. Pretty rawesome when it works right, and unless he was dreaming, he and Anubis could now hear each other's thoughts. How cool is *that?* Not that Anubis ever has any cool thoughts, but still. Oooh, I hope he didn't hear that.

"HMMPFT," Anubis sputtered, looking at Alex.

"Really? Now?" Alex asked. Anubis turned away.

"I'll leave you to it then," Odin said. "Until our destinies cross again, young Alex."

"Fo shizzle, Odizzle," Alex responded, trying to act cool in the hope that the others wouldn't notice the tears forming in the corners of his eyes.

"Word," Odin replied. Alex laughed.

"WORD," Anubis boomed. A cat shrieked in response somewhere in the night. Alex shook his head.

"Too much, dude," he scolded.

"HMMPFT," Anubis said. With that, Odin slowly turned and walked out of the room. There was no grand exit, no pounding of the staff, no vanishing act as before. He was simply gone.

Alex walked over to the edge of the bed and placed the journal down on its soft covers. He took one last look around. Visions of this journey's events floated through his mind. They were of giants, of the battle-hungry Valkyries and their terrifying screams, of the great wolf Fenrisúlfr and his sister Hel. A picture of the giant snake slithered by, and Alex shuddered. Yeah, him I can do without. His mind drifted to Zach and Loki, of Odin and of goats. Goats?

He shook free of this rather odd ending to his trip down memory lane and turned to his large friend. Before he could open his mouth, Anubis spoke.

"WE TRAVEL TOGETHER," he boomed.

"Hmmnft," Alex said with a laugh. It's possible Anubis will never know the importance of that statement to Alex. It felt as if his heart swelled, and it made him warm inside; quite warm, in fact.

His hands were sweating. When he opened his palms, the pendant was glowing softly. It was time. Somehow *it* knew it was time. He let it drop to his chest, and he snatched the journal. Anticipation grew inside and he became anxious; not of what was to happen, but of where it would take him next. He desperately wanted it, needed it, to be home.

Stroking the words engraved on the spine, he thought of Ms. Flowers. She always spoke of how powerful the written word could be. Man, she had no idea, Alex thought.

"Ala-Kazaam," he joked. "Hmm, nothing." Anubis stared down at him in disbelief.

"Just kidding. Sheesh, have a sense of humor," Alex said. He cleared his throat and spoke those all too familiar words.

"Through time and space I will travel to mend the deed unraveled."

The room filled with the familiar pulsing blue glow that grew so intense it startled the two ravens perched on the balcony just outside the room. As they fluttered off, the wind picked up and funneled through the open balcony doors. The edges of the bed linens flapped violently. Thunder rolled in the distance and he thought of Thor.

The wind swirled inside the chamber, creating a vortex, forcing the door to the hallway to pull open and slam shut repeatedly until it was yanked from its hinges. It sailed across the room, only to finally be sucked out beyond the balcony and into the night sky.

Once again, Alex's chest felt like it was burning. The pain was unbearable. He looked down to see the pendant spinning out of control. The dark space was suddenly ablaze with symbols cast from his necklace. They danced and flicked wildly on every surface.

The bed, as heavy as it was, lifted from the floor and spun about the room, smashing into the far wall. The fire in the chamber had long since been blown out. The two friends held their ground. All that was happening around them didn't matter compared to the task at hand. Alex looked at Anubis. It's now or never, he thought. He took a deep breath and shoved the pendant deep into the recess carved into the cover of the journal.

Without warning, something took hold of his body; he was no longer in control. It jerked him cruelly, twisting and contorting his limbs beyond possibility. Bone stretched painfully against his skin, trying to break free.

A single intense blast of noise flooded the room, so concentrated that he believed his brain had liquified. When the noise finally subsided, he pulled his hands away from his head and they were red. Blood seeped from his ears. Yep, liquified, he thought.

The blue from his pendant pulsed far up into the night sky like a beacon into space. It was pure, and Alex had become a part of it; or rather, it had become a part of him. Looking down, he realized that it wasn't the pendant radiating. In that moment, he somehow connected, merged with it. He'd become raw energy.

"Well, *that's* new," he said.

He held his breath, remembering what came next. It didn't help much. His stomach pushed outward and its harsh acid filled his throat. He felt numb as his power grew. In a sudden surge, Alex flashed like a nuclear explosion.

He watched helplessly as the wooden pegs that held the massive roof to its walls pulled loose; the roof spun off wildly into the darkness and disappeared. Without support, the walls suddenly collapsed inward on him, then reversed and exploded outward into oblivion. Everything was gone. No chamber, no hall, not even Asgaard nor Midgard remained; just emptiness, black and silent.

He floated almost lifelessly in this tranquil sea of strange new darkness. A single thought pushed into his mind; Anubis. He searched frantically for him, but found nothing. His friend was a fading memory, but before a single tear could form, the space around him was torn open and a blinding light penetrated from beyond.

An eruption of chaotic sound passed through the opening, pulling at him. He disappeared downward in a snap of light, then there was nothing.

THIRTEEN

When next he woke, Alex's neck whipped upward in a start. He'd blacked out once again. Drool had dried at the corner of his mouth. As he wiped at it, he heard laughter.

"Mr. Chronos, are you quite rested?" Ms. Flowers' voice stabbed at him sharply from the front of the class. Alex rocked forward in his chair. Looking around the room at all the familiar faces, he wanted to believe it. His heart fluttered. It was his class, his school. He was home!

A yardstick slapped hard against his desk, demanding attention. Alex was smiling.

"Well, I'm glad you find this amusing, young man. Perhaps a trip to see Crun, er, Principal Crunch will wipe that smile off your face." Her slip up sent a wave of giggles through the crowd, none any louder than from Jackson.

He didn't care about any of that. He was finally home. Alex snatched the pass from Ms. Flowers' hand so quickly it startled her, sending her backward and falling into Jackson's lap. It was hard to tell whose face had turned redder. Alex knew he'd pay for that sooner or later. Leaving a room full of laughter behind, he headed toward the office at the end of the hall.

The bounce in his step quickly faded when he realized he returned alone. Mixed emotions slowed him to a crawl. He was excited to finally be home, but saddened his friend wasn't with him. I should've held on to him, Alex thought.

YOU ARE NOT ALONE, a voice inside his head thundered. He recognized it immediately and ran to the hall window, pressing his face against the glass. His eyes searched the distant tree line.

Nothing; all was quiet.

I know I heard it. I couldn't have imagined it, he thought. Anubis is out there somewhere, speaking to me. We can do that now.

"Come on, you overgrown Chihuahua. Tell me where you are," Alex pleaded as he banged on the glass in frustration. All of a sudden a dark shadow popped up from beneath the window, catching Alex unsuspecting. Its figure was so large it blocked the sun from shining through the window. Alex stumbled backward in fright, tripping over his feet and sending him to the ground sputtering.

"HERE," Anubis bellowed. When Alex was finally able to put his heart back into his chest, he stood, rubbing his backside. It's true, Anubis was here. But how? Alex wondered.

"I was worried. We were separated," Alex said.

"NO. NOT HERE. TOO MANY HUMANS," Anubis thundered. Alex understood.

"You're still exposed. You need to hide somewhere. Quick, someone's coming. I'll find you later," Alex whispered to him. A look of indignation formed on Anubis' face. Alex knew hiding wasn't in a warrior god's nature, and sensed the obvious reluctance in his friend. Anubis grunted, reverted to all fours, and headed for the trees.

"And take that silly armor off," Alex shouted after him. "The only battle you'll get into around here is with Mittens. On second thought, maybe you'd better keep it on."

Ringing unexpectedly filled the hall. It screeched loudly as it entered his ear canals. The floors vibrated beneath his feet. Every door in the hall burst open in unison. The space filled with the electrically charged hormones of hundreds of teenagers. Alex had no idea what was happening. We must be under attack, he thought, until he realized that not a single person looked afraid. In fact, some were smiling and laughing.

A second ringing plucked at his already sensitive nerves. The school bell, he thought, feeling rather embarrassed. He relaxed and let it all soak in, every locker, every brick, and every face. He was home. His face split with a toothy smile. It may have been a bit too soon.

From through the crowd a massive figure pushed its way toward him. Alex saw a flash of fist and heard, "Where you been, Chronos?"

His heart leapt. How long have I been gone? Centuries, I'm sure; but there's no way this lunkhead could know. "We missed you last period," Jackson continued mockingly.

The fist landed, knocking Alex to the ground in front of the brute and his entourage. A chorus of laughter ensued. Jackson stood, on the ready.

Rather than returning blows, Alex simply smiled.

"What are you smiling at, Chronos?" Jackson asked angrily. He was obviously expecting quite a different reaction.

"It's just good to be home," Alex responded, patting his swelling lip.

"Freak," Jackson replied. Seeming disappointed, and likely to get no further satisfaction, Jackson and his peers turned and left for class.

"You've no idea," Alex muttered. He looked down at the slip still in his hand. Yep, sure does feel like home, he thought, rubbing his jaw.

Alex pushed open the heavy wooden doors that led to the principal's office. It was just as he remembered it, dark and dusty.

Stacks of books and papers teetered on every flat surface available. The birdcage in the corner was covered, and there were plenty of candy wrappers strewn about, but one thing was missing.

"Principal Crunch?" Alex spoke. "Hello? It's me, Alex." The room was quiet and still. Alex liked the principal; he was a good enough fellow, heavy-set and jolly; still, being sent to his office wasn't exactly Alex's favorite thing, but he didn't want to go back to class either. He walked behind the over-sized desk and sat in the large chair behind it.

"Oooh, that's nice," Alex said as he sank into the softness of its cushion. It'd been broken in perfectly. All I need to do now is to wait here until Crunch gets back and I'm home free, literally. It was different sitting on this side of the desk, he thought; not just the view, but the perspective. He sat up a little straighter out of respect for the position the chair held, or rather the person who usually sat in it.

So there he sat waiting and bored. It'd been some time, and he started getting restless. He leaned back in the chair and put his feet on the desk. When he did, something underneath fell to the ground. He sat up quickly. The last thing he needed was to get caught messing around in here.

He dove under the desk to retrieve whatever it was and had every intention of returning it to its rightful place. Feeling around blindly, his hand brushed over it and he snatched it up.

Crunch's desk was covered with papers. In fact, his whole office was covered in papers. He took no real notice of the folded one in his hand, yellowed and worn. That was, until he read the name written near the bottom corner.

It wasn't possible, he thought. Alex slumped down against the desk. His hands trembled. Every cylinder in his brain was firing, telling him no, but his heart kept telling him yes. It can't be the same one. It has to be a coincidence.

If it were any other name, it would mean nothing, but it wasn't. Here? Now? he wondered. His curiosity piqued. He needed to know what was inside. His fingers shook so that when he tried to open the corners and peel them back, he failed. Alex took a deep breath. Relax, Chronos, you've seen stranger, he thought.

"Gerry," he whispered, making sure it was real. That name, rolling over his lips, haunting him from beyond; it was pulling him in. This guy's like a bad penny, Alex thought. He tried again, this time able to grab the tiniest bit of corner. He shook it open furiously. As his eyes adjusted, his heart pounded and his breathing became heavy and labored. He dropped the paper.

His hands began to sweat, and he started to feel clammy and nauseous. Instinctively, he looked down at his chest, but saw no blue light, felt no heat. It wasn't his pendant this time.

Slowly, he reached for the paper again and carefully laid it out on the floor in front of him. He studied it for what seemed like hours. Running his forefinger over the familiar lines, the symbol in the corner, endless possibilities flooded his mind once again.

He'd first seen it in the marble chamber beneath the sand. Their discovery of this place had been unintentional, accidental almost; or maybe it wasn't, he suddenly realized. Perhaps, as Odin would say, it was his destiny all along.

It was an exact duplicate, only smaller; as if someone had been lying where he'd lain so long ago and drew what he'd seen. Strange lettering adorned the edges of the paper, but he recognized the symbol, the one with three wavy lines. Definitely not a coincidence, he thought.

He knew it was impossible, but on that paper, the one he held so

Loki's Wrath

tightly in his hands, was more than just a coincidence, more than a simple drawing.

"Atlantis!" Alex whispered loudly. He turned the paper over; there was nothing else, just Gerry's name on the one side, the drawing on the other. But how? he wondered. How did it get here? How did Gerry's name get on it? And, most curious of all, *how* did it get under Crunch's desk? Did he know?

Alex looked again at it. It was the same as the one etched into the gleaming white marble ceiling from Egypt. He rubbed the paper between his hands. It felt different to him, foreign. In fact, it felt old.

The handle of the door rattled and turned. Someone was coming. He hunkered down, pulling his knees up close to his chest, desperately trying to make himself smaller. Holding his breath, he waited in silence as the door swung open.

Hushed voices spilled into the room. Alex recognized Crunch's voice immediately and started to crawl out from under the desk until he heard someone else speak.

"I told you three never to come here. It's too dangerous. The boy can never know," Crunch said forcefully. His voice seemed out of place to Alex. He never heard Crunch speak in that manner.

He needed to see who Crunch was talking to. From between the cracks of the desk's frame, Alex could make out three others with the principal. They were oddly dressed and spoke with a heavy thick accent. Alex shifted slightly for a better vantage and almost gave away his hiding place when one of the men turned.

It was the Greek! The old one from the docks. In fact, it was all three of them. Alex crouched even smaller. What are they doing here? With Crunch? he wondered.

The first time he'd seen them, it was down at the harbor. An

237

unassuming older gentleman and two younger men, sailors; the Captain had told him they were Greek. Alex hadn't paid much attention to them until they noticed his pendant.

He had no idea what they wanted, only that when they saw his pendant it set them off, angered them. They chased him down the docks and through town. If he learned anything from his relationship with Jackson, it was if someone chased him, he ran.

He remembered bounding from roof to roof keeping ahead of them, out of sight. It was only after he reached the safety of his home, the old wooden shed in his yard, that he lost them. It was the same shed where it all began. Gods, demons, Egypt, even Anubis; all started in that shed. Alex's mind drifted back to his current situation.

Crunch said it was dangerous, Alex recalled. What was dangerous? What boy was he talking about? Alex's mind reeled with possibilities.

He knew one thing for certain; he wasn't going to move until they were long gone. Lucky for him, he didn't have to wait long. All four men walked into the hall and disappeared.

Alex slowly pulled himself out from under the desk. He folded the map up and placed it inside his journal, then tucked the journal deep down into his back pocket. Wait until Anubis hears about this, he thought.

The final bell rang signaling the end of another grueling day for the students of PSA. Alex cautiously tiptoed to the door, peering out. The men were gone. Entering the hallway from Principal Crunch's office would've seemed particularly uneventful, if it weren't for what just happened.

As he merged with the rank and file, he realized that here at school he was just another faceless being in a sea of facelessness. It

238

wasn't like that out there, he thought. Out there, he'd made a difference, but here, nobody even knew he existed. Well, nobody except maybe Jackson on a slow day.

Walking through the crowded halls, he moved in a daze. He only had one thing on his mind; to get back home and check on Anubis, preferably without incident. Pushing his way through, deep in his own thoughts and not paying attention, he barely heard the others talking about the latest news.

A new student had enrolled in PSA, late in the year. He hadn't seen her yet, but could care less. I'm a bit busy doing this little thing I like to call *saving stinking history*.

He overheard one of them say how beautiful she was, and another asking her if he could carry her books, and yet a third asked about the hair care products she used. How lame, Alex laughed. She'll probably fall in with Jackson and his mob anyway, he thought. They usually do.

The mass of student body pushed as one. He was caught in the slipstream. They were all heading in the same direction, toward the main quad. There, gathered in the middle, was Jackson and his crew. All others remained on the fringe, hoping to get a glimpse.

Alex hugged the walls, trying to squeeze by unnoticed. Think wallflower, Chronos, he told himself. Hold your breath and avoid eye contact at all costs. They looked hungry and could pounce if they felt threatened in the least. Too late, the crowd parted ever so slightly, and he looked up out of the corner of his eye.

Alex saw what all of the commotion was about. Well, actually, he saw the back of her head and long brown hair. That was about it. Several people in the crowd noticed his glance and shot him nasty looks.

He began to sweat and quickened his pace. He just wanted to get past. The faint hint of Jasmine wafted by, and his thoughts drifted to Tad. How he missed her, her dark skin, much like the new girl's. Her laugh, too, was similar to Tad's.

It was then that Alex overheard the perfect ending to his day. Jackson asked her out. Saw that coming, Alex thought. The crowd hushed, then suddenly split open as Margaret Stimpson pushed through and stormed off. *Yikes.* Note to self, avoid Margaret for a while.

"No, thank you. I'm already spoken for," the new girl responded to Jackson politely. She turned toward Alex, her face beamed with a smile. Alex stopped dead in his tracks. It was Tad!

He could've asked all of the obvious questions. How? When? Why? How, again? But for once, Alex didn't question, didn't try to make sense of things. He just smiled, and before he could say anything, Tad ran up to him, threw her arms around his neck, and kissed him. It seemed she too had missed him. Alex was quite certain that if it hadn't happened to him before, time was definitely standing still for him now. He was okay with that.

The entire crowd of misfits stood and gawked as this unnatural scene unfolded before their eyes. Silence blanketed the hall. Someone in the back of the crowd yelled, "Alright, Chronos, you dog."

"Ooh, maybe not a dog," Alex said. Both he and Tad laughed. The crowd began to clap and cheer. It was as if they'd been waiting for something like this their whole lives, something to upset their normal routines, upset the balance of nature.

"Is this some sort of joke, Chronos?" Jackson's voice cracked in uncertainty. The crowd slowly left his side and started circling Alex and Tad.

"Not a joke," Alex responded, looking into Tad's eyes; "destiny."

For once, Alex was happy, extremely happy. Still, somewhere buried deep inside his subconscious, he couldn't help but wonder how long it would last. *Was* this his destiny, or was there more?

As they walked out of the school holding hands, he looked back. He thought of all those moments that'd brought him to this one. It would be the last time he'd look back, he thought.

It was as Odin had said, history can always be changed. The future, Alex thought; now that's a journey worth taking.

THE END

Ves heill and many thanks to Jeffrey Rigdon, *Hersir* of the *Vikings of the Valley* for his keen insight on all things Norse. May you dine with Odin someday.

www.facebook.com/thehoundsofset
www.thechronosseries.com